"All men dream, but not equally. Those who dream by night in the dusty recesses of their minds wake in the day to find that it was vanity; but the dreamers of the day are dangerous men, for they may act their dreams with open eyes, to make it possible. This I did."

—T.E. Lawrence

# Prologue

It was hot. Unbearably hot. That was the single notion that kept invading my thoughts. A blistering heat that encompassed all my thoughts and mind. Never had I known a desert—or any place, for that matter—as this. It was all I could think about. What I wouldn't give for just a little shade and the smallest sip of water.

*Water.*

The lifeblood of Earth. Seventy percent of the planet was covered in that beautiful stuff, and here I was without a drop for endless miles around me. But I had to keep my head; I couldn't afford to lose my mind now.

She needed me.

She?

Who was I thinking about? Emma! How could I forget? What was wrong with me? Was I losing my mind?

Probably, I thought with a smirk. I suddenly recognized the beginnings of heat exhaustion, my mind beginning to wander. I tried to focus, take my mind off the heat. Or maybe it was a concussion, either way.

Even though it had been several hours since I had last opened my eyes, I knew the scenery hadn't changed all that much beyond my sweat-drenched blindfold. The only thing worse than the nasty piece of cloth, which I'm guessing had never been washed, was the fact that my wrists were tightly bound.

I could barely feel them at this point; somebody clearly had some mommy issues.

But the absolute worst bit of my predicament was my complete loss of time and lack of knowledge. How long had I been tied up? Where the hell were we going? And who were these men working for? My list of questions had only grown longer since the start of this crazy adventure.

I had spent the first few hours of my captivity trying to loosen the hold of the rope on my wrists but without much success—unless you count the blood now flowing slowly down my fingers. Of course, all the movement of the camel hadn't helped. Come to think of it, maybe my captors did know what they were doing—practice does make perfect. Had there been any saliva in my mouth, I would have gulped. I was really tired of people trying to kill me.

I must have passed out at some point from the heat (or the concussion). What had happened since the alley?

Lost in my dark thoughts, I almost fell off the camel as it slipped down a dune before recovering.

I had already fallen off the smelly thing several times when I wasn't paying attention, especially in the last hour or so (this heat really had a way of getting to you), and had no desire to do so again.

I especially didn't want my captors stopping to throw me back on. One of them—I called him Grumpy (because the others yelled at him a lot and made him do all the grunt work, so naturally he took it all out on me)—wasn't the gentlest creature when he had to stop and throw me back on. And "he had an absolutely horrid smell about him," to quote Emma (it seemed like a lot of things smelled out here—go figure). But then, maybe it was all of them. Or maybe it was just him.

In fact, the only improvement to my situation was the rapport I was developing with my camel. The endless hours on his back had allowed me to fall into a natural rhythm with the camel's movements. He did smell a bit, but he was starting to grow on me (at least he didn't yell at me). It was only when I passed out that I would find myself on the sand or being thrown back on by Grumpy.

I didn't really care about falling off, but the heat was really starting to take its toll on me. I was having trouble thinking clearly, let alone keeping my mind off it. Not to mention I could feel the warm blood coming from my wrists with all the struggling. If anything, my struggles had only tightened the rope further into my flesh.

No, I would have to wait for my opening, probably when—or *if*—this damn blindfold was taken off, I thought with dismay. It had better be soon, before my waning strength was completely gone.

It was just after noon, if the burning sensation on the back of my neck was any indication. Even the camels must have been wishing they were somewhere else by now. I imagined the desert must look just like those pictures in *National Geographic* I had seen; hopefully I would still get the chance.

Unfortunately, pictures can never convey the unbearable amount of heat. No shade, no water, barely any animal life except those few that have evolved over millennia to survive. The ultimate survivors in my book, and no place fit for a human being.

Sure, it may look all pretty in pictures in your air-conditioned house with cold running water, but no words exist to describe a sun that literally burns through your clothes and into your very heart. It literally cooks your brain slowly and evaporates every ounce of sweat as it escapes your body, and the reflection of the light in the sand burns your eyeballs. Endless sand dunes that reach as far as the eye can see, offering no escape, no withdrawal, a prison with no walls. This must have been Satan's backyard growing up.

The Sahara. Man's very own hell on Earth.

for Alexis

CHAPTER ONE

# SCHOOL DAYS

*Max Taylor was an interesting young man in many respects. For one thing, he much preferred being called by his nickname instead of his proper name. For another, his mind was always wandering. He rarely focused on whatever dismal thing he was doing and would spend his time daydreaming of far-off monasteries in some forgotten mountain or some hidden temple deep in some nameless jungle.*

*He preferred sleeping outside under the stars as opposed to a proper bed and eating a fish that he had caught in a stream instead of a three-course meal with all the trimmings.*

*If you were to pass him in the street, you wouldn't give him a second thought. He had no real discerning qualities, nothing that would separate him from the masses.*

*In fact, Max Taylor was just your ordinary college student at Asher University, soon to be college graduate. He was no different than any other college student in any other college in the entire world for all but maybe one small way. You see, Max Taylor had a secret.*

*He wanted to travel the world, and not just stop at all the regular tourist destinations like everybody else, there was nothing unique about that. Max wanted nothing more than to just get out* there. *He wanted to camp out in the Amazon for months at a time, climb through the Himalayas, and trek across the African safari. He wanted to spend time with the indigenous peoples of the world and learn their languages, customs, and cultures. To climb the tallest mountains, hike the longest trails, hunt and fish for his next meal. To live and be free from all of the modern world's turmoil and stress. To see things that most people have never seen or will see, to live harder in one year than most people live in their entire lives. But Max, unlike most people, always had a way of getting what he wanted and accomplishing his goals. He had a uniqueness about him. Some called it focus. Some called it drive or ambition. Max always thought it was something deeper, something in his soul, a passion, no, a need. To prove himself, to go over the next hill, the next challenge, the search for glory...*

Suddenly, the dream ended as I awoke from that nameless place between sleep and the waking world. Almost as quickly as it came, the memory began to fade—something to do with ice boulders and a pack of husky dogs.

As I sat up in my bed, rubbing the sleep from my eyes, I took a moment to survey my surroundings and let my eyes adjust to the new day.

Like most college dorm rooms, mine was small, but I think I had done a good job decorating it and letting my personality show.

My eyes wandered to the well-used surfboard leaning against the wall, barely hiding the scuba tank behind it, both of which had been had been squeezed between the wall and the desk.

I smiled as my eyes lingered above my desk. In fact, all around my desk and on every available space on the wall above it—heck, even on a good portion of the ceiling—I gazed at my growing obsession: pictures and posters and even torn pages from *National Geographic* showing mountains, canyons, deserts, oceans, forests, and jungles from all corners of the globe; tribes from Africa, the Amazon, desert nomads, and Buddhist monks; and scores more of other barely known or seen exotic and far-off locations around the world.

Photos of my exploits were scattered around the desk wherever there was a free place to be found. Memories frozen in time reminding me of my childhood and days spent growing up in preparation for my freedom. Times spent with my father camping and hunting, skydiving, scuba diving. Still another showed me mountain climbing (a small mountain but I considered it a mountain none-the-less), and even one with me beside a small Piper aircraft that I had learned to fly. I suppose you could say I was not the couch potato type.

I continued to look around as I sat in bed, not really wanting to get up yet (not that I had to), and for the hundredth time reminded myself to buy another bookcase. A bookcase by the bed was crammed full of travel and adventure novels including the likes of Tolkien, Tolstoy, Goodkind, Homer, and, naturally, even some by Cussler and the occasional book about Indiana Jones stuffed in somewhere.

My thoughts were suddenly interrupted by the alarm clock and a moan from the bunk underneath me, followed by the unmistakable sound of a fist hitting the clock. I wondered how many more days that poor thing had before it had to be replaced *again*.

My gaze was then captured by something by the door, and my eyes lingered for a few moments on the piece of black lingerie hanging on the doorknob that I had *somehow* managed not to notice the night before.

If it was even there the night before, I thought with a smile and a shake of my head.

Jayne Fielding, my roommate for about three years now and the probable explanation for the *other* side of the room, where stood a growing pile of dirty laundry that I was about ready to throw out the door before the odor started to reach me. That is, if I managed to make it over all the clothes that had failed to make it that far *and* not break a toe on the random football gear (one especially filthy undergarment in particular) on Jayne's side of the room.

Standing at roughly 6'4", Jayne truly was an impressive specimen to behold. Perhaps it was some subconscious fear at having a girl's name (which would be your funeral if any mention of the fact was ever made to his face), or maybe it was the constant grind of football since his early childhood that had produced such a towering bulk of muscle that Jayne wasn't shy about showing off.

Further adding to the effect was Jayne's buzz cut and the thin-line beard he had recently grown, which enhanced his intimidating look that resulted in few men ever giving him a hard time.

Over the years that we had known each other, I still didn't know how Jayne had become the way he was. Maybe no one ever would. Maybe it was just how he was raised, or maybe he had watched too much television as a child (too much MTV and the like can have a strong influence on a child), or maybe, as I suspected (but was too adverse to ask), it really did have to do with his name.

True, I had almost gotten used to Jayne's sometimes uncivilized and arrogant manner (especially toward women), but he still sometimes managed to surprise even me with some random comment (ironically those were also usually directed at women). To sum up, Jayne was one hell of a character.

For roommates, I bet there's no better example of opposites, I thought with a grin. And why not, when you look at all the posters of models and celebrities, and a bookshelf, which unlike my overflowing collection, contained mostly *Sports Illustrated.*

Jayne and I may have been about as far apart as you could get, but you would have been hard pressed to find two closer friends. I served, in many ways, as a buffer to Jayne's more *eccentric* habits. His habits, if you couldn't tell, tended to revolve around partying and "let's have fun." In fact, many people who knew both of us tended to agree that if it weren't for me and the small amount of positive influence and control that I managed to enact over him, Jayne probably would have failed out of Asher long ago.

Deciding that it was time to get up, I threw back the sheets and hopped down from the top bunk, being careful as always to avoid stepping on anything while making my way to the dresser.

Looking in the mirror by the dresser, I noticed the light five o' clock shadow I was sporting and thought that it was probably about time to shave again (something I didn't bother to do every day). Though I did look pretty good with a bit of facial hair, I thought. My mother would have probably said otherwise. Although I decided to skip the shave this morning, I did try to flatten down my short, dark brown hair (which stubbornly refused yet again to comply with my wishes), which the sun, after many weekends out and about, had managed to bleach to a light chestnut.

As I started to change, Jayne managed to drag the sheets off his face.

"Max," he moaned. "It's like nine o'clock. Go back to bed." He turned under his sheets. "It's not going to kill you to miss a class," he finished before placing his pillow over his head.

I looked at the sleeping mass. "I think you already proved that theory to the world."

As I finished buttoning my shirt, Jayne replied sleepily, "All the better to follow my excellent example."

As I rushed over to his desk to grab my backpack (a substantially easier task now since my space by the window was much tidier than Jayne's side), I looked back at Jayne. I figured I should be the responsible one (which I usually tended to be; and by "usually," I meant always), especially today.

"So it's safe to assume that you're not coming to class today either?" I asked, opening the door to leave.

"Take notes for me today, will you?" Jayne answered before turning over again under the sheets.

Having waited as long as I could, I figured it was probably time to break the news as I walked out of the room. Sticking my head back in the room and with a devious smile on my face, I broke the bad news to the poor fellow.

"Well, it'll be kind of hard to take notes today, what with there being a test," I said before slamming the door closed behind me.

I wasn't positive, but I was pretty sure I heard a small yelp followed by an unmistakable thump of someone falling out of bed as I walked down the hall toward the exit feeling particularly good about the upcoming day.

Too bad he wasn't on the top bunk, I thought happily.

"You know, you could have told me we had an exam," Jayne called, running to catch up. I stopped and waited at the bottom of staircase outside Le Conte Hall with a small grin on my face, savoring the small righteousness of the world.

Asher University, acknowledged by many to be one of the top private research universities in the country, was located in northern Massachusetts outside of Boston.

Considered to be a beautiful and exquisite campus by all respects, Asher, like so many New England colleges, combined the Gothic architecture of Oxford with the local landscape to establish a unique American Collegiate Gothic style—or so it said in the brochure. It occurred to me (I think it may have been my second day) that this was another attempt by Asher (and most colleges like her) to be more respectable and sophisticated like her British counterparts.

Le Conte Hall, where I had most of my classes these days, was one of the main engineering buildings and located almost dead center on campus.

"Serves you right for cutting class for three straight weeks," I said as Jayne caught up to me.

"More like two weeks actually," Jayne retorted.

"My mistake," I finished with a grin. We stared each other down for a few seconds before breaking into laughter.

Most of the stupid things I got in trouble for were Jayne's ideas, and to be fair, I only listened to them when I got bored (which seemed to be happening a bit more often lately, according to the dean). Maybe I wasn't as good of an influence on Jayne as I had thought; maybe it was the other way around.

"Come on, let's grab some breakfast," I said.

"On you?" Jayne asked. I only smiled as he took off.

We set off in silence, with Jayne leading as we crossed a bridge over a small half-frozen creek before coming upon Proctor Hall, one of the campus's dining halls.

I, not being able to resist and knowing the usual bull answer, asked, "So how do you think you did?"

Looking partially distracted and not paying attention to me, Jayne answered, "Probably would have failed if I wasn't such a genius."

"I guess you won't mind buying then," I responded.

Jayne just continued smiling. What was he up to? A bit of revenge?

We came before Proctor Hall. It had been a while since I was here. In fact, I used to come here all the time to eat. It was a charming enough place. By that, I mean it's about what you would expect from a campus dining hall, if your idea of a dining hall were something of a mix between a cathedral and an English manor.

This part of Proctor housed the food preparation and some administrative offices on the upper levels. Of course, the building (or the entire university, for that matter) wouldn't complete the Old English effect (or copy it, as I liked to think) it was going for without the odd turret or two attached at the end.

I always liked the inside of the hall the best; it had always given me a comfy, cozy feel, unlike the outside. It was lined with four long tables for students with large chandeliers overhead.

Once inside, Jayne, still in the lead, led me across the dark green tiles scuffed from years of use toward the front corner of the dining hall.

I felt as if I should have seen this coming. How could I have been so stupid? Hadn't I avoided coming here for at least a month, and now Jayne had led me here without my realizing it?

Ignoring the salad bar on my right and without even taking a look at the large selection of cereals and fruits available, Jayne, heading like an arrow toward his target (if only he took his studying as seriously—not that I did either, but at least I went to class and studied when I had to), walked straight to the small omelet bar in the corner where a short blonde was manning the counter.

As soon as she spotted Jayne heading toward her, she looked left and right, as if hoping she might be able to make a quick getaway. Failing that, Katie reluctantly looked back at the approaching predator (he really could be sometimes). It took a second for her to notice that Jayne wasn't alone, and upon seeing me, her frown immediately turned into heavy blushing (I really wished it wouldn't).

Katie Finnegan, an attractive blonde with one *slightly* negative quality (slightly being perhaps a little generous in my opinion). Over the past few weeks she had taken quite a liking to me and had developed an annoying habit of turning up whenever I had a few moments to myself.

Despite my best attempts, which included avoiding my favorite place to eat where she just happened to start working, and that she seemed to pop up in more than one of my classes (despite the fact that I was quite sure she was a psychology major), she hadn't taken the hint that I wasn't interested. Some people might consider these things nothing more than a coincidence, but I didn't believe in coincidences.

And Jayne definitely didn't help the situation. Having what he'd call a crush on Katie (who didn't he have a crush on, for that matter) resulted in something of a classic love triangle. But then, Jayne always did seem to have a new love interest every week—until he conquered that mountain, as they say.

I was never one to have many girlfriends. In fact, my last steady girlfriend was in high school, and that wasn't anything exceptional either. It wasn't that I didn't like girls or anything, mind you, but I never found the right one. I wasn't looking to get married or anything, but I was looking for something—I don't know another word for it except…special.

It took me a few seconds before I realized --with Jayne still talking on about something—he hadn't noticed that no one was listening to him or even *looking* at him for that matter—someone was staring at me.

Upon my noticing, Katie immediately looked away, her cheeks once again deepening to a dark red. And it wasn't until then that *she* noticed that someone was talking to her.

"Earth to Katie," Jayne repeated, his face only inches from hers.

Having come back to Earth, Katie jumped back with surprise, not realizing how close she had let Jayne get. Like most of the girls on campus, she knew not to let her defenses down around Jayne for even a second and looked relieved that he hadn't thought to take advantage of her moment of weakness. Actually, she looked to be more surprised than anything.

"Hello, Katie," Jayne said with a devilish grin.

"Hi, Jayne," she said quickly and indifferently. "Hi, Max. How are you?" she asked cheerfully, turning her full attention once again on me.

"Goo—" was all I managed to get out before Jayne interrupted.

"So, you miss me?"

"You know the manager said you're not allowed to bother me when I'm at work. But I'd prefer if you *always* followed that rule," she finished, clearly hoping against all hope that that would be enough to finally stop Jayne's endless attempts at asking her out. I had to admit, though, that he was one determined guy.

"But I'm not here to bother you. We're here," Jayne replied, grabbing me tightly before I had a chance to slip away, "for some breakfast," he finished victoriously.

After several painful minutes with Jayne questioning an agitated Katie about the menu, I managed to drag Jayne away by the scruff of his neck (almost literally).

Talking a seat at the massive table, I nearly collapsed with exhaustion. That was nothing more than utter torture. In fact, come to think of it, I would almost rather wrestle a bear than have to endure anything like that ever again. Jayne, looking slightly upset over another failed attempt at winning Katie's heart, decided to take it out on his omelet.

Still worn out from our little escapade, I wasn't terribly hungry anymore and decided to pass the time watching Jayne gulp down the three omelets he had made Katie make for him (knowing Jayne, this was probably so he'd have an excuse for round two). Needless to say, watching this had an even more adverse effect on my stomach.

Having finally taken his eyes off of his food, Jayne looked at me, a few words of wisdom ready to leave his astute tongue. He had a little something hanging from the corner of his mouth.

"I thfph sfe lihf me," he said. I just smiled at my friend, amazed that any sound had come out at all.

"What?" I asked a few seconds later when I was sure the laughter in my head had died down.

Jayne swallowed. "I said, 'I think she likes me.'"

"Really?" I replied with raised eyebrows. "And what gives you that idea?"

"Well, she can't take her eyes off me for one."

Not believing him, I turned around to look for myself, catching Katie looking away, her cheeks once again turning red.

"Told ya," Jayne said triumphantly.

Shaking my head with a grin, I decided it was best not to argue with him and started eating my eggs (interesting how Jayne could make one lose his appetite and regain it just as quickly).

A few minutes passed before Jayne went to help himself to seconds, which involved less omelet and more Katie.

"You're hilarious, you know that?" he said, dropping his plate.

"Why?" I asked perplexed.

"You could have told me that I had something on my face. The whole time I thought she was laughing at my joke about the baboon and the priest"—I really didn't want to know that one—"and she was actually laughing at the piece of pepper clinging to the side of my face."

I couldn't help but laugh a little. "Well, it's a little funny," I said, finishing my eggs.

"Yeah, freaking hilarious," Jayne answered, barely touching his fresh omelet.

A few more minutes passed in silence during which Jayne grumpily resumed eating his fourth omelet before asking me, "So what's up with you lately anyway?"

Being a little confused and thinking that Jayne was still upset about the omelet incident, I asked the obvious question: "What do mean?"

"I don't know. You've been a little quiet lately, dude. Bit more than usual I think. Depressed or anything?"

Truth be told, I was a little touched and surprised at Jayne's concern.

"Yeah, I'm fine," I answered honestly. Well, *almost* honestly.

It was true that I hadn't been in the greatest mood lately, but I wouldn't go as far to call it depressed. Maybe a little tired…but from what? I couldn't put a finger on it.

Jayne, showing a level of insight I had never known existed, didn't believe me. Maybe there was more to the man than I gave him credit for. Then again, it would probably take a lifetime to fully understand Jayne.

"You know what'll get you out of this funk you're in?"

I smiled, raising my shoulders. "No, what?"

"Spring break!" Of course, how could he forget? Maybe there really wasn't more to Jayne than everybody thought; maybe what you saw was what you got. Sorry, Earth. Spring break was pretty much the reason of Jayne's existence. Well, that and girls of course. "Think about it, the surf, the sun…the women."

Maybe a break was what I needed, but somehow, I didn't think Jayne had the solution.

However, against my better judgment, Jayne had talked me into going on a little trip to the Bahamas for the break a few weeks back. Still amazed that I had accepted the offer (it must have been in a moment of weakness), Jayne couldn't stop talking about it for the last month.

"You know there's still a week before we leave, right?"

Jayne just waved me off, grinning. "Right around the corner."

"You know we have our midterms, right?"

"I thought we just took it," Jayne replied.

"No, that was just a test. Which you would know if you went to class." Even this news barely diminished Jayne's newfound happy mood.

As Jayne got up with his empty tray, he added, "I think I'll go see if Katie has any plans."

CHAPTER TWO

# THE SWORD IN THE SAND

The following week was nothing less than what I expected. I had spent the week, like most of my classmates, studying hard (well, harder than usual) for my upcoming midterms before the break, and thankfully I hadn't had much difficulty in any of my exams. Jayne, naturally, had gotten a *slightly* later start than everybody else at his studying, if you count the night before as slightly later.

But at the end of the day, we had both emerged from our last exam together, an advanced engineering class, exhausted but pleased that our long-awaited break had finally arrived.

And Jayne, of course, felt the exam was a breeze. Some people thought Jayne was nothing more than a big brute, but I knew appearances could be deceiving. Jayne, in fact, was rather smart, a bit lazy perhaps (at least when it came to school), but he definitely didn't have a bad head on his shoulders. Nevertheless, even he looked relieved that exams were over.

But soon the day came to an end, and after a restless night, the kind most people get before a trip, Jayne and I woke up early for our flight. Dressing in silence in the early morning, we grabbed our packs and headed out. Being too early for Proctor Hall to be open, we headed down the steps and let our sleepy feet carry us to the bus terminal two blocks from campus.

Along the way we passed a few other early students, most likely traveling home or to Miami or some other destination. Outside the station we met up with Matthew Brooks, a mutual friend of ours and fellow traveler to Nassau. I silently shook hands with Matt before heading into the terminal.

Even at this hour, the station was rather busy with travelers rushing around looking for their bus before it departed. Already running a little late, the three of us immediately headed to the large overhead departure board and looked with bleary eyes for the bus that would take us to the JFK airport.

"Platform thirteen," I said, being the first to catch it.

Without another word, we headed off in the general direction of the platform. After a ways, we exited through a door at the side of the terminal onto a wide boardwalk with an overhang. Large silver Greyhounds were lined up, waiting to depart for their destinations.

We had emerged before a large Greyhound that was backing out of its spot with a big plastic eight hanging above the platform. Seeing number seven to its left and nine to the right, I took the lead and headed right, looking for the thirteen bus to JFK. Checking my watch and seeing that we only had five minutes left, I urged the others to hurry up. Missing the bus would be a sorry way to start spring break.

After rounding a slight corner past the number twelve, we stopped before our nearly full bus.

"Great. Now it'll probably smell like old people," Jayne remarked. I silently wished we'd stay quiet for a little longer (a few hours at the very least).

After showing the driver our tickets, Matt and Jayne took the remaining empty seats in the middle. I headed toward the back of the bus, placed my bag in the overhead, and took one of the last seats beside an elderly chap.

Not ten seconds after taking our seats, the bus driver started the engine and closed the door, and we rolled out of the platform. I let out a sigh that I wasn't even aware I had been holding in and smiled at the thought of having a whole hour to rest my eyes while the driver took me to the airport.

Barely a minute had passed before I was jerked awake.

"Roasted peanut?" asked the elderly gentleman sitting next to me. He shook the brown paper bag in front of my shocked face to reiterate his point when I just stared back at him.

"No, no, I'm fine. Thanks," I said, closing my eyes again, thinking that the conversation was over and the old man hadn't meant to wake me.

"So where you headed, son?" he asked. I, deciding that trying to grab a quick nap was out of the question until I had at least entertained my seatmate for a little bit, turned my head to get my first good look at the older gentleman.

Older was indeed a stretch. Ancient was the first word that first popped into my mind. It may have been the early morning light, or perhaps my impression was caused by a combination of his clothes, which consisted of an old brown suit with individual threads coming loose, a worn-out wool coat, and an old yellow tie. Or the fact that the entire outfit was topped by a shabby old fedora hat that gave the man a depressing and melted look.

I answered his question with a sudden curiosity in the man. "Nassau, sir."

"Hmm, sir? Oh, forgive me. Leroy Williams," he said, holding out his hand.

I instinctively shook it before realizing the man was still staring at me.

It was the eyes that got to me. His pale blue orbs felt as if they were staring through my very soul, if such a thing were possible. Unlike the rest of him, they looked sharp and alert, almost youthful, as if they took in every detail, eyes that had seen a lot in its day—both good and bad.

"And you are?" Mr. Williams asked, breaking me out of my reverie.

"Sorry," I stammered. "Max. Max Taylor, nice to meet you," I replied, releasing Mr. Williams's hand. He had a surprisingly strong grip.

"Nice to meet you as well, Maxwell."

"No, just Ma—"

"So the Caribbean, huh," Mr. Williams interrupted, repositioning the small leather bag on his knees.

"Yeah, the Caribbean."

"Been there myself, you know, in 1961. Petty Officer Second Class Williams. Long time ago, but you won't be interested in any of that," he finished in a quiet voice. Mr. Williams turned to look out the window, seemingly lost in the past.

Nearly an hour had passed in silence before Mr. Williams spoke again.

"Funny place, the Caribbean."

Not being able to hold my curiosity, I asked, "Really? Why's that?"

Mr. Williams looked over at me with a jolt in his pale blue eyes, as if he had forgotten I was sitting next to him.

"Oh, I was just thinking back to my tour. I was a diver you know—lots of wrecks in that area. Hurricanes," he answered to my questioning look. "They churn stuff up when they pass. Lots of debris, old wrecks—some even a couple hundred years old, if not older. You must have heard some of the stories, Maxwell, right? About sunken ships filled with treasure and all that?" Mr. Williams asked with a sparkle in his eyes.

"Yeah, the ones filled with stolen Incan gold and all that," I replied, choosing to ignore the incorrect use of my first name.

A sudden excitement seemed to fill the old man, who didn't seem quite as old as he had an hour ago. "Oh, there's more than just gold in those waters, long before any Spanish, and you can take my word for it," he stated matter-of-factly.

The bus pulled to a sudden stop. Mr. Williams stood up suddenly, surprising me (the old man was faster than he looked and more than a little mysterious). He then squeezed by me, clutching his bag to make his way into the aisle. he turned around to offer me his hand.

"Nice meeting you, Maxwell," he said with a twinkle in his pale eyes before heading out with the crowd. I grabbed the bag of peanuts he had left on the seat to return them.

I never did meet the strange old man again.

* * *

I would have given almost anything to be back on the plane after spending the day chasing after Matt and Jayne. I couldn't help thinking about the plane ride, nice and peaceful, and all the peanuts I wanted. Anything had to be better than this; it was like trying to keep two rabid monkeys still.

I had expected them to run around all the local tourist hotspots in Nassau, but I never wanted to be their chaperone. Since when was I the responsible one?

After following the pair around to a flea market, more pubs than I could recall, and even being asked to leave one of Nassau's many famous beaches (something involving Jayne, a girl, and her towel—best not to ask), I nearly collapsed on my bed in the small hotel we were staying at.

Lying back with my body spread out comfortably, I thought it was about time to call it a day until Jayne walked out of the bathroom.

"You guys ready?" he asked, looking from me lying on the bed to Matt sitting at the small table fishing around in his bag.

"For what?" I exclaimed, sitting up.

"Don't know. Want to go to the pub downstairs?"

"Sure," Matt replied with excitement.

"Max?" Jayne asked expectantly.

"No, you guys go. I think I'm going to call it a day," I said, lying back down and closing my eyes. I was thankful just to get a few hours of rest (which was the point of a vacation, wasn't it?).

"You sure, Max?" Matt asked in disbelief.

After they left the room, I decided to spend the following day on my own, leave early and explore some of the more remote parts of the island. I had a sneaking suspicion that the Bahamas had more to offer than just your average tourist traps, if you just knew where to look.

Guessing correctly that Jayne and Matt wouldn't be back until long after midnight and would spend the morning a *very* deep sleep, I had no problems sneaking out, making sure to grab my aviators before I left.

Stepping out of the hotel, I took a deep breath of freedom and turned left. I had spotted a small business the other day that rented scooters, and I figured that I might get one and explore some of the more isolated, locals' only spots. Maybe do some snorkeling while I was at it.

After paying the owner a rather overpriced rental fee, I took the keys for an overused, slightly rusted red Vespa. I turned the ignition and gunned the little electric motor for all it had, taking off down the busy street. Not much power but you couldn't buy this kind of freedom (well, technically you could—it cost $25.50 an hour—but I didn't think it was necessary to include that, and besides, after a bit of haggling, the owner had let me borrow some snorkeling gear free of charge).

Exiting the city, I couldn't think of anything better than driving down the coast, hugging roads outside Nassau, on the little Vespa. Sometimes you just need to get away and be on your own for a little while. I couldn't help smiling at the thought as the warm tropical air pelted my hair and my white button-down shirt flapped in the manmade wind.

After nearly an hour cruising down the coast enjoying my newfound freedom from Matt and Jayne, I figured it was time to break out the snorkeling gear and check out some of the local wildlife. Without seeing any sign of life on or off the road for the last ten minutes, I reckoned I was about as far from civilization as possible on the small island. I had never really minded being alone and was quite used to it these days; sometimes I even preferred it.

After rounding a rather tight bend a bit too quickly, I emerged with a breathtaking view of the ocean before me. Guessing that this was as good a spot as any, I pulled the Vespa over, skidding slightly in the sand by the road, turned off the little whining engine to give it a well-deserved break, and headed down to the deserted shore after kicking off my shoes.

Enjoying the sand between my toes, I stripped off my cargo pants and shirt and flopped down on the morning sand. Riding the Vespa was fine, but even at this time of day, the climbing sun still managed to make me sweat almost immediately.

I had only lain on the sand for a few minutes before my stomach started growling. In my haste to sneak out of the room quietly and unnoticed, I had forgotten to grab some breakfast. A silly mistake, but not one that I felt like correcting now that I was here. Deciding to take my mind off my hunger and with the sweat now clinging to every pore on my body, I grabbed the snorkeling gear in my bag, annoyed that the flippers were a bit tight (I made a mental note to be more patient), and headed out into the clear, warm waters of the Caribbean.

Looking out to the endless expanse, I was glad that Jayne had persuaded me to come along. Fixing my mask and snorkel on, I dived in. Being an experienced scuba diver, I was familiar with the ocean world, but it was still an amazing and enjoyable experience.

Having never dived in the Caribbean before, I was

astounded at the diverse wildlife swimming in and around the shallow coral reef—clownfish, angelfish, sergeant majors, lionfish, needlefish, and even a small eel poking its head out from behind some brain coral. The sheer amount of color and life was remarkable.

The sun was directly overhead when I first saw it.

Or thought I saw it—something shiny, like metal, glinting in the sand far below. Looking in that general direction I saw nothing…

Until yes, there, maybe twenty feet down at the very edge of the small reef. Swimming out farther, I took a deep breath and dived down.

Coming to the edge of the reef where I thought I had seen the reflection, I looked around. There was nothing out of the ordinary here, just sand (being now too deep for coral) stretching out in the deep.

With the need for air quickly overtaking my brain, I decided to wait a few more seconds before surfacing, just in case a slowly passing wave overhead managed to reflect the sun off whatever it was, probably nothing but a piece of trash. God knows man has thrown enough of that into the world's oceans.

Right before I was about to turn and head for the surface—there—I saw it!

Four feet in front of me and on my left, definitely a piece of metal, a little metal ball maybe, about half the size of my fist.

Swimming toward it and ignoring the need for fresh oxygen, I reached out for the little ball of metal. Digging my hand into the sand, I gripped what felt like a handle.

What on earth was buried here?

With my lungs burning for oxygen at this point, I gave a good tug and pulled out—I couldn't believe it—a sword!

What on earth was this doing here?!

I let out several large bubbles of air in surprise.

Bad mistake.

With my lungs now screaming for air, I swam for the surface, the sword awkwardly clutched in my right hand against my chest and momentarily forgotten.

Kicking hard and using my left hand as best as I could, I swam desperately for the surface overhead. What was I thinking? Why did I stay down so long? I could have dived back down. This was not the way I had planned to meet my end.

As the corners of my vision began to darken, I broke the surface and breathed in a mixture of air and salt water.

It was the best taste in the world, I thought—that is, until I began coughing out the salt water I had inhaled. But I didn't care. I was alive.

And I had the sword.

The sudden realization hit me like a ton of bricks as my oxygen-deprived brain began working again.

The sword.

Swimming sideways with one arm and the other still clutching the sword, I made my way to shore. I was exhausted to say the least, and I would be lying if I said nearly drowning hadn't scared me.

After several minutes, I kicked my flippers off and made my way back to shore. Throwing myself down on the soft sand, I took a deep breath to steady my nerves; I suddenly noticed my hands shook.

Sitting up, I looked over at the sword I had let drop beside me carelessly. Picking it up with both hands a little more carefully, I took my first good look at it.

Looking at it now, I was surprised my brain was able to tell what it was down there. The sword was double-edged with a dull, tapered point and about seventy-five inches long, the blade itself maybe sixty inches. The knobbed hilt and the ball at the end both appeared to be made out of a different metal than the blade itself, but unfortunately, being in the ocean for so long had corroded the entire sword (and the slimy barnacles and seaweed covering it didn't help uncover its secrets).

Suddenly I heard a truck engine coming steadily toward me down the road and decided (for reasons unknown to me) that I would rather not have anybody know about my discovery just yet.

Carefully wrapping the sword in my towel, I just barely managed to squeeze it into my backpack as a couple of locals packed into the bed of a small pickup rolled by. I waved to them, being careful to keep my treasure hidden behind me, just in case.

Getting dressed quickly, I revved up the scooter and took off back to the hotel. A small towel covered the bulge sticking out of my backpack.

After an hour of swerving traffic, which nearly involved hitting a tourist bus in Nassau, I, upon returning the scooter and grabbing a sandwich at a street-side shop, headed back to the hotel.

I hadn't bothered to bring my laptop to Nassau, but luckily for me, Jayne didn't like staying in anything but four-star hotels, preferably five (they were both a bit too fancy for my taste, especially since they screamed, "I'm a tourist, come rob me," but I had to admit, not a bad change of pace from time to time). And most four-star hotels had a business center, complete with a computer and Internet connection.

I wasn't entirely sure what I was looking for as I started up the Internet browser, but I was sure that I had something pretty important, if not valuable. And I was sure *somebody* on the island would be able to help me *quietly*. I wasn't looking for some media frenzy.

A sudden memory of the old man I had met came back to me: "Oh, there's more than just gold in those waters, long before any Spanish, and you can take my word for it."

After several minutes of perusing numerous websites and quite a few old articles, I discovered a link to an old newspaper clip from *The Nassau Guardian,* dated about fifteen years ago. The headline read:

## Ten Years Hunting For Junk?

Jack Kelley, 38, treasure hunter or junk collector? Mr. Kelley, being a noteworthy doctorate graduate of UC-Berkeley in the field of underwater archeology and currently residing at the Nassau Yacht Haven Marina on his yacht, *Quaero*, has once again astounded the world with his latest find.

The treasure hunter, having spent years fruitlessly searching the waters of the Bahamas, flabbergasted (some would say conned) the world by claiming to have found the famous lost wreckage of the *El Dorado.* The ship sank on July 4, 1502, with nearly all hands and her $3 million horde, including the legendary solid gold table of Bobadilla, weighing in at 1.5 tons.

After making the claim and letting the world hold its breath for several days, Mr. Kelley had the audacity to hold a public hearing to apologize for making a mistake and not finding the lost treasure.

Several of Mr. Kelley's close colleagues, who chose to remain anonymous, claimed that, "Jack's been slowly losing it for years," and "He's become obsessed with finding something for years…I don't think there's anything he wouldn't do to finally make his name."

When questioned repeatedly by reporters as to what he did find, the recently divorced Mr. Kelley reluctantly said, "It was the wreck of an old shrimp boat."

Mr. Kelley's financial backers pulled out shortly after his announcement, leaving Mr. Kelley humiliated in the eyes of academia and archeologists. He is now without any financial backing and utterly broke.

The article included an old picture of Jack Kelley in front of *Quaero*, a modified sixty-foot sea trawler. I vaguely recalled from my early Latin classes as a child that *quaero* meant "to search," a fitting name.

The yacht had a large elbow pipe at the end, big enough to fit a man inside, and only a little rust on her otherwise pristine blue steel hull. The picture must have been taken before the *El Dorado* disaster, I figured, since the Kelley in this photograph was smiling with his healthy, clean-shaven face.

My instinct told me this was someone who might be able to give me some answers *and* was not likely to go blabbing to the press. I hated the press. I had hated them ever since I was ten, and I had the feeling that Jack Kelley didn't have much respect for them either.

Failing to find a current address online or with the help of the hotel's concierge, I decided to try the marina listed in the article as a last resort before I looked for someone else to help me identify the mysteries of the sword.

It was too late to head over to the marina today so I decided to go to bed and hit the marina early the next morning. I had a sneaking suspicion that Jayne and Matt weren't going to be back until the early morning again so I didn't think I would have any trouble sneaking out again.

After a restless night filled with lost treasure and swordfights, I awoke early the next morning to find I had the bedroom all to myself. Clearly my two friends were still having a good time (a very good time most likely, unless they were in prison) somewhere in downtown Nassau. I pulled back my sheets revealing the sword, still wrapped in my beach towel, lying just where I had left it beside me.

After a quick breakfast in the hotel's dining room, I headed outside with directions in hand to go rent my favorite red Vespa. The owner looked quite happy to see me, but then, what storeowner didn't mind return paying customers (especially when they rented an hourly bike for a whole day). If only he knew how many close calls I had had yesterday, I thought, paying the happy Nassauan.

Situated next to Bay Street by the busy Nassau Harbor, the Nassau Yacht Haven Marina was one of the larger marinas in the Bahamas.

Parking my scooter next to the dull yellow, two-story yacht club, I made my way to the rear entrance next to the harbor. The numerous piers in the harbor were filled with scores of motor and sailboats all of shapes and sizes from around the world. I wondered where to start my search.

"Can I help you?" someone asked in a heavy French accent, making me jump. I looked up and saw a small, shirtless man leaning over the blue railing of one of the small personal balconies that lined the club's second floor.

"Hey, yeah," I said with some uncertainty. "I'm looking for Jack Kelley. Does he still live here?"

He took a casual puff from his cigarette. "Yes, he does, pier trois, last boat on the end," he said, holding up three fingers and pointing to the left.

"Thank you," I replied, setting off for pier three.

After walking to the end of the pier, I finally saw the *Quaero* behind a large catamaran.

Rucksack over one shoulder, I stood before it, examining what was left of the once proud vessel.

The boat had indeed seen better days. In the newspaper picture, the *Quaero* looked almost brand new. Now she was in desperate need of a paint job, showing clear signs of long neglect; her steel was mainly composed of rust. I was amazed that the sea trawler was still afloat, considering that her lines were rotting away and there was enough garbage scattered around the deck to fill a small Dumpster.

My eyes lingered on the ship's faded name, *Quaero*.

Before I had the chance to call out and see if anybody was onboard, a voice interrupted.

"You lost, kid?"

I turned around, surprised that anybody could sneak up behind me so quietly; but then, being barefoot had a few advantages.

I took a second to study the man. This was clearly a much different Jack Kelley than the one from the paper. Now in his early fifties, he looked much more worn down than the young, enthusiastic treasure hunter in the newspaper article. It probably didn't help his appearance that he was in need of a shave and a good bath. The man had a rather unpleasant smell about him—or that may have been his clothes. His dirty wife-beater was almost rags, and his shorts weren't in much better condition.

"Are you Jack Kelley?" I asked hesitantly.

Kelley looked me up and down once, seeming to take me in as well, before he walked past me and jumped onboard to disappear below deck.

"Well, you coming?" he called.

Hesitating for only a moment, I decided to take my chances. Grabbing onto the rusty railing, I hopped onboard to follow the mysterious Jack Kelley into the belly of the beast, as it were. I smiled at my little joke and silently hoped I would end up in better hands than Jonah.

Climbing down the worn steps into the saloon, I saw evidence that the *Quaero* was indeed once a proud and pristine ship in its day. It's a shame that Kelley let the ship go like this, I thought. Numerous old books were thrown around the ship, and even more nautical charts and maps, every now and then covering a filthy garment. Didn't the man ever bother to do his laundry?

The ship was revealing itself to be a small treasure trove of reclaimed artifacts from the world's oceans. As I looked around, I saw handmade necklaces hanging from the ceiling, a few old coins thrown around, a restored Spanish conquistador helmet (I wondered where that was from), and numerous pictures and newspaper clippings with a much younger Jack Kelley—a man trapped in his glory days.

There were pictures of Kelley receiving his PhD from Berkeley, finding some coins (probably the very same ones that were now thrown carelessly around the cabin), and countless others of a young, smiling archeologist shaking hands with locals, academics, and heads of state. Another time, another world.

Suddenly, Jack Kelley emerged from the bow wiping his hands on a dirty rag. That answered the laundry question.

"Well, what do you want, kid?" Kelley asked in an accusing voice.

I hesitated a moment before answering. Could I really trust this man?

Well, what choice did I have?

"I was wondering if you could help me, Mr. Kelley. You see—"

"Just Kelley," he interrupted.

"Sorry, Kelley then," I retorted. The man's lack of manners was starting to raise my temper. I counted to five in my head before continuing. "I understand you're an archeologist, or a treasure hunter if—"

"Well, you heard wrong then," Kelley interrupted again.

"Sorry?" I asked, slightly confused.

Kelley threw the dirty rag onto the bench beside him and looked out the port hatch to the harbor.

"You need to find something to be either," he said quietly, not looking at me. The fight had suddenly gone out of him.

Deciding that now was as good a time as any, I carefully removed my pack and pulled out the sword, which was still bundled up in my beach towel.

Kelley, breaking out of his reverie, looked at me as I placed the bundle on his small, littered table.

"What do you got there?" he asked, overcome with curiosity as to what I had brought onboard his ship.

"Open it," I said simply with a small smile.

Seeing my resolve, Kelley unwrapped the bundle, revealing the degraded sword. I couldn't help but smile at the sight of Kelley's mouth hanging open.

After several long seconds, Kelley asked quietly, "Where did you get this thing, kid?"

"Actually, I found it off the coast at—"

Interrupting me for the third time in as many minutes, he said, "Give me a minute." Then he disappeared into the bow of the ship.

He was definitely an interesting fellow, I thought before Kelley returned with a cardboard box. He swiped the table clean, sending books and maps tumbling to the floor. Turning on an overhead lamp, Kelley then pulled a magnifying glass out of the box and began examining the sword up and down.

Several minutes passed in silence as Kelley looked the sword over carefully, with only the occasional "oh" and "ah" breaking the silence. I had no idea what the man was looking at. I had spent half the night studying it in my room, trying to figure out its secrets, but the blade had stubbornly refused. It was so badly corroded and covered with smaller barnacles that it was impossible to tell anything about it. And I wasn't about to start cleaning it and risk any damage to it.

In all the drama and excitement that had ensued, I hadn't noticed how warm it was on the *Quaero*. I backed away from Kelley to lean by the steps; a slight breeze cooled me, but only a little.

"So come on, Kelley, what do you make of it?" I asked irritably after several more minutes passed. Honestly, would it kill the man to put some kind of air conditioning on this boat? The humid Bahaman air was starting to make me sweat.

"*Hmmm*. Interesting," Kelley said quietly as he stood bent over the small table, still examining the sword.

"What's interesting?" I exclaimed impatiently. Realizing the heat was starting to affect me, or maybe it was just Kelley, I took a deep breath to regain my composure. I was always good at keeping my head and wasn't about to let one man ruin that. "So what do you think?" I asked a little more calmly.

Kelley glanced over his shoulder at me with a slight smirk on his face before turning back to his examination of the sword. "Here's a free piece of advice, kid. If you want to get into the archeology business someday, you are going to have to learn a little patience."

After about a minute during which I stared at the back of Kelley's head with an increased amount of annoyance, I was starting to wonder if this guy really was the expert that I had thought he was. I was considering leaving and trying my luck elsewhere before I remembered that Jack

Kelley really was my only chance.

I couldn't risk passing the sword through customs, and after reading the article about Kelley, I knew the press definitely wouldn't keep quiet if word got out from another expert on the small island. And I was assuming Kelley had no love for the paparazzi.

Quite suddenly, Kelley laid his magnifying glass on the table beside the sword. Placing his hands on either side of his small examination table, he leaned over the sword, seemingly in deep thought. He then let out a long sigh before speaking to me.

"Where the hell did you find this thing, kid?" he asked rather quietly.

Somewhat taken aback at this new, quiet attitude, I promptly answered his question. "On the northeast side of the island, at the edge of the reef of all places." I wasn't quite ready to place all of my trust in Kelley in case I was wrong about him, but a small lie about where I had found the sword shouldn't cause any problems.

"I was doing some snorkeling when I saw something shimmering on the sea floor. Frankly, it was a miracle that I even saw the thing, considering that most of it was buried in the sand. You can imagine my surprise when I pulled it out of the sand," I finished with a smile. Saying it now reminded me of the tale of King Arthur that my mother used to read to me as small child; it always was one of my favorite stories.

When Kelley didn't say anything and resumed his examination, I figured now was as good a time as any to ask the big question. "So what do you think it is? Looks like some old European sword to me."

It took a moment before Kelley replied. "I agree actually, but that's not the weird part."

I stood up to get a better look at his perplexed look. "What's the weird part, Kelley?"

Kelley looked over at me and said, "Well, this isn't some fifteenth-century Spanish or French blade that you would expect to find in the Caribbean. This looks older—a lot older in fact—and unless I'm mistaken and my history is totally out of whack, it looks more like…early Roman, second or third century. Hard to tell until we get this blade cleaned up some more."

"Roman," I repeated in surprise.

Kelley continued as though I hadn't said anything.

"Nothing like this should be anywhere near the New World," Kelley said as he stood up and began pacing the small cabin.

"How the hell this thing ended up way out here, on the wrong side of the Atlantic, is anybody's guess. Frankly, I'm amazed it's in as good of condition as it is. You may have something really valuable here, kid, if it proves to be authentic, of course. I reckon there'll be more questions than answers unfortunately." Kelly paused for moment. "I wish I could tell you more about it, kid, but frankly this looks to be out of my time period. I have a friend, old colleague really, who may be able to tell us more about it, maybe answer some more of those questions for us. So what do you say, kid? Feel like going on a trip?"

"Trip? Where does he live?" I asked with rising excitement.

"Oxford," Kelley replied matter-of-factly.

"England?"

Kelley threw me a look that said, *No, Texas, genius.*

"Can't we just call him?"

Kelley laughed. "No, we can't *call*. It has to be examined in person."

It only took a few seconds for me to think about it. "Hell, why not."

I could afford to cut my Caribbean break short to solve a two-millennia mystery. It wasn't like there was anybody to object.

I looked up to find that Kelley had returned to his examination of the sword and was attempting to carefully clean the blade above the hilt.

"What's your friend's name?" I asked. Kelley stopped his work to look at me.

"Oh. Wilson. Dr. Edward Wilson," he said with some distain. "He's a professor of archeology at Trinity College. Brilliant, arrogant, and he definitely likes the finer things in life," Kelley said with a grin. "Anyway, the man really knows his stuff, got to give him that. Tries to research a very broad area of archeology, which is why he's a good place to start. Course, I don't know how much help he'll be. He might be able to point you in the right direction though. I'll give him a call if you want, see if he's interested, but I guarantee you he will be. He can't resist a good mystery, if I recall right."

"Sure, give him a call." I couldn't help noticing that Kelley had started using "you" instead of "us."

"You're not interested in coming?" I asked. Without realizing it, I had taken a liking to Kelley and could use his help.

Kelley looked rather touched at the question but said, "Sorry, kid, I had my shot. This is your adventure."

*Adventure.* The magic word.

"Wait here a minute. I'll go find his number," Kelley said as he headed into the bow, expertly maneuvering through the crowded confines of his swaying ship. I suddenly wondered how many years he had been living on this ship alone, searching for his fortune, *his* adventure.

Kelley was still talking from the forward cabin, but I wasn't paying him any thought as I turned my attention back to the sword still lying on the table. More specifically, I was focusing on the spot where Kelley had cleaned the blade.

The sword had been filthy, but Kelley had carefully cleaned off some of the crud to reveal a strange assortment of characters on the blade. Most were still covered and indiscernible from the corrosion, so I had no idea how far up the blade they went.

They were a bizarre collection of lines and circles with some small Latin characters thrown in, and what I recognized as possibly some Arabic symbols, but I couldn't be sure.

It may have been a language, but it was like nothing I had ever seen before. My instincts told me, although I didn't register it at the time, that this was something new and important, and these characters only added to the mystery of the sword.

Suddenly Kelley reemerged triumphant from the next room, holding up a crumpled piece of paper. "Knew I had it somewhere, though I think it might be time to finally clean this place a little."

I was too taken with the sword to comment, so I simply asked, "Kelley, what do you make of these markings on the sword?"

"Oh, those? Honestly? I have no idea. Hell, kid, it could be a treasure map for all I know."

CHAPTER THREE

# THE WILSON DILEMMA

After another plane ride, a bit longer than the last one to be sure, I arrived at London Heathrow airport tired and a little jet-lagged but excited. After a short call by Jack Kelley to Dr. Wilson telling him in only the vaguest terms what I had found, Dr. Wilson had arranged for a meeting with me two days later at Trinity College.

Dr. Wilson must indeed have some pull in the archeological world, I thought, because I had no trouble getting the sword through airport security and customs, which he had promised would be the case on the phone.

After waking Matt and Jayne up upon my return from Kelley's, I told them I was going home because of a family emergency. Jayne, looking suspicious, was about to ask me what sort of family emergency I could possibly be having before seeing the sharp look I gave him, and he held his tongue in frustration. He could be quite observant when he wanted to be.

I deeply trusted my close friends, whom I could count on one hand, especially Jayne (for reasons I still didn't understand), but a warning from Kelley left me not wanting to involve my two friends.

Holding on to my shoulders, Kelley had said, "Listen, kid, don't make the mistake I did. Keep that sword to yourself, and keep it secret—from everyone. Don't even share it with your own mother if you don't have to. Good luck, kid," he finished, shaking my hand before I left.

I was sorry to go. Despite our awkward beginning, I had taken a liking to the retired archeologist and was sad at the life the cards had dealt him; if anything ever became of this sword, I swore to myself that Jack Kelley would reap some of the rewards.

So I took Kelley's advice to heart and told no one. I knew my two friends would be hurt that I had lied to them (especially Jayne) and would have gladly come with me if I had asked, but for reasons I didn't fully understand, I needed to do this alone. They would be all right with out me slowing them down.

I was slightly nervous at GBIA when security had asked to see what was in the duffel bag I was carrying, but before I could start arguing, whatever pull Dr. Wilson had chose that moment to arrive in the form of an anxious-looking security officer carrying a printout. I had no idea what the sheet of paper said, and before I could ask, I was whisked through security to my departure gate, no questions asked. It was all very unusual. I wasn't even asked to go through the metal detector or to take off my shoes—not that I minded of course. Just what kind of man—an archeologist, of all people—has that kind of influence?

But those thoughts were quick to leave my head because I was soon immersed in the excitement of England. As enthusiastic as I was to explore London and some of its surroundings, I decided that the old axiom "Work before play" was the best route to take here.

So with a brief sigh I boarded the Oxford Tube for an hour-long bus ride for none other than the academic heart of England—Oxford.

After checking in to a small hostel and grabbing a

few much-needed hours of sleep (luckily the hostel was empty during the day), I headed out into the late afternoon sun for my meeting with Dr. Wilson.

I thought I'd stretch my legs a little and take in the sights on the few miles to Trinity College.

I'd always loved Europe. I felt at home here. The sights, the people, the culture—I loved it all. I hadn't been on the continent since I was a small boy with my parents, but I remembered parts of it well, mainly the smell. I smiled; something in the air just smelled special to me. I was probably imagining it, but I didn't care.

"The city of dreaming spires." Oxford truly live up to its motto, I thought as I made my way down the famous High Street.

Looking up at the arched oak doors of Trinity College, I took a moment to appreciate the sixteenth-century neo-classical walls before entering the main entrance. The porter directed me across the campus's expansive quadrangle to a small, worn door at the rear of the courtyard marked in small, bunched letters:

DR. EDWARD WILSON
PROFESSOR OF ARCHEOLOGY

I hesitated for a moment, not knowing what to expect, before knocking quietly. I wasn't sure, but I could have sworn I heard a soft grunt followed by quick shuffle of papers as if someone had suddenly woken up. After a few seconds with no reply, I knocked a bit harder.

"Yes? Enter," the deep voice said.

Upon entering, my eyes darted from one corner of the office to another. The office was small, and the rich, dark oak walls were beginning to show their age, but neither of these facts had slowed the good doctor down.

The office reminded me of Kelley's boat with the numerous old books and texts scattered around the room and there being no more room on the bookcase that covered the entire back wall behind the desk. The room also featured an impressive collection of ancient artifacts from all over the ancient world, ranging from African ceremonial head masks to a preserved bronze statue of the Hindu god Vishnu.

However, unlike Kelley's floating laboratory, Dr. Wilson also chose to decorate his office with some of the finer points of life.

An expensive collection of fine liquors filled a small table in the corner of the room next to the bookcase. Framed articles and various awards covered the walls wherever they managed to find a space among the delicate artifacts and a painting by…I wasn't an art expert, but it looked like a Van Gogh. Surely a fake, I thought.

Unlike the rest of the office, the large executive desk with its deep maroon tufted chair was nearly spotless, except for the small green lamp in the center and a glass of what looked like scotch. The desk had dozens of rings set in the woodwork that would probably never come out from dozens of strong drinks over the years.

"Well, are you just going to stand out there?" the deep voice with a clear English accent asked.

I looked at the large (plump was the actually the word that first came to mind) man in a dark blue Armani suit standing behind his desk. The buttons on the vests strained from the burden of containing the man's mass and looked to be on the verge of failure. I held a laugh at the comical sight.

"Sorry," I said as I walked to the center of the office. "I'm Max Taylor, a friend of Jack Kell—"

"Ahh, yes, yes, so you're the young man Jack sent over," he interrupted through his thick mustache. "Absolutely wonderful surprise," Dr. Wilson said as he lumbered over to pour himself a drink. "Wonderful surprise that was. How is old Jack? Old, he's younger than me actually." He laughed before taking a gulp of his scotch. "I apologize. Would you care for a drink?" he said, pointing at the small table with his free hand.

"No, Doctor. I'm fine."

"You sure?" he asked before sitting down heavily in his century-old chair that creaked with the strain. I doubted the chair was ever designed to carry the weight.

"So," Dr. Wilson said after he made himself comfortable, "still hunting down silly treasure in the middle of the Atlantic, is he?"

"I don't really know. I was only there to—" was all I managed to get out before Dr. Wilson interrupted me again. What was it lately with people cutting me off midsentence?

"Well, that hardly matters anyway. Nice to see that he finally got over that silly little grudge of his anyway," Dr. Wilson said, taking another large gulp of scotch. The man was starting to turn red.

"Grudge?" I asked.

Dr. Wilson stood up to refill his glass before answering. "Oh, nothing serious. Just a little bit of harmless fun, nothing really. I honestly don't even remember." I doubted that. "It was over ten years ago, some silly joke about shrimp boats or some such thing during my presentation to the Archaeological Institute of America's annual conference, and he goes and storms out of the hall. Very embarrassing. Haven't seen him since actually." He took a drink. That probably explained why Kelley was so reserved during his short call with Dr. Wilson.

"But where are my manners now? Come, sit, sit," Dr. Wilson said, indicating the small inexpensive chair.

I took a seat before his desk, feeling very low to the ground and small, but then that was probably the point, especially with a man like Dr. Edward Wilson.

"Are you sure you wouldn't like some? Single-malt scotch made in Ireland, aged twelve years. Far better than that watered-down American stuff you must be used to."

"I'll take your word for it," I replied.

"Your loss," he said, taking a seat once again. "Well, enough pleasantries, I think, down to business. Jack said you found something very interesting, although he wouldn't give me any real details. Something about an old sword. You must have found something quite interesting to force Jack to call me." He smiled. "Well, come on there, let's have it."

I hesitated a moment before opening my duffel bag, suddenly looking up at Dr. Wilson. For just a split second, I could have sworn I saw a deep, almost longing look on his face before he noticed my gaze. The good doctor took another drink from his half-empty glass to mask the exchange.

Happening all too fast to be sure, I ignored my gut and opened the duffel bag to pull out the carefully wrapped sword. Luckily, it wasn't wrapped in my beach towel anymore; Kelley had been kind enough to rewrap it in several protective cloths for the trip. He had preferred to ship it but remarked that it was probably for the best if I kept an eye on it. I didn't think twice about it then, but I was starting to wonder if all this secrecy was necessary. Archeology might be more of a brutal game than I had thought.

I placed the sword on the desk in front of Dr. Wilson, who drained the rest of the glass (at least the second since I had arrived) and unwrapped the sword.

"Well, let's see what we ha—" Dr. Wilson stopped midsentence and stared at the sword. Carefully, he picked it up and turned it over to reveal the few distinguishable characters. He traced his fingers over them.

"Whe…where," he stuttered. "Excuse me," he said, quickly recovering his composure. "Where did you say you found this piece?"

"Near Nassau," I answered. Dr. Wilson already knew that from Kelley's call, so there was no point in lying. "What do you think of it?" I asked.

"Well, Maximilan."

"Just Max," I corrected.

"It is definitely an interesting piece, very early French."

"French!" I exclaimed in disbelief. "It looks more

Roman to me—and Kelley."

"Well, I'm afraid you're both mistaken," Dr. Wilson retorted, almost savagely. "But you must remember the Roman Empire did have a very large influence on modern-day France's territory. So, of course, there would be many similarities, such as in weapon design."

"And the markings?" I asked.

"Yes, I would say they are the personal markings of the French family who owned this blade," Dr. Wilson replied indifferently. It appeared the effects of the scotch had worn off quickly. "Similar to writing your name on a treasured heirloom, you could say. Handed down through the ages, father to son. I suppose it must have been lost in a shipwreck at sea."

"Are you sure?" I asked, hoping this was a joke. What a waste this little *adventure* was turning out to be.

"Quite," Dr. Wilson said, maybe a little too quickly.

"Not much value, I'm afraid. Poor metal, it's already corroded rather well."

"Really?" I replied. "Kelley said it looked to be in remarkably good condition, nothing a bit of cleaning couldn't fix."

"Are you an expert in artifact restoration?" Dr. Wilson asked coldly. "No?" he said sarcastically. "Well, if you were, you would see that this cheap metal wouldn't survive *any* restoration attempts. It would just fall apart."

At this point, I noticed the hairs on the back of my neck were standing. Why was he being so defensive? Was there more to this sword than he was letting on? Probably. French heirloom, my ass.

"Remember, if the hairs on the back of your neck start standing, start running." I couldn't remember where I had heard this, but I was ready to believe it.

"I'd be happy to buy it from you. The university is always looking for old relics to display. You would be given credit for its discovery of course," Dr. Wilson said, interrupting my thoughts.

"Umm," I said, caught off guard. "Thanks, but I think I'll hold on to it for a while, if that's all right."

Dr. Wilson looked slightly annoyed by the news but just smiled and said, "Of course. Why, it's your property now. What is that American saying? Finders keepers," he finished with a hollow chuckle.

I just smiled in reply and began rewrapping the sword before Dr. Wilson's now poorly masked hungry eyes.

"Well, thank you so much for your help, Doctor. I apologize if I took up too much of your valuable time," I said.

"No, no, not at all. Quite happy to help," he replied indifferently as I placed the sword in my duffel.

"One moment, Maximilan," he said seconds before I walked out door.

It's Max! I thought angrily, wishing I had been a little faster out the door. But I bit my tongue, turned on my heel, and answered politely, "Yes?"

"Where can I reach you? In case I should happen to think of anything else of interest," Dr. Wilson said.

"I don't know the number," I answered skillfully, wanting nothing more than to get out of there.

"That's fine, the name will do," Dr. Wilson replied lightly.

"The Stag Inn," I replied. It was the first hotel that came to my mind. I remembered passing it on the way to Trinity.

"Oh, excellent. Just down the street. I'll leave a message with them if I think of anything over the next few days."

I swore at my own stupidity. If I had to make up the hotel I was staying at, couldn't I have thought of something a little more remote and harder to check? I was glad I was at least quick enough not to tell Dr. Wilson my real address. Just what was so special about this sword? Maybe it was worth a fortune and Dr. Wilson wanted the money for himself. I'd have to find another expert who could be a little more honest.

"Until we meet again then," Dr. Wilson said as I left.

My first impulse was to get as far away as I could, but I decided to play it smart and wait a few seconds against the door I had purposely left ajar. Maybe Dr. Wilson would let something slip, give me some sort of clue about his motive. That decision turned out to be one of the best I had ever made. In fact, it probably saved my life.

Just before I was about to call it quits and leave, I heard the old tufted chair creak as Dr. Wilson stood up.

From the sound of glass striking, I was pretty sure the good doctor was pouring himself another drink.

Suddenly I jumped back, afraid that Dr. Wilson had caught me snooping. Then I realized he was talking on the phone.

"It's Wilson. Yes, yes, I know, unless it's important," he said. "Will you shut up and listen? I found it…*the key*!"

Key? What key, I thought. Maybe this had nothing to do with my apparently worthless sword. I decided to listen in a few more seconds before departing.

"Well, no," Dr. Wilson continued. "I don't have it. Some stupid kid has it."

Stupid kid! I bit my lip. It was probably best not to be discovered right now.

"Yes, do it….The Stag Inn, but I think he was lying….Yes, do that….Good, call me when's it done and keep it *quiet.*" Dr. Wilson hung up the phone.

"Shit," I whispered.

I didn't like the sound of that. I turned quietly and high-tailed it off campus as fast as my legs could carry me. Was the sword really that valuable? Who was Dr. Wilson talking to? What on earth were they going to do to me *quietly*? Mug me? *Kill* me?

Just what was I getting into?

* * *

Deep inside a certain country, in a certain city, there was a certain room. Inside this room was a short rectangular table with seven chairs—three on either side and one at its head.

This was a room unlike any other. It had no windows, no electricity, and remained sealed for several years at a time. But not today. Today the room was full—well nearly. All but one chair was occupied. The only light in the otherwise pitch-black room came from a single candelabrum set in the center of the table casting a faint glow onto the room's occupants. The room was otherwise unadorned.

Secrecy was paramount. For millennia the council had maintained secrecy and exacted great pains to maintain it in this technological age. No electric devices were *ever* allowed in this room except for the bug sweepers. No cell phones to prevent eavesdropping by some unknown agent; no windows to prevent an optical bug; no electrical wires in the wall to hijack its power for long-term reconnaissance in anticipation of the day when the room may be occupied. No aides knew of this room. Even the men in the room had been required to succumb to strip searches in case of infiltration. In short, this was, with the possible exception of a nuclear missile silo, the safest and least suspecting room in the world.

Its building, hidden in plain sight in one of the world's holiest cities, likely housed one of the oldest and most secretive societies in world. It sat only a few hundreds yards from the pope himself.

In fact, had there still been a window—the original had been sealed up more than fifty years ago on the advent of electronic surveillance—it would have provided an amazing view of St. Peter's Square and the impressive Egyptian obelisk at its center as well as the more inspiring basilica rising over the square.

As it was, the view was long covered up for

paranoia's sake. A blank wall stood in its place, shrouded in the obscure darkness and repugnant musky odor of a room sealed and neglected for far too many years.

The candlelight did little to pierce the room's darkness, barely extending its reaches beyond the table's center to reveal six tailored designer suits, their owners' identities just beyond the illumination.

"Really, I don't see the point of these searches," a deep voice said, breaking the silence as he replaced his eighteen-karat cufflinks. "I feel like some common criminal."

"It's not like any of us is going to reveal what goes on in here," a second voice said.

"And what are we doing here?" a third older, raspy voice asked. "I don't like being woken up for nothing. After thirty years, I've only been here three times, and each time it's another dead end. I'm getting too old to waste my time on a child's fantasy."

"This is no fantasy," the second voice said. "We're part of a society that has been—"

"What?" the old voice interrupted. "You're still young, hopeful. I'm realistic. We haven't found a single clue since—"

"Enough," the man at the head of the table said. They all came to eerie silence. "And I'll remind you, gentlemen, that the security measures are in place for a reason and will *not* change." There was no argument; his word was law.

"And as to why we are here," he said, looking at the old man immediately on his right, everyone's face still hidden in shadow. "We have a lead. Wilson," he indicated the empty chair at the end of the table, "has come through, despite some of your previous…" He paused, searching for the right word. "*Misgivings* about him."

"Misgivings." The old man snorted quietly. "I still think it was a mist—"

"*Enough*," the voice yelled, slamming his fists on the table. Only the cracking of the candles' wicks broke the eerie silence that once again settled upon the room.

"What news then?" the second man asked after several seconds. "What has Wilson found?"

The man leaned back in his chair to regain his composure. "The key has been found."

The men gasped and looked around at each other, even though their gazes couldn't discern their own noses through the darkness.

"Is he sure? Why didn't he bring it?" the old man asked, regaining his nerve after the rebuke.

"He hasn't acquired it yet," the voice answered simply.

"What!" the old man exclaimed. "Then where is it?"

"Please, if you would let me explain," the voice said. He took the room's renewed silence as confirmation that he should continue. "It turns out, despite all of our searching and financial resources, that the key has been found, quite by accident in fact, by a boy."

"Where?" the second man asked curiously.

"Where we long suspected, I am happy to say. It turns out the story is true. The key was banished to the depths of the ocean far beyond the reaches of any who might ever try to discover its secrets. The key eventually found its way to the Caribbean until this boy," he paused, trying to recall the unimpressive name, "Max Taylor, found it and eventually brought it to Wilson to inquire of its origin."

"Strange that he made no mention of its discovery to the media," the second voice remarked. "It would have long been in our custody by now otherwise."

"That doesn't answer the question as to why *Wilson* hasn't brought it here now," the old man said in contempt.

"Because he let the boy leave with it," the voice answered. The gasps echoed around the room.

"Do you mean to tell us," the old man asked, "that he *held* it in his fat fingers and then just let him leave?"

The voice smiled, even though he knew the others couldn't see it. "Indeed." More gasps echoed around the room.

"I told you! I told this council we should never have let a *simpleton* like him have a seat on this council," the old man said.

"No matter," the voice said. "He had the foresight to at least contact me moments after the boy left, if not the prowess to retrieve it from him. The problem has been rectified, and I have already dispatched men to retrieve the key," he finished.

"And what if they are caught or fail?" the old man asked.

"Or realize what they have?" the second man chimed in.

"They won't," the voice said. "And *if* my men are caught or *fail*," a word he disliked using on his expensive and privileged tongue, "which is a rather large *if*, then they will have to be dealt with." He smiled again in the black. He was not used to failure or incompetence; both were dealt with severely and equally.

"And what of Wilson's failure?" the old man asked, already knowing the answer.

The voice smiled again. "Of course, old friend." It was as close as he dared to use the man's name in case any new, high-tech surveillance devices were in use (you could never be too careful in today's ever-changing technological world). "I will leave him up to you to deal with as you wish. His joining was, after all, always against your wishes and more experienced judgment," the voice said, appealing to the old man's ego. He had been right after all. Commoners had no right to be involved directly in this council, even ones as intelligent and connected as the late Dr. Wilson.

CHAPTER FOUR

# THE COLLISION

*I* hadn't gotten very far before hearing the screech of rubber behind me. Running, running, always running; I felt as if I'd been running all day, or at least all afternoon, but it must have only been a few minutes, a couple of miles at most. It was amazing how your perception of time could change with just a little running. A few minutes could feel like an hour. No time to think about that, I thought as I dodged a passing biker, the sound of rubber closer behind me in the crowded streets of Oxford.

After visiting the traitorous doctor, I had made a quick stop at the hostel to grab a few essentials, mainly my passport, which I had forgotten. Stupid mistake that I vowed never to let happen again.

After unceremoniously switching the sword into my old rucksack, I left as quickly as my legs could carry me, not even bothering to check out. Unfortunately Dr. Wilson's guys were better, far better than I had guessed (I supposed they did this sort of thing often).

After only two blocks, I was sure the black Audi was following me. Sure enough, the second I stopped to *tie my shoe* and check behind me in the display glass of a

Bloomsbury's, two men exited the car and walked toward me.

Just who was Dr. Wilson? What was so important about this stupid sword? And what on earth were those men (I wasn't even sure how many were watching me from behind the tinted car windows) planning to do to me?

Maybe I should just let them have the sword.

No. On second thought, maybe not.

I got up and started walking down the street, then rounded the nearest corner. I chanced a look behind me and noticed the two men, both wearing black suits (very cliché in my opinion), were closer than they had been moments before.

I picked up the pace, but it didn't help. The two men were nearly running, trying to end this as quickly and quietly as possible.

They were nearly on me, only a few feet away. I knew what I had to do, my feet carrying me before the thought had even entered my head.

And here I was now, running, running quite possibly for my life. I could feel the men gaining in their pursuit. Quite sad, I thought, considering they were wearing expensive Italian loafers. But impressive too.

Passing a trash can, I grabbed it and threw it to the ground, never losing an ounce of speed, hoping for anything to slow my nameless pursuers.

Hearing a crash behind me, I knew the desperate trick had worked, but I didn't take the chance to spare a second look. My second pursuer was still hot on my trail.

Suddenly, I felt a hand on my rucksack.

*The sword*!

I stopped unexpectedly, surprising my pursuer and causing him to bump into me. I momentarily hoped the sword was all right, but I had other things to worry about at the moment. The sudden stop had confused my pursuer, and I used his hesitation to my advantage, delivering a clean right hook squarely to the man's jaw.

The man was trained military—I had no doubt—but the sudden stop of his prey coupled with the unanticipated punch caused him to hit the ground hard like his associate. Oddly, the crash sounded very similar to the one his partner made, I thought with a smile.

Unfortunately, to my dismay, I wasn't able to enjoy the small victory. The man, who was built like an ox (just how could he run so fast?), started to rise, and I, once again, started to run. I didn't like running away from a fight, but I knew the odds just weren't in my favor today, especially with his buddy coming back to play.

"The little bastard!" the man screamed, getting back up as the Audi came to a screeching halt beside him. The door closed after him before he even finished the sentence.

Luckily, Oxford was a pedestrian's city and an automotive nightmare. As long as I didn't let them trap me in some dead-end alley, I'd be safe. Or at least I'd have a chance. They may have had speed, but speed wasn't part of the equation in Oxford, with its endless alleys barricaded against automobiles. But I was a stranger in the city, while the driver of the Audi clearly wasn't. Every time I came out of a crowded alley, I spotted the Audi aggressively turning the corner at the end of the street.

Running down the busy street, my heart pounding, I could hear the Audi's engine roaring right behind me. Surely they weren't going to run me over on a crowded street and risk damaging the sword, I thought. But then, if someone punched me in the jaw, I might want a little payback too.

An alley!

I bowed into it at the last second. Not a moment too soon, I thought, taking a precious moment to let my lungs breathe.

My short-lived break came to an end with the sound of heavy braking just past the alley. Why wasn't it ever that easy? Then I saw that the alley—the one I was standing in, the one that had quite possibly saved my life a few seconds ago—was also just wide enough for the black Audi to follow! My nightmare quickly becoming a reality, I gasped in horror as the Audi shot into view. The driver aggressively backed it into position, pointing the car right at me! Then I did the only thing I could do. I ran.

Halfway down the alley, I spotted a side street. Turning down it, I looked behind me to see the Audi race by. It was an impossible turn for them. That was close. They were getting—

Suddenly I smacked right into someone. I flipped over and landed on my back—thankfully not my head, I thought, which wasn't feeling too good at the moment. Cursing myself for not looking at where I was going, I rolled over to pick myself up. Shaking the stars out of my eyes, I looked to see if my unexpected victim had fared worse than me.

"Are you all r—" I stopped, momentarily lost for words, not really caring about the men chasing me, the sword on my back that was probably in a thousand pieces, the conniving Dr. Wilson, and all the other concerns that had besieged me over the last few days.

"What's the matter with you?! Are you blind?!" the tall brunette yelled in an English accent. Luckily, she seemed to be all right as she picked herself up from the ground and turned to her fallen scooter that I couldn't recall knocking over.

"Well, are you just going to stand there?" she asked harshly.

"Oh, right…sorry," I said awkwardly, helping her pick up the scooter. She seemed to be about my age and, judging by the textbook that still laid on the ground, a student in Oxford.

Suddenly we both looked up to the sound of brakes squealing at the other end of the narrow alley. Two men exited the Audi and started running toward me.

I was tired of running. If I couldn't get away on foot, than I was just going to have to borrow a ride. I noticed the keys were in the scooter's ignition jumped on.

"Just what do you think you're doing?" the girl asked, probably thinking I had some nerve.

One of the men pulled out a Glock handgun and fired a warning shot that echoed down the alley. I knew he was still too far away to get a clean shot, but I didn't want to still be here when he was close enough. I especially didn't want anyone else to get shot by accident because of me. Time to get out of here.

"What did you do?" the girl asked, realizing the warning shot was meant for me.

"Nothing," I replied, starting the scooter.

As much as I would have liked it, now wasn't the time for a lengthy conversation. Frankly, I was just glad these guys wore Italian loafers with their suits—must've made chasing someone a real pain.

"*What did you do*?" she asked again more forcefully, spinning me around by my shoulder to look me in the eyes.

"I'm telling you, *nothing*," I yelled back, all patience gone. "Let go!"

It was enough. I don't know why she did it. Maybe she saw the look of sheer terror in my eyes. Maybe she knew they would kill me if I were caught. Maybe she figured what chance did this American boy have in the congested streets of Oxford. But whatever her reason, she made the decision.

"Slide back," she yelled, surprising me.

I did it without complaint. There was no time. A bullet struck the ground before us, my pursuer realizing what I was about to do.

She gunned the little motor for all it was worth and headed back the way I came, burning rubber in the process.

"Hang on," she called back as an afterthought, the sound of bullets pinging off the ancient walls of Oxford.

Nearly falling off, I grabbed hold of the mysterious girl's waist as she gunned the poor scooter for every ounce of power it had.

I didn't care who she was or why she was helping

me. All I wanted was to rest, just for a second, to clear my head. I was falling into a daze, maybe even shock. They were shooting at me. Those men, in their expensive Armanis, were actually trying to shoot me in an alley and rob me. What was this—a movie? I just wanted it to end; this was not my idea of an adventure. *Adventure*. Who needed it? For the first time in my life, I would rather be at school.

Suddenly the scooter roared by the amazed shooter, who was changing clips, and pulled out of the alley back onto the busy street. Who was this girl? Was she crazy? It was one thing to run back toward the gunfire, but weaving in between cars, double-deckers, and bicyclists like a lunatic was another.

I tightened my grip on her waist as we drove between two Peugeots; it was a *very* narrow gap. Her hair flapped around my face. Shouldn't she be wearing a helmet? She drove like evasive driving was her life. After nearly running an old woman off the crosswalk, I spared a moment to see if the Audi had managed to follow us.

Nothing.

After a few more minutes of Audi-free pursuit, my mysterious heroine abruptly pulled over, giving the little scooter a much deserved break but idling the engine just in case.

She turned around, her blue eyes taking me in before she spoke.

"Now who are you, and why did I just risk my life for a criminal?"

"I'm not a criminal," I said irritated. "Do you think cops just go around trying to run you over and shoot you? And nobody asked you to help. I just wanted the scooter."

She smiled, catching me off guard. "We both know you'd never have been able to lose them without me," she said rather smugly.

It annoyed me.

Our heads twisted forward as a black Audi abruptly power-slid onto the street, heading straight for us.

"You sure about that?" I whispered into her right ear with only a hint of smugness.

She looked back at me, her gaze unwavering. "Do you trust me?"

"You suicidal?" I responded.

She smiled, her eyes meeting mine. I noticed they were an attractive shade of deep blue.

"I guess we're about to find out," she said, taking off straight for the Audi!

Just what on earth was she doing? Maybe she really was a nut job.

"What the hell are you doing?" I yelled in her ear over the increasing wind. "You can't play chicken with a four thousand–pound car!" If I was about to die, I might as well know what plan was.

"Get ready to jump!" she yelled, seconds before the imminent impact.

"What!" I screamed.

She really was a nut job. What were the odds?

"On three," she continued, ignoring my outburst, never taking her eyes off the Audi.

I knew I had no choice. Either take my chances with them or die with her. Well, at least I had some chance with her. This was just like jumping out of a plane, I told myself, except it wasn't. I knew that, but I wouldn't admit it. Pavement tended to hurt a lot more in this scenario.

"Two," she counted down.

Two? When had I missed one?

We were yards from each other. Neither driver was backing out of this dangerous game. A few pedestrians on the street were staring, the realization of what they were witnessing just starting to sink into their brains.

Only a split second separated me from having my brains scattered all over the Audi's windshield.

"Three!" the girl screamed.

I threw myself from the moving scooter as hard as I could, the ground rushing up to meet me. Luckily, instinct (and probably my skydiving training from a few years back) made sure I rolled, displacing my momentum and the energy of the jump.

Unfortunately for the occupants of the Audi (well, I wasn't going to lose any sleep over it), they hadn't fared so well. After seeing us jump from the scooter, the driver had panicked and swerved to avoid the motorbike. Had he stuck to his training and remembered his high school physics, he would have ended up with nothing more than a good dent in his bumper from the scooter.

But he had panicked, and the scooter had gone under his left wheel, causing the Audi to flip onto its roof, sliding until a steel light pole brought it to a grinding stop.

This chase was over.

I sat up on the pavement. I must have rolled over twenty feet and my head hurt, but I was all right, despite the bruises that were sure to appear by morning. I looked to where my apparent savior was sitting across the street, looking at me as if nothing had happened.

I picked myself up, as did the girl, and I met her in the middle of the confused street. We watched the people crowded around the Audi for a second before I broke the silence.

"Pretty sure I could have gotten away without crashing into them," I said.

We looked at each other and laughed.

She held out her hand. "I'm Emma."

I shook it. "Max. Pleased to meet you."

We looked back at the new commotion coming from the wreck and saw a man crawling out. I recognized him immediately; he was the man I had punched earlier, the same man who had also tried to shoot me in the alley before Emma saved me. I had to give it to him; the man could take a beating.

"I think it's time to go," I said, the distant alarm of a siren in the distance adding to the situation.

Emma offered no argument. "I think you're right."

Nightfall had set in before we stopped wandering the endless maze of Oxford. We were both tired and more than a little worse for wear, but I wasn't about to put my guard down until I was sure we weren't being followed.

Emma had followed me for over an hour, zigzagging through narrow alleys, losing ourselves in crowded streets, and even grabbing a few buses around the city. All the while, I kept checking over my shoulder for a glint of metal, the tap of Italian leather, the swish of Armani fabric. Emma might have considered telling me I was being paranoid, but didn't I have a right to be after all I had been through?

"Come on, we can rest in here," I said, directing her into the nearest pub.

"You're not trying to get me intoxicated are you?" Emma asked with a weary smile.

I was too exhausted to respond and plopped down at a secluded table in the back.

Taking a seat, Emma noticed me warily eyeing the door.

"I think we finally lost them," I said.

"I think we lost them a while ago, Max, especially after that accident," Emma responded softly.

I just grunted, my eyes glued to the door as a middle-aged man walked through for a drink at the bar.

Emma placed her hand over mine.

"*Max*," she called, breaking my trance. "Calm down."

I looked at her, then down at her hand. Emma pulled away, blushing slightly.

"Now, will you tell me why I just risked my life for you?" Emma said, trying to change the subject.

"My irresistible smile," I responded with a grin.

Emma laughed, the awkward tension gone as quickly as it had arrived.

"Seriously, Max. Please tell me you're not a serial

killer."

"No, I'm not a serial killer."

Emma waited. Looks like I wasn't getting off that easy.

"No," I said slowly. This was it. Should I tell her? Could I tell her? Could I *trust* her? After all we'd just been through, after all she had done to help me, to *save* me. She deserves to know, I thought. She deserves to know why we were chased and shot at across half of Oxford, what they wanted so badly. I made up my mind.

"They want this," I said, tapping the rucksack resting on my lap. I was scared to open it. Scared that after everything I, *we*, had just gone through, the sword was nothing but a pile of broken shards. After hundreds, maybe thousands of years in the ocean, how could it survive running around the city all day, let alone jumping off a speeding scooter?

"Drugs?" Emma asked in all seriousness.

"Dru— What? No!" Did I really look like some common criminal to her? Honestly, a thief, a serial killer, and now a drug runner. I suddenly rethought my decision.

"Actually, it's probably better if you don't know." I started to stand up. "Listen, I appreciate all of your help, really I do, but I've got to get out of here."

"Wait!" she yelled. Several customers looked over. What did a man have to do to get a quiet drink? "Wait," she asked a little more gently. "I risked my life, nearly got run over, got shot at, my scooter is destroyed—"

"That was you," I threw in.

"At least you can tell me why," Emma said, ignoring me.

I sat back down, placing the rucksack on the table before us. "Fair enough," I said.

I took a quick, discrete look around, just in case any Suits had walked in. Satisfied, I unzipped my pack and prepared to show her the sword, silently praying it was undamaged after all we'd been through.

I grabbed some of the wrapping and pulled it halfway out. Well, it felt solid enough, I thought.

"Well, it's not drugs at least," Emma said with a smile. "Not exactly worth dying for though, is it?" she asked, delicately touching the metal ball on the hilt that had started this crazy mess. "So how did we get mixed up in all this?"

I told her everything, starting from the beginning.

* * *

"And I thought I'd be dead before our next meeting," the old man wheezed as the council took their seats. "A second meeting in as many days; never would have imagined. Can't say I missed those strip searches though. Somebody's security has very cold hands," the old man added as he made himself comfortable. Some of the less important members laughed quietly at the end of the table.

The man seated at the head of the table simply smiled in the darkness of the room. In his old age, the old man's amusing outbursts were usually tolerated; he did deserve it in a way. He had been on this council longer than any of them and was getting on in years. The man's sources had informed him of the old man's failing health, and he deserved a bit of respect, especially after all he had accomplished in his long life. He had always looked up to the old man; he had been quite the business mogul in his younger days, ruthless, and a fact well known considering he was easily the wealthiest man in the room. And that was saying something, considering billionaire status was required to even be considered for an empty seat on this ancient council, with the exception of Wilson of course (and look at what a mistake that had turned out to be; commoners simply had no place in seats of power).

He glanced over at Wilson's empty seat.

Something would have to be done about that, or perhaps not. Perhaps after millennia of waiting, they would finally succeed. Perhaps this council, which had always consisted of wealthy, powerful men, would finally be at an end.

He folded his hands on the ancient oak table, the light from the candelabrum reflecting off his manicured fingers.

"I thank you all for meeting again on such short notice," he began. "I've just received word from Oxford." He paused for dramatic effect.

"And?" the man on his immediate left asked. He always was an impatient one. "Have they retrieved the key? Is it here?" he asked hungrily.

"No," he replied. "Unfortunately, the boy proved to be more troublesome than we expected. He managed to evade my men and disappear with the key."

The room was silent.

"Not very competent then, are they?" the man on his left replied nastily. "They can't even catch one boy."

The man was prepared for this. His authority was being challenged, and that was unacceptable.

"It appears we may have underestimated him. Of the four men sent, somehow he managed to kill two and critically injure a third."

"Not bad work for some kid, eh? Maybe we should hire him," the old man threw in.

The man smiled; the old man always had a way of breaking the tension. He supposed tension was bound to arise among powerful billionaires used to getting their way; *he* certainly was.

"And if your man talks? If word of this gets out?" one of the men at the end asked.

"Officially, there were no survivors," he responded.

"And unofficially?" the man asked nervously.

"I suppose you can say there's no difference," he replied with a shallow grin. *Fool*. By now every man here should know the price of failure. Maybe it was time for a major review of memberships.

"The problem we have now, gentlemen," he said,

"and why we are here, is how to find the boy."

"He's on a plane headed for Rome," the old man said. Several members showed their surprise at this news. What was the boy doing in Rome? Did he know he was heading toward danger? Did he know he was bringing the key right into their midst? Impossible. How could he have left the country without the head of their organization, the man with nearly infinite resources, knowing?

"Are you sure?" the man asked. He wasn't surprised. The old man had his sources as well, probably more than any of them knew. What did surprise him was how *his* sources hadn't known. They were usually quite reliable, and it wasn't as if getting past airport security was very easy these days.

"I'm afraid so," the old man replied. He was clearly enjoying telling *him* news. The man would make sure someone would pay for this embarrassing blunder, maybe his security chief.

"Yes," the old man continued, "he boarded a plane with an attractive little brunette. Apparently, it's because of her your men are dead. They were seen leaving the area, but I think you already knew that," the old man said to the man at the head of the table.

He did know the details, but hadn't wished to divulge *how* his men had failed.

The old man went on. "They had turned on airport facial recognition, but it turns out our young pair acquired some false identification." The old man chuckled at their resourcefulness. "But since no one got a good look at them, no alarm was brought up."

The man wondered how the old man knew the details of the pair's escapade; perhaps his men had been followed or some cameras hacked.

"And you just let them go?" another man asked.

"I felt quiet was the best way to proceed. We can't afford to draw any more attention to ourselves," the old man answered.

"I agree," he said. It was a smart move, but then, the old man didn't get to where he was today by being stupid. "So where are they now?"

"Ahh, yes." The old man hesitated. "I'm afraid we lost them after they landed in Rome, but *my* men are searching the city. We'll find them."

"I trust there won't be any more failures." He didn't bother mentioning Oxford was his failure.

"No, I think we all know that price is a little high," the old man said in the darkness.

"Good." He leaned over the table, his face entering the faint candlelight, which flickered off his almost black eyes. "Soon, gentlemen, the key will be within our grasp. Even now it works its way closer. Soon our long wait will be at an end, and that insolent boy will pay for all the trouble he caused…him and his little girlfriend."

CHAPTER FIVE

# THE KEY TO AN EMPIRE

Rome. The heart of an empire that had ruled a quarter of the known world only to be beaten down by the endless corruption and the pressures within its world. A city forever trapped in the mists of the past, where the shadows of emperors still ruled and gladiators fought like lions to the death.

Despite all we'd been through, I was determined to see this mystery through to the end, no matter where it led. I just hoped it didn't end up somewhere I didn't want to go—the end of the line, as they say.

A smile came to my face as I watched Emma come back with a pizza *–real Italian pizza–* from one of the many pizzerias the Italians were world famous for.

Another thing puzzled me as I watched Emma approach. Not many people would have risked their necks for somebody they didn't know, a complete stranger. Fewer still would have willingly gotten involved in a dangerous, potentially fatal chase. And practically no one, *no one*, would *volunteer* to keep going with the risk of death following your every step.

Watching her walk toward the fountain where I was waiting, her long brunette hair waving gracefully in the light breeze (strange, that was something I had never noticed before), I wondered what her game was. More than once I had wondered whether she worked with the men who had tried to kill me. *Kill me*. I still couldn't believe it. The words were almost foreign in my mouth. I was just your ordinary college kid on spring break. Why was this happening to me? Just what was so special about the sword that it was worth killing for? Was Emma some kind of spy? It was possible, I thought.

No, I decided, it was just too much trouble for…whoever they were. I would never have gotten away without her, as much as I didn't want to admit it. If Emma was a spy, then all she would have had to do was stop the vespa and let those guys grab me or shoot me as Jaw Face had tried to do in the alley. Besides, what were the odds that I would run down that specific alley and try to take *her* scooter unless…I had been led down that specific street, like herding sheep into a pen?

No. Again it was just too much trouble. There were easier ways, and there had been plenty of times Emma could have killed me in my sleep or at least knocked me out or stolen the sword when I wasn't looking. I had to admit, I had kept my eyes on it like a hawk—I even slept with the thing—but there were a few times when my attention had wandered.

And if it weren't for Emma and her *contacts*, I would never have gotten this fake passport. Frank Ford, from Georgia? Honestly? What was she thinking? Did I look anything like a Frank? Emma seemed to think so when I asked. I'm pretty sure she was holding in a laugh with that one.

Of course, I was almost sweating bullets at Heathrow when they had checked my passport at security, but they had just waved us on. (With a fake passport and a pretty girl on your arm, you could get a way with murder). Naturally,

Emma had seemed perfectly at ease using hers. I guess archeology students have a lot of experience sneaking into countries. Frankly, I was just glad I didn't get arrested. And how many people know a forger who will make a fake passport for one hundred pounds apiece? There was definitely something *different* about this girl.

The fact was, I just didn't get her. There weren't many people who would drop everything and go on a dangerous adventure with a complete stranger. Actually, I had thought I was the only one, but I was starting to doubt that I would have if *our* places had been switched. People can be full of surprises. For now, I decided, I would trust her. She had helped get me this far after all.

It never even occurred to me that Emma was just like me: restless, searching for an adventure.

We had come to Rome after much deliberation, and against my better judgment, I had agreed to meet with an old archeology professor of Emma's. Frankly, I'd had about as much as I could take from professors at this point. I'll confess, I had wondered if this one would try to kill me too. Suddenly the entire world of academia was full of psychotic killers who would rather run me over and mug me. I shook my head at the ludicrous thought. That was just crazy talk; I knew the world was filled with, on the whole at least, generally good and decent folks who just wanted to live happy and fulfilling lives.

But after what had happened, I wasn't that excited about Emma's plan. Truthfully I didn't have a better one. It would be too risky to go back to Kelley's; even though Kelley had no part in it, Dr. Wilson might send some friends to visit him too and, god forbid, our family and friends. Luckily, after a few quick, cryptic calls from a payphone, I confirmed that everyone back home was all right. Looks like our friends wanted to keep things nice and personal (fine by me—minus the bullets and death and all).

Suddenly my world went dark. My heart rate shot up before a soft, feminine voice filled my ears.

"Guess who?" Emma whispered playfully, removing her hands. How had she snuck around me without noticing? I really did have to focus and pay better attention to my surroundings.

"Funny," I said. "You almost gave me a heart attack." Emma just laughed as she sat down on a step below me and handed me my slice.

"Your not still upset about that car chase, are you?" she asked.

"Upset isn't exactly the word I would use," I replied. "You know we made the news, right?" I showed her the paper I had snagged from the trash. The article was brief—international news wasn't of much concern to the Italians (God bless them for that)—but still, I wasn't too happy about seeing a blurry image of the two of us running away from a car crash.

Emma skimmed the article. "Relax. We're not even mentioned by name, and they'll have to do better than some bad cellphone picture. Besides, we're out of the count—" Emma paused.

"What?"

"Looks like there were two fatalities and one critical, still unidentified. Another unidentified man was seen running away, only to be found dead in a Dumpster six hours later," she replied softly.

"What's wrong?"

Emma hesitated before responding. "Someone *died*, Max. Because of me."

"Hey," I said, sliding a step lower to sit beside her. "Listen, it's not your fault. If it wasn't for you and your crazy driving—which was amazing, by the way—we'd probably be dead. *I'd* be dead. You wouldn't want that now, would you?" I said, bumping my shoulder against hers.

Emma gave a small smile in return. "No. I wouldn't want that," she said, resting her head against my shoulder for a minute.

"Besides," I continued while surveying the crowd, "it

sounds like they killed that one who survived, the one who crawled out of the car that nearly had me."

"Jaw Face?"

"Yeah," I replied grimly. "Looks like failure has a heavy price for these guys. Imagine, going through all that just to wind up in a Dumpster. Makes you think what would have happened to me."

Emma didn't say anything, so I thought I'd try a different tack. "So, remind me again, what's the plan?" I asked, trying to take her mind off the men. Unless she came to her senses and went home, I needed her to stay focused, not that she seemed like the kind of girl to start crying.

Emma sighed and raised her head from my shoulder. I had almost forgotten it was still there. *Almost.*

"*We* are going to go see my old archeologist professor, Professore Giordani, to see if he can tell us something useful about this sword of ours."

"*Ours*," I said.

"Yes, *ours*." She smiled. "You still owe me a new scooter, remember? And I'm not leaving until you pay me back."

"Hey, I never told you to crash it into a speeding car," I pointed out for hundredth time. Emma ignored the rebuke. *For the hundredth time.*

"Maybe he can tell us what's so important about that old sword and why people are trying to kill us."

"Still not much of a plan," I said.

"Well, it's the only one we've got unless you have a better idea."

"Well," I said, standing up and holding out my hand, "let's get going then."

"Just what makes this guy an expert anyway?" I asked as Emma led me through the Roman baroque building toward the professor's office. I stopped by a window for a moment to marvel at the Tempietto di Sant'Ivo and the amazing dome surrounded by towering pinnacles and topped with the cross. Sometimes I think I should have been an architect. There really was no place like Europe.

"Max! Come on!" Emma yelled from the end of the hall. I still wasn't happy about this. The last time I had asked a professional, he'd very nearly gotten us killed, but I couldn't fret over that forever. Best to remember the lesson and move on.

"Are you going to answer my question?" I asked, catching up and matching her long strides.

"This *guy* just happens to be one of the world's foremost experts about Roman history, and we both agree this sword looks like something out of the movies. And *Professore* Giordani just happens to have a particular interest in Roman military history, so naturally that includes—"

"Weapons," I said, finishing her sentence.

"Exactly," she replied smugly.

"Fine," I said defeated. "We'll see what he has to say, but the second I start to feel something's up, we're out of there. Agreed?" I asked.

Stopping outside his office, Emma turned. "Just let me do the talking, okay?"

I grabbed her arm before she opened the door. "Emma?"

"Okay," she said. I don't think she really meant it, but it made me feel better.

Emma knocked on the open door as the Italian professor looked up from his work. He looked to be the complete opposite of Dr. Wilson. His cheap gray suit closely matched his graying beard, and unlike Dr. Wilson, his office was barely larger than a cupboard.

It was so cramped that there was barely enough room for the desk and the chair that was squeezed before it and the door. Somehow the archeology professor had also managed to squeeze in a small bookcase that was so overloaded the bent shelves were being supported by the books below it. Not much respect for the "the world's foremost expert," I thought, but I immediately lightened up to the old professor.

If the prosperity of a man's office was a sign of his intentions, then that made Dr. Wilson a man to avoid and Professor Giordani someone who *might* not be a psychotic killer antiques collector/archeologist. I smiled. That close miss in Oxford had shaken me up more than I cared to admit.

The untidiness of the small office also reminded me of Kelley's boat. Why is it that geniuses are almost always slobs?

"Miss Atherton!" the professor said, looking up from his work. "What a pleasant surprise! How are you? Back from Oxford already?"

"Hello, Professore," Emma replied. I noted the mesmerized tone she had used to address the professor…or *Professore* as she so elegantly used. I wondered for a moment if there were any other reasons besides the professor's so-called qualifications, that had caused Emma to lead us here.

"And who's your young friend?" Professor Giordani asked.

"Oh, sorry. Max. Max Taylor," I said, squeezing past Emma into the cramped office to hold out my hand.

The professor reached over to shake it. "Pleasure," he said. Giordani was a smart guy and seemed to sense this wasn't an ordinary house call.

"Emma," he continued, looking at her, "what's wrong?"

She hesitated. Maybe after all that had happened Emma didn't want to put her old archeology professor at risk. She clearly admired the guy; maybe she wasn't as tough as she looked. I figured I'd cut in and take the lead, at least for now.

"Actually, Professor, Emma and I are having a little bit of a problem, and we're hoping that you could maybe help us out," I said.

Giordani looked at Emma for a second. His curiosity had definitely bumped up a notch. It wasn't often one of his best students showed up out of the blue *and* didn't have something to say.

"Of course, of course. Any friend of Emma's is a friend of mine. What can I do to help?"

I exchanged a glance with Emma for a second, as if to voice my objection at getting anyone else involved with the sword (too many people knew already), but where else were we going to go? I deferred to Emma's judgment in the matter, took my backpack off, and removed the ancient blade that had already cost four men their lives (hopefully the sword wouldn't be claiming my own in the process).

The second I unwrapped it with the strange symbols facing up, Professor Giordani's mouth dropped. I knew we had a winner.

"So I take it you know what this is?" I asked. There was no way he could hide his reaction now, even if he wanted to. The man's eyes had almost come out of his head in shock (which would have been quite the sight).

"Yes," he replied quietly, the shock barely waning. That was all the confirmation I needed. He had definitely not expected this to come through the door today, unless the professor was also an actor on the side. I could rule him out as one of the bad guys (and if he really was, maybe they should pay him more).

"It's not some old French heirloom, is it?" I asked sarcastically. If Giordani said yes, then Emma and I would be out that door faster than a jackrabbit on caffeine (actually that would be an interesting sight—where do I get these analogies?).

"No," Giordani said with a small laugh, as if he were only half listening.

I decided to give the professor a few moments to get over his initial shock and examine the sword, but soon the moments turned to minutes and, if we had let him, I was pretty sure those could turn into hours. Quite frankly, I was sure he had forgotten about us and had entered his own world. Emma and I exchanged another look before she broke the silence and asked what had been on both of our minds for the past several days.

"So what is so special about this sword, Professore?" she asked.

"It is worth more than all our lives put together, I'm afraid," the professor said, reaching for a book on his overflowing shelf.

I couldn't suppress a snicker at his answer. "That much we know," I replied.

The professor didn't miss the comment. For a man in his late fifties, he was pretty quick at picking things up, even when he was engrossed in his work.

"What do you mean? What has happened?" he asked, looking at Emma and me in turn.

Emma beat me to the punch; I wasn't quite ready to trust the professor with a rundown of our exploits just yet. Emma, of course, trusted the professor completely.

"Some guys tried to kill us in Oxford two days ago," she answered. "They were ready to shoot us in order to get this sword from Max."

The professor's curiosity increased even more—if that were possible. "What did these gentlemen look like?" he asked with a hint of—what?—despair.

Emma looked at me for a second; maybe she hadn't wanted to tell her old professor everything. Perhaps she didn't completely trust him like me, or *maybe* she didn't want to worry her favorite professor and possibly place him in harm's way. My money was on the latter.

"Well, it's tough to say. We never really got much time to get a good look at them. They were all big, muscular, short-cropped hair, I'd say ex-military, and they all had really nice designer suits," she said. The professor didn't move a muscle; he just sat at his desk with his hands folded under his chin lost in thought.

Of course, girls would notice that kind of thing and give a vague description, but then, I couldn't give a much better one, even after coming toe to toe with Jaw Face.

Suddenly it dawned on me.

"How do you know they were designer suits?" I asked.

Emma gave me a look that said, "Please, are you serious? I am a woman after all." I decided right there that I would never underestimate a woman's sense of fashion.

"Are you two all right?" he asked with real concern. "How did you get away?"

"Well, they tried to run us over, but…" Emma smiled mischievously. "Well, you've seen me drive before Professore."

The professor laughed loudly. "Yes, I do, and thank the gods that you do. In fact," he paused for a second, staring at Emma hard, "I do remember reading about a deadly accident in Oxford this morning. Two suspects fleeing the scene and only a bad picture captured. *And no registration* on the scooter," he said sternly. "I thought they took your license away, young lady?"

Emma blushed. "Maybe," she mumbled.

"Wait," I said. "Are you telling me that you were driving without a license that whole time?"

"Hey, it was my *driving* that saved *your* life," she replied. "And I don't seem to remember you complaining earlier."

Professor Giordani laughed. "You two certainly had a bit of an adventure getting this sword to me. And I won't ask any more. Somehow, I think the less I know, the better off I'll be," he said through his Italian accent.

"So you won't help us?" I asked. Now where were we going to go? Maybe I should just throw this thing back in the ocean and hope that would be the end of it.

"No, I never said that," the professor said. "Just the less I know about your well-dressed friends, the happier I'll sleep tonight."

"So what can you tell us about the sword, Professor?" I asked, my excitement rising. Finally some answers.

"Very little at the moment, I am afraid," he answered

with his head hovering a few inches above the blade. This was not the answer I had been hoping for.

"The symbols near the hilt that have been partially cleaned look mostly Latin. This symbol half covered by the grime might be Arabic. An interesting mix if that's the case. These strange lines I am unsure about," he said.

Kelley had told me pretty much the same thing. At least I knew he hadn't lied about that. I wasn't sure what I had been hoping for, but maybe some idea as to what was so important about this thing that was worth killing for. This wasn't just some private collector looking for his latest piece. I also wanted to know what I should do with it.

"No," he said, lifting his head to look at us, "there is not much I can tell you right now, I'm afraid."

My heart sank even lower.

"The lab," Emma said simply, as if that explained everything.

"The lab," Giordani repeated with a smile.

What lab? I thought.

After several hours of careful scrubbing and soaking in a variety of acidic solutions in the professor's lab, which was located in the basement and had seen much better funding than his office (at least his priorities were straight), most of the blade's markings were finally becoming distinguishable.

Professor Giordani, although happy with the results, continued to object to this utterly ridiculous pace that Emma and I were setting.

"Honestly, you two, you'd think your lives depended on this. An archeological find of this magnitude requires very careful conservation. I still think we should take the time to properly preserve it. Why are the young so impatient?"

"How long would that take?" I asked. He had clearly forgotten that our lives did depend on this, but I chose not to remind him in case he changed his mind, but somehow I didn't think the old professor would do that.

"Well, some artifacts recovered from the world's oceans take years to properly preserve, but," he said after seeing the look on my face (maybe he hadn't forgotten), "something a bit more realistic is possible. For example, I would recommend about twenty days for mechanical removal of encrustations, about two hundred and fifty days for a good electrolytic cleaning, several days for rinsing, another fifteen days of dehydration in alcohol, and a further two days soaking in a microcrystalline wax to avoid further corrosion of the metal."

Emma and I just stared at him with an "I don't think so, Professor" look.

"Well, let's see how well this last solution worked," Professor Giordani said defeated as he placed his gloved hands into the dirty tank to remove the sword. He placed it cautiously on the table, and the three of us leaned in to look at the newly revealed blade.

"Very good metal, astounding really. This was very well made," Professor Giordani said, the archeologist coming out.

Although many of the symbols and markings were now clearly visible, they still didn't shed any light on the sword's mysteries. While Professor Giordani recognized a few of the symbols as having Arabic origins, he was unable to translate them, which was very frustrating considering he was fully fluent.

"Very good metal," he said again. The thing almost looked new with its gleaming metal blade. "Amazing it survived so well if it's as old as we think it is. These seem to be Arabic above the hilt," he said, pointing at several markings along the blade's center. "However, I don't recognize any of them. Perhaps it's a dead dialect or one from the desert nomads. It could be years before—" He stopped midsentence, his eyes lighting up.

"Years before what, Professore?" Emma asked.

"Years before...*anyone* understands it," he finished

slowly. Emma and I looked at one another (we seemed to be doing that a lot).

Slowly Professor Giordani turned the sword over for the first time. Kelley had never cleaned any encrustations on this side, not wanting to damage the metal with his quick cleaning. However, the professor's soaking solution revealed a clear message etched deeply along the blade's center:

CLAUSTRUM ACQUIESCO CUM VIRIS DE SPQR

"Do you remember your Latin, my dear?" Professor Giordani asked Emma quietly.

"The key rests with the might of the Senatus Populus Que Romanus," Emma translated.

"The Senate and people of Rome," I finished. My Latin was a bit rusty, but I had seen enough movies to know what that meant.

"Yes, close enough. You see here," Professor Giordani said as he turned the blade over to show the side with the strange markings, "this mark." He pointed to a small symbol closest to the hilt and isolated from the others. It was different from all of the other unknown Arabic characters and strange symbols. "You see this? What does it look like?" he asked, as if this were just another one of his classes (too many years teaching tend to have that effect, I suppose).

"A tree," I replied.

Professor Giordani smiled. "Yes, but what kind of tree?"

"A date palm," Emma answered.

"Yes, very good. I'm glad you paid such good attention in my class."

Emma blushed again.

"The Judean date palm, to be precise. Extinct since 70 AD, the date palm was a large commercial fruit tree exported from Judea, or Israel as we know it today, and shipped all across the Mediterranean. After the Second Temple was destroyed by the Romans, the venture was lost, and the palm became extinct. It was a symbol in Judea for grace and elegance, and became the main symbol for the man who destroyed the Holy Temple: the future emperor, Vespasian, and his son, Titus Flavius, who had crushed Israel and the First Jewish Revolt. The date palm was used alongside a weeping Jewish woman on a special bronze coin at the time to celebrate Vespasian's conquest and to commemorate his coronation as emperor," Professor Giordani finished.

"What was the revolt about?" I asked, overcome with curiosity.

Professor Giordani looked down at the date palm sadly. "It was about money mostly, and power, as with most wars. You see, the Jews felt overtaxed by the empire and underappreciated. The Romans, after the great fire that destroyed much of Rome and being ruled by several emperors over a very short period, needed leadership and money. General Vespasian and his son saw their opportunity in Jerusalem, and they took it. The revolt was short lived against the might of Rome. Four legions, with at least ten cavalry squadrons, another fifteen to twenty auxiliary cohorts, and even a fleet of warships killed more than a million Jews, imprisoned another hundred thousand for the gladiatorial games back home, and crucified or sold into slavery thousands more. The iron fist of Rome could not be resisted," Professor Giordani said with a sigh.

"It was a very sad time in Italy's history. Emperor Vespasian sacked the city of everything of worth. We know from the writings of Flavius Josephus, a Jewish commander who turned traitor for Vespasian, that it was a landscape of death and destruction, the coming of Armageddon on Earth. Imagine looking out at the great city of Jerusalem, the holiest place on Earth, and seeing it consumed in flames, shooting black smoke of a burning temple into the air. The air reeking of burning human flesh, a few Jewish revolutionaries fighting back but no defense against the storm and the bodies. Can you imagine the sight? Hundreds of crucified

Jews groaning, screaming into the night for mercy; thousands more, famished without a morsel of food for many days, being taunted by the Romans with food and beer. A bloody time in history, but then, things haven't changed too much, have they?" he asked.

"But what does this have to do with the sword, Professore?" Emma asked.

"*Il mio dio*!" Professor Giordani exclaimed in the Italian he loved so much. "It has everything to do with this sword. Have you forgotten what the back says? 'CLAUSTRUM ACQUIESCO CUM VIRIS DE SPQR.' The might of Rome!"

"But what does it mean by 'the might of Rome,'" Emma asked.

"Blood," I answered. On seeing Emma's perplexed look, I elaborated. "The might of Rome lay in the sword – conquest. Blood, in other words."

"A good answer," Professor Giordani said with a smile. "But conquest, or blood as you put it, was just the means. The real strength of Rome lay in gold, and Jerusalem reeked of it. Rumors had persisted, and still do, that the Second Temple was stuffed with the most fabulous and rarest treasures the world had ever known. Only the high priests knew the extent of the Temple's wealth, and they weren't willing to give it up. What was well known was that nearly the entire interior was plated in gold and precious stones."

"They don't build them like that anymore," I said. Emma shushed me to let the professor continue. It was turning into quite the story. I was starting to see why Emma liked the old professor so much; his classes must have been something.

"Quite right," Professor Giordani said with a laugh. "But that was only the beginning. The secret storerooms held the wealth of several empires. Josephus wrote that the Temple overflowed with thousands of vast chests of gold and the rarest jewels, the finest works of art in paintings and sculptures, piles of the finest silks and garments, and hundreds of years of offerings from the humblest farmer to kings. Even the priests and aristocrats stored their personal wealth in the sanctuary because it was both fortified and no man would dare to steal from the resting place of God—or so they thought.

"But these treasures were nothing compared to the religious objects revered by the Jews. Inside, the Romans took all of the sacred seven-branched candelabras, the gold cherubim within the holy sanctuary, the holy trumpets of truth, seventy-seven tables made of pure gold, including the sacred Table of the Divine Presence, and even the exquisitely woven veil separating the Holy of Holies from the impure outside world. They also took the priests' robes off their backs and quite possibly the Tabernacle itself, the resting place of God! The atrocities that man can achieve," Professor Giordani exclaimed.

"Some rumors claimed that even a few of the riches stolen from the First Temple, made by Solomon, if he existed, over five hundred years earlier, survived! Sought-after treasures included the crown and ring of Solomon, the Ark of the Covenant with its mystical power over armies, the sword of Muhammad, maybe even a Holy Grail—not that any archeology evidence ever existed for one, mind you. Just imagine the allure this must have had for a city in ruins and a man with visions of leading an empire!" Professor Giordani finished.

"But Professore," Emma asked, "what ever happened to all that treasure?"

"Well, naturally some was spent. A few villas for the emperor and his descendants, of course, but surprisingly much was spent on Rome for its people. The Arch of Titus, for one, built by Rome to commemorate Israel's destruction. The immense Colosseum, which Romans today are so proud of but ignorant of its history, was paid for by Emperor Vespasian to house fifty thousand spectators in the grandest arena ever seen in the ancient world. Some was spent by the emperor as propaganda, including coins depicting him as a bearer of peace and others marked 'Judea Capta' for his capture of Jerusalem. These feature the date palm, that we see here on your blade, and the weeping Jew underneath it that I mentioned earlier," he said.

"But it wasn't all spent?" I asked, even though I already suspected the answer.

Professor Giordani smiled. "No, it's well known that most of the treasure survived through the Flavian Dynasty, which ended with Titus Flavius Domitianus or Domitian in 96 AD, I believe. However, what became of it after his death remains a mystery. Some say it was all spent by the time Domitian died. I find that a little hard to believe. Some say it was hidden in the farthest reaches of the empire; still others say it's hidden to this day in the Vatican's underground storerooms . In fact, many Israelis believe that even to this day and continually request the Vatican to return what was stolen from them all those centuries ago."

"What do you think, Professore?" Emma asked.

"Personally, I think it may be a little of all three," he said with a laugh.

I, being deeply impressed with the story, wanted to get back to the business at hand.

"So what do you think is the purpose of this sword, Professor? There is more to it than just monetary value, isn't there?"

Professor Giordani paused for a moment, as if considering his next words carefully. "Well, there is one other symbol I recognize besides the date palm."

Emma and I leaned further forward over the lab table; we were already on the edge of our seats.

"What," we both asked.

"Well, it is actually three symbols superimposed on one another right above the date palm. I almost missed it until it just came to me," said the Italian joyfully, enjoying the rapt attention he was receiving from his audience.

"A monogram?" Emma asked.

"Yes," he confirmed. "The first two symbols are a six-rayed star on top of a crescent moon. Do either of you—"

"The symbol for Islam?" I interrupted.

"Another good guess and normally so, but remember this sword is at least two thousand years old. It predates Islam, which did not emerge until the time of Muhammad in the seventh century. The crescent moon and star have been seen as ancient celestial symbols for several thousand years in Asia and Siberia in the worship of sky gods. But this sword isn't quite that old, and it is completely the wrong style for those parts of the world. Judging by the time period and style, I would have to say this represents the city of Byzantium or Constantinople, as the empire later knew it," the professor said.

"Istanbul," Emma said, more to herself than to either of us.

"Yes, as it is known today," the professor confirmed. He was clearly in lecture mode now, but I didn't mind; the man taught some good history. "By about 340 BC, the Byzantines were under siege by King Philip of Macedon…"

He was Alexander the Great's father, if I recalled correctly. I was no history major, but I had a deep respect for men who had made their mark on the world. By twenty-five, Alexander the Great had conquered nearly a quarter of the known world. Talk about ambition. But with a father like Philip, I suppose he had no choice.

"And on one particularly rainy night…" Giordani had obviously kept going as I daydreamed about being an emperor at my age. "…his surprise attack was thwarted by the appearance of a brilliant light in the sky, most likely a meteor. Hence, the symbol of the city being the crescent moon and six-rayed star."

"What's the third symbol?" I asked before the professor could continue on about the history of Constantinople. Not that I wasn't interested, but frankly, I was getting hungry. We had been in that basement lab for hours already. Emma could probably have listened all night long, but I hadn't forgotten about the bad guys. If they could find us in Oxford easy enough, then I doubt any fake passport would hold them off for long. Best to get as much information as possible from the good professor, figure out my next move (for better or for worse), and keep moving.

"Hagia Eirene," Professor Giordani answered.

"Ahh…bless you?" I said. The professor gave another small laugh at my misunderstanding.

"No, Hagia Eirene is the third symbol." He laid the sword on the center of the lab table. Looking above the first symbol, the data palm, I could now see the three symbols superimposed on one another. The star, the crescent moon, and what resembled a cross with a tiny three-step pyramid below it. The level of detail on the blade was truly extraordinary. I thought only a laser could make lines this fine. Clearly I was wrong.

"I have heard of Hagia Sophia in Istanbul but never Hagia Eirene," Emma said after looking at the three symbols. If only we knew what all the other ones meant.

"I'm a bit surprised really. The Church of Holy Peace, as the name translates, is not quite as well known as Sophia, but they are quite near each other. It is still a popular tourist spot to see on the outside."

"Outside?" I asked.

"Yes." The professor smiled. I was starting to feel like a little kid in school at this point. "It is usually closed to the public, even though it is located on the outer courtyard of the Topkapi Palace."

"Oh, now I remember," Emma said. "It was the first church built in Constantinople by Emperor Constantine's order. Supposedly it sits on a pre-Christian temple, if I remember right."

"You do, but no excavation was ever done to prove that story," the professor said. "The church was completed a good deal earlier in the fourth century before the much grander Hagia Sophia was finished, sometime in the 530s I believe."

"And how do you know that this cross is from the Eirene?" I asked.

"Simple," the professor answered. "I have seen it before." Emma and I looked at the professor. "I have only seen this great cross with the three steps below it in the half-dome above the main narthex in Hagia Eirene. The star and crescent moon help confirm that the church is in Istanbul."

This sword was becoming more and more of a mystery. It was almost as if it were leading us somewhere. Leading us. *Where, though?*

"Professor," I started, "do you think these symbols may be leading us somewhere?"

"Leading?" he asked. "What do you mean?"

"The first symbol, the date palm, led us to talk about the destruction of the Second Temple and the lifting of the Jewish treasure in 70 AD."

"Yes," Professor Giordani said.

"Then the second symbol or symbols above it point almost three hundred years later to the first church built by the most powerful Roman emperor for at least a hundred years in his new capital. And let's not forget the front of the blade: CLAUSTRUM ACQUIESCO CUM VIRIS DE SPQR, the key rests with the might of the Rome."

"So," Emma continued, following my train of thought, "what if this sword is a kind of map to 'the might of Rome,' as in treasure!"

"But what is the key?" I asked her. We both looked at the professor.

"I don't know," he said. "And I think a treasure hunt is a bit unlikely. No one makes a treasure map with X marking the spot. This isn't some game, you two."

"Well, those guys following us sure do want it badly for being nothing more than a simple antique," I replied.

"But where do we go from here?" Emma asked, her excitement quickly ebbing away. "That church has been there for over a thousand years. There was never any treasure there."

"Perhaps they didn't look in the right place," the professor said.

"What?!" we both exclaimed.

"What do you mean, Professore?" Emma asked, her excitement rising again.

"I have seen this cross in only one other place in the Eirene."

"Where," we both asked.

The professor hesitated for a moment, clearly deciding if he wanted to tell us. Whether for our safety or so we wouldn't waste our time on what could turn out to be a wild goose chase or maybe because he wanted to go see for himself—possibly all three.

"Directly below the great cross in the apse is a single tile with a small cross with the three steps on it. I remember seeing it on my private tour of the church when I was writing my dissertation, and thinking it only decorative, I never gave it a moment's thought. However, a church would be a good place to hide something since *no one* would *ever* think of desecrating a church, *especially* one so old." He looked at the two of us. He definitely suspected what was on our minds.

Another clue to the sword or possibly hidden treasure! This would be an amazing adventure if the goon squad got off our backs.

Suddenly, the phone rang. Emma and I jumped. The excitement and danger (not to mention being locked in a basement for several hours) had put our nerves on high alert. The professor exchanged a few words on the phone with his secretary, his face showing growing concern with each word exchanged.

Professor Giordani hung up the phone and turned to us. "There are two well-dressed gentlemen on the way down. My secretary said they were quite impolite, so she called to warn me and security," he said.

I grabbed the sword at "well-dressed gentlemen" and

was wrapping it back up, preparing to take my leave of the good professor.

Giordani grabbed my arm. I looked at him, my worst fears about him coming to reality.

"Not that way. Take the back exit to the streets," he said. My increasing heart rate dropped a small degree.

Professor Giordani led us toward a small, unseen set of stairs that led to the back door. Before we reached it, I turned around to thank the professor for all of his help, but Emma beat me to the punch.

"Professor," she said softly with tears starting to form in her eyes.

"I will be all right, my dear," he said as they exchanged a quick hug. "You two are the ones I am worried about. Take care," he finished, releasing her.

Giordani and I simply shook hands not, knowing how things were going to turn out. We shared unspoken words as our gazes met. "Take care of her," his eyes seemed to say. "I will," I conveyed as we released hands.

"This is not worth your lives. If you need some help, please just ask," he said as I turned the doorknob.

"We will and thank you," I said as I poked my head out into the alley. Not a soul in sight. Something about abandoned alleys I never liked, but it was this or through the front door.

We turned at the sound of a bang from the lab. It sounded like someone trying to break down the door, followed by shouting. I grabbed Emma's hand. It was now or never.

"Good luck," Professor Giordani called in a hoarse whisper as he closed the door.

I hoped he didn't try anything foolish with those guys. They weren't the type to play nice, especially with people who got in their way. Giordani was a good man. I hoped he had enough sense to play dumb and hide.

Emma and I ran down the side alley quickly but cautiously. I think she had the same thought as I did. If these guys really were ex-military and were able to find us as easily as they had (which I still hadn't figured out how), then they wouldn't be so clumsy as to leave the back door wide open with no eyes on it. Something was up.

With Emma following me, I peeked around the corner to a rather busy street at the end of another short side alley. My mistake.

One man with short-cropped sandy hair grabbed my shirt and pulled me in before I could register what had happened. We were so caught by surprise that Emma had barely gone two steps before a shorter man grabbed her from behind and held her next to me.

My captor pulled me close to his face. "You've caused us a lot of trouble, boy," he said in a German accent. "Killed a few of my friends too, you did." His breath smelled of onions, or at least I think it was onions. Maybe it was sauerkraut or something. Whatever it was, it was enough to make me sick. Maybe if I threw up on him, I might have a chance to free Emma and make a run for it. I couldn't believe we had walked into that obvious trap. So much for the back door.

Suddenly Emma kicked Shorty in the groin *hard*, sending him to the ground. Smart girl. I saw my opening and head-butted Sauerkraut when he wasn't looking.

"Ouch!" I yelled. That never looked like it hurt that badly in the movies.

"Max! Come on!" Emma yelled. We ran down the side alley toward the busy street before more Suits showed up. Really, they would be less conspicuous if they didn't stand out so much. Obviously their employers had never heard of camouflage and blending in to the environment a little.

Turning right onto the busy street, we saw two more Suits spot us and start running after us. They were quickly joined by Shorty and Sauerkraut (hey, if they weren't going to tell us their names or who they worked for, then I was just going to have to give them names of my own).

"Max! That one," Emma yelled over the roar of a particularly loud passing bus, pointing at a young Italian teenager parking his scooter in front of us.

"*No*!" I yelled, grabbing her hand to keep her moving as she slowed down to hijack the poor kid's Vespa. There was no way—*no way*—we were going to go through with that again. I may have survived her driving once but not again, no way. She didn't even a license anymore (I wonder why). I stole a quick glance behind me; the four Suits were too close for us to hot wire a car (nothing I had practiced, but I was willing to bet that Emma might have a little experience; she was proving to be a jack-of-all-trades), so we would have to grab one with the keys inside.

Suddenly there she was—a red Porsche 911 being dropped off by the valet in front of the hotel.

"The Porsche," I yelled to Emma as I grabbed the keys from the valet's hands, much to the shock and outrage of the owner, who was rushing out of the lobby at the commotion.

Emma hopped in (it was even a convertible; how perfect was that?), and I started the motor, popped it in first, and took off, wheels spinning. The fingertips of one of the Suits grazed the spoiler.

Emma threw her hands in the air, screaming joyously, as I swerved past a taxi and threw the sports car into second gear. I may have done a bit of screaming as well.

"Now we're even," I yelled to Emma over the roar of the engine behind us. And with a bit more style, if I do say so myself, as I eased our speed and headed out of Rome as quickly as I could without drawing any additional attention to ourselves. The faster we got out of Rome and ditched the car (as much as I wanted to keep it), the better off we would be. I didn't want to deal with the police as well. But for now, I sat back, threw on the designer sunglasses I found in the car, and enjoyed the little break from my newfound life as a fugitive.

I looked over at Emma; she smiled affectionately through all the hair blowing around her face, and that was enough for me. I threw the sports car into third gear as we hit the motorway, heading toward the Italian countryside.

As the day approached sunset in Tuscany, we started to look for a little place to stop for the night and refresh ourselves before starting anew in the morning. I had to admit though; I was starting to see the allure that some people got from grand theft auto. The top down, the wind in your face, the engine humming around you, and the adrenaline rush from *borrowing* a car (an expensive one at that, judging from the interior) that wasn't yours. I don't plan to start a life of crime, but this little treasure-hunting adventure (still hoping that's what this was all about) had me doing a lot of things and crossing a lot of lines that I didn't think I'd ever cross.

First things first, it was time to be smart and dump the car (I guess the Italian police had better things to do since we had yet to see one) and find a quiet place until we could grab a plane in the morning.

I looked over at Emma. Frankly, I didn't think she was quite ready to stop for the night (for that matter, I wasn't either) as I watched her gaze out at the Italian countryside with that same blissful smile she wore when we first took the car. No, I don't think she regretted my decision not to take the scooter. Scooters—if I never saw one for the rest of my life, I would die a happy man.

All of a sudden a black helicopter flew overhead. There must be an airport nearby for it to be flying so low, I thought. We both looked up at it as it made a wide circle back toward us.

"Where do you think he is going?" Emma asked uninterestedly, still relaxing in the comfortable seats.

"No idea," I said. "But wherever he's going, it looks like he's in a hurry," I added as it flew over our heads again. Unless I was mistaken, this pass looked a little lower than before.

"You don't think it's the police, do you?" Emma asked, pushing the hair futilely away from her eyes. She craned her neck to see where the helicopter had gone.

"It's coming back!" she yelled to me.

Great, I thought. So what if it's coming back? What am I supposed to do about it? If it is the police, then that's it—we're going to jail. If it's the Suits, what am I supposed to do? Outrun a helicopter? Activate the hidden controls and fire my stinger missiles from under the headlights? Okay, that last one would be cool.

Besides, what's the worst they could do? Call their buddies? Fly around us all day?

Then the bullets came.

Maybe it was a warning shot or maybe the idiot didn't know the engine was in the back (somehow I doubted it), but when those first bullets pinged off the hood, I knew we were in trouble. This was not a situation I could solve from the ground and *not* something Emma could just kick in the groin.

Assuming it was just a warning shot, I took the only action I felt we had. I threw my foot down. If we stopped and let them take the sword and us, I knew we were dead. I assumed we had seen way too much for our own good and had caused way too much trouble to be left alive. I just wished Porsches were bulletproof.

"He's coming around again," Emma yelled over the growing roar of the helicopter. A helicopter! Seriously? Who were these guys? I was just glad the Tuscan streets were empty so no one else would get hurt. Seriously, where was a cop when you needed one?

I could hear the distinct ping of bullets hitting the rear bumper as the helicopter took up a perfect position directly behind us. The gunner hung out of the open left hatch, trying his best to end our lives.

I kicked up our speed to give the back bumper a break as a hail of bullets carved a sweeping curve into the road. This was intense!

"These guys sure don't quit easy," I yelled to no one in particular.

"Shit," I yelled, throwing my head to the right. Suddenly, the side mirror I had been looking into was shot off as the gunner re-aimed. A small piece of shrapnel flew toward my eyes. Luckily my borrowed sunglasses took most of the impact. Unfortunately, I wouldn't be returning the sunglasses anytime soon, let alone the car for that matter—and you can forget mint condition.

"Are you all right?" Emma yelled as bullets hit the road in front of us.

"Yeah!" I yelled back.

"Max!" Emma screamed as more bullets struck the hood right in front of her. They were getting better, I thought, as I threw the car into a lower gear taking another one of Tuscany's tight winding turns. The bullet strikes traveled down the right side of the car before impacting the side of the roadway. I was amazed Emma was all right.

Enough of this, I thought, throwing the car into neutral and pulling the emergency brake.

"Hang on," I called to Emma as I sent the car into a spin. The helicopter overshot us. The pilot was already starting to bring the bird around again. I needed something to bring him down.

"You could have given me a bit more warning," Emma said, rubbing the side of her head.

"Sorry," I said. "We're in trouble unless we can shoot that thing down."

"Too bad we can't just throw a tree at it," she said, shaking the pain from her head.

"A…tree," I said slowly, looking at the large one right next to me as an idea came to me.

I threw the car into first, wheels spinning, smoke flying. Time to see what this car is made of, I thought right before the bullets started flying again.

And then I saw it in my rearview mirror—a trail of

fire following us.

"Max," Emma said in a worried tone. "There's a trail of fire following us." She seemed rather calm, considering the situation, the pain in her head momentarily forgotten.

"They must have hit the gas tank," I yelled, taking a broad left turn much too quickly. They must have ignited the gasoline with all of the gunfire.

"What if they hit us?" she asked.

I didn't bother answering as I concentrated on my driving. Emma knew the answer. If I didn't keep our speed up, then that was it. Game over.

Time. That was all I needed. Time to find the right spot and carry out my plan. It was a long shot, but it was our only chance. The pursuing flame was only another variable to the equation.

More bullets pinged off the hood. The chopper was tight on our tail. Nothing could stop it.

"Keep your head down," I yelled, swerving left and right trying to avoid the hail of gunfire. Next to us, in front of us, off the hood, even the rear (I hope Porsche engines were made to endure a little punishment), bullets set deep holes in the bodywork. We were traveling too fast, too recklessly. But what could I do? Death from above and from behind in close pursuit. The devil was working overtime today.

But we were still alive! In a car covered in bullets, leaking fuel, but we were still alive!

Why did I have to pick a convertible?

All of a sudden climbing over the green hilly landscape, I saw it—a beautiful vineyard before us on our right and a bare field on our left. The field looked like it was getting ready for planting. It looked fairly dry. I hoped it would be enough. In the middle of the small field was a group of large Tuscan Cypresses, maybe twenty-five yards high.

It was perfect.

This was it, I thought. My plan was either going to

work or it wasn't.

"Hang on," I yelled to Emma over the sounds of the helicopter, hopefully for the last time.

I swung the car to the left onto the field, heading straight for the line of trees.

Emma looked over at me, gripping her seat and the door arm. "Max? What are you doing," she hollered.

"Trust me," I said, maybe too quietly for her to hear. Emma's knuckles turned white. I guess she heard me.

The Porsche's suspension was not made for off-road maneuvers, I thought as it sent clumps of dirt and dust up behind us. Hopefully the owner of the field hadn't planted anything yet, or else I would feel really bad about what I was about to do.

Luckily, though, the trail of fuel we were leaving behind had stopped following us. Probably because of all the little airborne maneuvers the Porsche was performing in this field. Haven't they ever thought to make these things flat? I thought as my brain flew up and down inside my skull.

Unfortunately, because the Porsche wasn't made for off-roading we were losing a lot of speed. Our well-dressed pilot was taking advantage of our handicap by flying lower to give his friend a better chance of finishing us. But maybe that was a good thing, I thought as I stopped a few yards away from the tall cypresses. The helicopter flew over us, circling for another pass.

"Max? What are you doing?" Emma asked.

I looked over at her—maybe for the last time—the bellow of the chopper getting louder as it approached. Her eyes held only a slight hint of panic. I hoped mine displayed more confidence than I felt in my plan.

"Trust me," I said, maybe more for my own sake than hers.

I threw the car into first gear and started spinning around and around, the level of dirt and dust increasing around us as we held our ground. The pilot and gunner must have been grinning wickedly at the stupid kid who took a sports car off-road and got stuck—or so they thought.

A few more bullets pinged off the Porsche's sides as the chopper came directly toward us before hovering over us and our cloud of dust. Within seconds the helicopter was engulfed in dust, the propellers continuing to carry more and more dust up toward them. The pilot, struggling to see, started swinging the helicopter around trying to find a hole in the dust storm.

I continued spinning, holding on to the wheel and keeping my foot jammed to the floor. I couldn't see a thing—my eyes were too teared up from all the sand and dust in the air.

Then I heard it, the increase in power as the pilot tried to fly out of the miniature storm.

"*Max! Go!*" Emma screamed.

I think she had figured out my plan. I just hoped I wasn't leaving the party too early (or too late) as I straightened the wheel. The contents of my stomach returned to their original position as I took off back toward the road.

Then I heard what I'd been waiting for.

A tremendous explosion erupted as the helicopter collided with the grove of ancient cypress trees and fell back to Earth where it belonged.

I swung the car to a complete stop to survey the damage. Nothing was left but a hunk of burning metal—a shame for the trees though. I could honestly say I'll never even think of cutting a tree down after this.

"Not bad."

I looked over at the girl smiling beside me. She was covered in dust, her hair was a windblown tangle, and she was bleeding from a cut on the side of her head. But somehow she still managed to smile.

I had never seen a more wonderful sight in my life.

"Now we're even," I said.

Emma laughed.

CHAPTER SIX

# CONSTANTINE'S CLUE

They sure don't make them like that anymore, I thought, looking at the palace from beside a tree.

According to the brochure Emma had picked up from the airport (not that she hadn't already had her fair share to say about it on the plane ride), the Sultan Mehmed II had built the palace in the fifteenth century after the Ottoman conquest of Byzantine Constantinople. Unlike most European palaces, it was comprised of an extensive complex of buildings and courtyards (four main areas) instead of one giant, monolithic palace. In fact, only a few of the buildings were more than two stories. The courtyards were filled with trees, gardens, water fountains, and Turkish military guards with guns—the usual stuff.

Seen from overhead, each courtyard fit inside the next. The Second Courtyard could only be entered through the Gate of Salutation, a large crenellated gate with two pointed octagonal towers on either side and ornately decorated with numerous religious inscriptions and monograms of the sultans.

That wasn't the bit that impressed me the most (or worried me, I should say). Right outside the gate was the famous Executioner's Fountain. According to Emma, who had spent the entire plane ride filling me in on the palace and subsequently made the trip fly by (pun intended), the fountain was used by the executioner to wash his hands and sword after an execution. I would live a happier life knowing that the practice was no longer observed.

Once past the gates, which only the sultan was allowed to ride through, the entire complex got much smaller and was used to hold the sultan's audiences and dispense justice. I really did feel like an expert after Emma's little lecture, something Professor Giordani would be proud of, no doubt. She'd make a good professor herself that one. Anyway, the Second Courtyard was filled with quarters, stables, the sultan's kitchens and harem (they sure knew how to live it up), and the treasury. The Imperial Council was also held here.

To get into the even smaller Third Courtyard, you had to be really high in the sultan's favor and pass through the marble Gates of Felicity. Inside this courtyard, where few ever entered, was the main treasury (yes, there were several), the Conqueror's Pavilion, galleys, the library, mosques, several privies, the imperial baths, oh, and a few hundred rooms for the sultan's consorts and concubines too.

The innermost courtyard (the Fourth and the smallest) was the most inaccessible, being the sultan's private domain. It contained numerous pavilions, terraces, the throne room, several kiosks, and chambers for the more important residents of the sultan's court. And, of course, it was the most difficult to get into.

Luckily, though, the Hagia Eirene was in the first courtyard, so it was only a matter of breaking into the church.

The First Courtyard was technically nothing more than a really high wall protecting the palace grounds and bordering the cliff by the sea. Being mainly a large park surrounding the Second Courtyard, it contained only a few buildings that had survived to the present day: the Imperial mint, several fountains, and the churches of Hagia Sophia and Eirene.

This was our first problem. Getting into the palace would be easy enough. We would just walk in as tourists. Unfortunately, because most of the buildings were closed to the public, we would have to break in to the churches—not something I condoned, but a necessary step. The trouble was that because the First Courtyard contained only a few trees for cover and the Turkish military was keeping an eye on things, it wouldn't be easy to sneak away from the tour group.

"Well, obvious question first—how do we get in?" Emma asked.

"That's simple," I said. "We go through the front door."

"I know *that*," she said, looking at me like I was an idiot. "Obviously, we'll just go in with the rest of the tourists, but how do we get into the church?" she asked me outside the Topkapi Sarayi Müzesi, the entrance to the palace.

Leaning against the building, still casually studying the guarded entrance, I answered her question for the second time.

"I told you, we'll go in through the front door," I said, looking at her with my most charming smile (at least I thought it was).

"Really? That's the best plan you have? You said you had a plan on the plane," she said, exasperated. "If I knew you were just going to wing it as you went along, then I wouldn't have come."

I didn't bother saying that her last statement probably wasn't true.

"You have a better idea?" I asked. Emma didn't say a word. "Look, the entire palace is surrounded by the Turkish military and a twenty-foot wall. I don't know about you, but I didn't bring any rope to climb over it or any shovels to dig underneath it. We're just lucky this is a tourist attraction now and the guards probably aren't the most alert. So we walk in with the rest of the tour, nice and simple, and then find a way to sneak off to the Eirene. Let's just get in, see what the layout is like, and then decide our next move, all right?"

I wished we hadn't chosen to have this discussion right outside the place. Somehow it was starting to feel more real, breaking into a guarded military site. Was I crazy for doing this? A week ago I would never even have thought of it. A week ago I'd still be in the Caribbean, I thought with a smile. Maybe Emma was a bad influence on me.

"Fine," Emma said, defeated. "It won't hurt to look. And I don't feel like digging," she said, taking off for the entrance.

I smiled, following her. I didn't feel much like digging either.

After paying the small fee and entering the palace grounds, I couldn't resist mentioning the fact to Emma.

"Did we just pay them to break in?" I whispered in her ear.

She shot me a smile that told me to shut up before someone overheard us.

"I just thought of another way," she said.

"How?"

"We could parachute in," she said seriously.

"Not much point now," I said quietly in case any of the tourists around us knew English (by the looks of it, quite a few) and overheard us. Better to be safe than to be held at Turkish gunpoint, I always say.

"Not as much fun," Emma said, looking at the peculiar hollow trees lining the broad path to the Second Courtyard. Frankly, I didn't want to go anywhere near that Executioner's Fountain. We would have to make our move soon, before we left this courtyard and entered the inner confines of past sultans (something all the tourists paid to see and not some smelly, rundown church).

Emma pointed to our left. “There,” she whispered.

And *there* it was. The Hagia Eirene. The Church of Holy Peace stood far to our left with a few trees around it (not many for concealment) and a couple of smaller buildings even farther away. The church itself wasn’t much to look at, at least compared with the cathedrals the Church later employed.

The church, comprised of brown brick –which had held up remarkably well, considering the age –was roughly rectangular, maybe a hundred yards long, with several arched windows covered with lattice grills. Like most of the palace buildings, it was about two stories tall, except for the large dome on top, reminiscent of so many Christian churches, no matter the time period.

It also looked like there was a small courtyard (these sultans really liked their courtyards), enclosed by a wall maybe five or six feet high, with a closed gate at the front of the church –we’d have to climb that, I supposed.

“What we need is a diversion,” Emma said, reading my mind.

“Already ahead of you,” I said as we dropped to the back of the small crowd.

“You’re crazy,” Emma said as she saw the small collection of fireworks I had purchased earlier that day from a street vendor.

“Crazy is as crazy does,” I replied, looking behind me to see if anyone was watching us.

“Do you even know what that means?” she asked.

“Honestly? It just seems to apply,” I said, lighting the firecrackers. The crowd had started to move away from us. Tourists! Honestly, they were the same everywhere, I thought as I threw the firecrackers as far as I could. Predictable.

*Pop! Pop! Pop!*

Emma was already gone. Dang, she was fast.

I sprinted after her, trying to keep the trees between

me and the crowd as best as possible. I hoped any guards on patrol would be drawn to the fireworks instead and just think it was some kids trying to be funny. No reason to raise the alarm.

I made it to the small gate right behind Emma. The last firecracker made its final *pop*. We had to get inside before everybody started looking around. The gate was about five feet; we easily climbed over it and ran across the small courtyard to the main doors of the Hagia Eirene.

They were locked.

"Huh," I said, looking at lock. I hadn't foreseen this. Suddenly I didn't feel so smart after my brilliant diversionary tactic.

"Forget something?" Emma asked, pulling a small bolt cutter (well, it wasn't that small) from her purse. The smug look on her face made me sick. The things girls kept in their purses was unbelievable.

"I would have thought of something," I said, cutting the bolt off the chained door. "Let's hope no one patrols an old, empty church too often."

"There are much more valuable things in the inner courtyards. I think we'll be all right," Emma said, closing the door behind us.

"You have a flashlight in that thing?" I asked, indicating her purse. It was getting rather dark in the church, but we had preferred to take the last tour of the day, desiring the cover of night and all (very James Bond–like, I thought—except I don't think Sean Connery ever broke into a church).

"You've got to be kidding me," I said in surprise as Emma pulled a small flashlight out of her purse. "What else you got in there? A clown?"

"No. No clown," she said. "I've got you for that."

"Oh, ha ha," I said as we exited the atrium.

We stood for a moment on the narthex overlooking the main nave. It may not have been the biggest church I had ever seen, but it may have been the oldest. The old church did have some charm, especially because it sort of stood out among the rest of the Ottoman architecture on the palace grounds.

Then, all of a sudden, the setting sun shot one last ray through the dome onto the great cross in the apse that Professor Giordani had mentioned.

"It's beautiful," Emma said.

"Yeah," I said quietly. Boy, the sound sure carried well in here. "Come on," I whispered, "let's get going."

As we made our way across the church, I looked around. A feeling of anticipation built as I continued; my stomach was in knots. My footsteps broke the eerie silence as they echoed across the nave and into the two aisles on either side divided by columns and pillars. The remaining light seemed to dance across the mosaics and frescoes decorating the church. I could see where the later cathedral builders had gotten their inspiration.

As we passed underneath the great dome with its twenty or so windows letting in the remaining light, I tore my eyes from the decorations and took my first good look at the apse. As we silently took our first steps onto the bema, Emma and I looked up. There it was—the great cross with the three steps painted below it.

"Look," Emma said, pointing at the floor. Her flashlight illuminated the tile Giordani had mentioned to us back in Italy.

We walked closer to take a better look. Yep, the exact same cross on the apse directly above us.

"Is it the same?" Emma asked, indicating the sword in my backpack.

I was getting quite used to carrying the thing around. After a quick check, I told her it was.

"Well, now what?" she asked.

"Well," I said, "I guess we'll have to see what's under that tile."

I held my hand out. "Crowbar?" I asked, looking at her purse.

"Sorry, I didn't think to pack that," she said.

"Huh," I said, looking at the small bolt cutter I still had in my hand, "Too bad."

Getting down on one knee, I tried to pry the tile loose with the bolt cutter (I wished I had brought a crowbar or chisel or something). After several minutes, sweat was forming on my brow, but only a small chink had broken off of the tile. This was definitely not working, but what else could I do? We couldn't break out and come back tomorrow (well, we could). And where was that light?

"Hey, Em, I don't think this is going to wo—"

Suddenly there was a tall metal candlestick by my head.

"Here, try this."

I shrugged and took the metal rod. What the heck, I thought; I didn't have a better idea. I slammed the metal rod into the tile as hard as I could; the echo vibrated throughout the room.

That did it. After only a few good strikes, I had destroyed the tile that had lain there for over a thousand years. I wondered if they would shoot me or just throw me in prison for the rest of my life.

I cleared away the broken pieces to reveal wood underneath.

"There's a door!" Emma whispered in surprise.

Sure enough, there was a handle right underneath the ancient tile I had just demolished.

"Quick! Break away the others," Emma whispered.

I looked around for a second. The acoustics were incredible in this church. Why hadn't anybody come rushing in yet?

"Where is everybody?" I asked Emma, voicing my concern, my voice echoing off the walls. I didn't even bother whispering. If my banging hadn't woken anybody up, then why would my talking?

"I don't know," she said, some concern now showing on her face. "Come on, let's hurry and get out of here."

After a few more minutes of prying up the surrounding tiles, the trapdoor was revealed. I had to admit it was a pretty good spot. Most people didn't like defiling a church like the two of us.

My heart rate was flying in anticipation as I pulled the handle, opening a door that had been sealed for close to two millennia.

A smell of old, stale air hit us as Emma pointed her tiny beam of light into the hole.

"I don't think those are built to code," I whispered, seeing the tiny, steep steps that descended beyond the flashlight's beam. I couldn't help but whisper in this place. The sun had set, and the eerie darkness and stillness were all around us, as if the church itself were holding its breath to see what mysteries were hidden from its upper depths.

Emma gave a little nervous laugh before saying, "After you," and handing me the flashlight.

"What ever happened to ladies first?" I asked, taking my first steps into the belly of the beast.

We had descended maybe halfway down the stone steps (I honestly didn't know if it was halfway) before I realized how quiet it was. It was an unnatural quiet. The air itself didn't move, and it became more difficult to breathe in the humid air as we continued our slow descent. The only sound I heard was Emma's soft, rapid breathing behind me, but I'm sure if I had stopped and focused for a minute, I would have heard my own heartbeat racing in the black staircase. Part of me was absolutely astounded by this discovery and brimming with anticipation as to where the stairs led. Maybe the treasure was here! Hidden by the Emperor Constantine all those years ago. My heart raced even faster at the idea.

But another part of me—and I have to admit it was the larger part—was scared out of my mind. Where did this passage go? Why couldn't security have found us banging away at an ancient church or even climbing the gate? Part of me wished to go home. But I couldn't. For some reason, I kept putting one foot in front of the other. I knew deep down this is what I had always wanted. This was, quite simply put…an adventure.

And then, there it was. The flashlight pierced the darkness and showed us the bottom of the hidden staircase.

"We must have gone at least thirty or forty steps," I said, looking back up the staircase. I could see a faint gray above us; too bad it wasn't daylight. "What do you think?" I asked Emma rather calmly (at least my voice managed to sound calm). "Keep going?"

I pointed the flashlight down the narrow passageway. Nothing pierced the absolute darkness.

"Yeah, keep going," she said.

I had taken maybe a dozen steps down the dust-covered passageway (the filth must have been at least an inch thick—when was the last time someone cleaned this place?) before Emma grabbed my shoulders and pulled me back.

"Stop!" she yelled as we fell backward to the floor and a stream of darts shot out from the wall. I was pretty sure one of them whizzed by my foot.

"Thanks," I said, helping her up. I pointed the light at the darts now incredibly buried deep in the opposite wall. "That would have hurt a little."

"Maybe more than a little," Emma said as I pointed the light to the other wall. A few small holes in the wall showed where the darts had originated. "Tough to catch unless you know what to look for," she said.

"I'm glad you paid attention." I smiled at her in admiration. Emma just smirked and shook her head, taking the light and the lead.

"Wait up," I called, catching up to her.

Emma suddenly stopped, causing me to bump into her.

"Careful," she whispered. Her flashlight was pointing at more dart holes in the wall.

"How is it triggered?" I asked. "Pressure plates of

some kind?"

"Most likely," she replied. "This is weird, Max. Do you know how few booby traps archeologists have come across?"

"What about King Tut's tomb?"

"No, that was a curse. Completely different," she answered.

"Not much different if you're dead either way," I replied.

I heard Emma give a quiet chuckle in the dark. "Well, *either* way, one of us is going to have to trigger it if we want to keep going." I had the suspicious feeling that she was looking at me, but it was hard to tell without any light.

I decided to do the smart thing. Better than risking either of our lives, I grabbed Emma's (giant) purse (it was heavy too) and dropped it in front of us. Another stream of darts flew in front of us and into the rock wall.

Emma picked up her black purse and pulled out a dart that had wedged itself in the middle.

"You could have asked," she said angrily.

"You said one of us had to trigger it," I replied.

"I really liked this one too," she said, surveying the hole.

"Come on," I said, grabbing the light back. "There's something reflecting the light up ahead," I said as I hurried onward.

"Max! Careful," Emma called, her anger about the purse evaporating as quickly as it came. "Let me have the light."

I gave it to her. She was better at spotting those little dart holes than me anyway. Somebody had a nasty sense of humor.

"Hey, Em?" I asked. "What are the chances those darts have poison on them?"

She looked back at me, shining the light in my face. "Just try not to get hit by one," was all she said.

Great, I thought, all I needed besides a dart in my ass

was a poison dart in my ass.

We came to another staircase descending farther into the earth. Emma pointed the light at the reflecting pool that rose to about the third step.

"End of the road?" she asked. It was tough to see into the water with the little flashlight. We could only see a step or two lower. There was no telling how far down this maze went. The sea may have flooded it long ago.

"I'm not sure," I said. I sat down on the first step and started taking my shoes off.

"What are you doing?" Emma asked like I was a mad man. "That water is too cold. You don't know what's down there. And you have no idea how far down that is."

Her voice got more distressed as I stood and unbuttoned my shirt and handed her my backpack. Now was the time to trust her with the sword. I knew it would be safe with her.

"If you drown, they might never find your body," she said.

"Oh, I don't know. It's not like there are many places to get lost in this place," I teased.

I didn't know what I was doing, but I had to make sure this was really the "end of the road," as Emma put it. We had come too far and gone through too much to turn back from a little water. I just wished there was a scuba tank in that purse of hers.

"That's not funny, Max."

"Just one quick little swim before we turn back and give up, okay?" I asked.

Emma sighed. She knew I was going to do it anyway. "How long can you hold your breath?" she asked.

"About two minutes. Less the colder the water is," I answered.

"Then, here, take this," Emma said, handing me her watch. The timer was set to one and a half minutes. "And this," she said, handing me the flashlight.

"Waterproof?" I asked. She nodded. "You really

came prepared, didn't you?" I asked, taking my pants off too. I could have sworn she looked for a second, but it was hard to tell by the little light. I would need some warm clothes after coming back from this. That water felt really cold.

"You going to be all right in the dark for a few minutes?" I asked her.

"I'll be fine," she said. "Just come back, okay?"

"Okay," I said softly. There was a moment's silence between us before I said, "Listen, if I don't come back, you—"

I never got to finish. Emma hugged me tightly. I don't know how long we stood in that dark, quiet passageway, but somehow I didn't feel alone. Suddenly that lonely place under the earth was all right.

"Good luck," Emma said softly, releasing me from the embrace. I almost didn't hear her.

I didn't say anything. Everything that needed to be said had been.

I took a breath and started down the staircase. The second my foot touched the water, I exhaled. That water was freezing! But I continued. The faster I got this over with, the faster we could get out of here. And the faster I could get warm.

By the time the water reached my chest, I was shivering, but still, neither of us said anything, and still, I continued. I couldn't take any more steps, so I took a deep breath and dived down.

I thought I had heard a sound from behind me right before I dove in, but it was probably just my imagination. And the cold.

I started my timer: eighty-seven seconds and counting. I started kicking downward, being careful not to hit anything. This staircase was just as narrow as the last one and probably just as long The light barely did anything to illuminate the darkness, but I was glad to have it. I could only imagine what Emma must be going through, sitting in the pitch dark with the silence crashing down on her.

Suddenly my ears popped. Seventy-five seconds left. At forty-five, the halfway mark, I had to turn back (not that it would be easy to turn around in this cramped staircase).

I keep swimming. Down and down I went. I tried to count the steps as they flew beneath me. I lost count somewhere after twenty-five. I was starting to have trouble feeling my fingertips. Maybe it was all just in my head. I wished I had some air. I couldn't remember the last time I had swam so long underwater. It had been a while. And never in such cold water. I kept going—no point turning back until I had to.

Then, all of a sudden, the staircase ended and turned into another straight passage like the one above. No need to worry about any pressure plates or poison-tipped darts here, I thought happily. The weight of the water must have set them off a long time ago. As if to confirm my suspicion, I swam over a pile of rusty darts on the floor. I guess there was some advantage to this water. I checked Emma's watch (that girl really did come prepared—nice taste in watches too): fifty-three seconds left. Plenty of time, if only it weren't so cold down here.

The passageway ended with another set of stairs. My spirits rose. These stairs went up! I swam with a newfound vigor, my lungs getting a little thirsty (thirsty for air—I know an interesting analogy; blame the cold—I do). If this staircase were just as high as the last one, then there would be air near the top.

I checked the watch: forty-six seconds left. Time to turn back; I swam on. I knew it was stupid, but I also knew that if this staircase continued, I would reach fresh air (the architects of this place weren't very creative in my opinion).

One arm in front of the other, kicking both feet madly up the small staircase. I had to see. I had to be sure this was the end. Thirty-five seconds left on the clock. My lungs were beginning to burn. I was using up too much oxygen, going too fast, working too hard. I had to turn back. I should have turned back twenty-five seconds ago. Ten seconds ago! Ten seconds ago! I had added wrong.

My head was starting to hurt. My heart was starting to slow; less oxygen was reaching my body. I was so cold. So cold. I had to keep going. I had wasted too much energy, too much time. I couldn't turn back now, even if I wanted to. I'm sorry, Emma. She must be worried sick, all alone in the dark.

Fifteen seconds left. This was definitely the stupidest thing I had ever done. Jumping in a freezing cold tunnel of water dozens of feet below an old church looking for…looking for what? I couldn't remember. Blackness formed around the edges of my eyes, or was it just this dark staircase?

I let out a precious bubble of air. I banged my foot against a stair. Stupid, stupid. Why hadn't I turned around at the forty-five-second mark like Emma had said?

Emma. Emma. The name stuck in my head. I heard a strange, dull beeping sound. It was her watch—time's up. She must be expecting me. Too bad I'll disappoint her.

I broke through the surface in surprise near the top of the staircase.

It was the sweetest breath of air I had ever taken. I breathed deep and coughed out a little bit of water. I had breathed in a little bit of water. Another stupid mistake. I didn't mind so much. It still tasted better than anything.

I'll never regret fresh oxygen, I thought, breathing in the stale air of the chamber. I didn't care; I had made it. The adventure wasn't over.

I climbed up the last two steps shivering.

"Great, now I'll freeze to death instead," I said through chattering teeth. Luckily, the chamber was rather warm, or at least I thought so. Anything was warm after that swim. I hugged myself, trying to warm up a little, but it didn't help much. Maybe a few push-ups might get some warm blood pumping. After about thirty, I felt a little better. I knew I had to get back and get warm as soon as possible; it was pointless to go through all of this only to die of hypothermia later.

I looked for the little flashlight. There it was, dangling from my right wrist. When did I let go of it? Since when was it strapped to my wrist? Emma, I thought, bless her. It would have been a shame to come this far only to be stuck in the dark. I wasn't in the mood to swim back with a dart in my butt.

It looked like this was a dead end. The light revealed the small chamber I was in. It was a six-by-eight-foot rectangle with barely enough room to stand up straight.

The tiny room was empty—almost.

I would have been really upset if not for the small picture painted on the wall in front of me. I walked up to it, my discomfort forgotten for a moment as I was overcome with curiosity. Here I was, the first person probably since the artist to swim here in more than a thousand years, and I didn't even have any pants on. I was starting to feel certain that the whole swim was another kind of ancient booby trap. The builders must have somehow worked out the level of the underground water supply and built that staircase to be flooded on purpose. I wondered how they did that. Clever, though, extremely clever.

I guess I was just crazy.

Actually, I couldn't be sure it was a picture now that I was standing before it. But there was nothing else in the room, just this small picture. I knew I had seen it somewhere before; I just couldn't put my finger on it.

All that was on the tan wall in front of me was a large, backward C and a bearded snake's head with a crown below it and a few, almost random curved lines below it. All of this was drawn with the left side being completely straight, as if the artist had only finished half of his work. Maybe he drowned. But I had seen no bodies or bones. I didn't get it. Any grave robber who had come this far thinking he was about to hit the jackpot must have been sorely disappointed.

I felt the walls with my shaking hands. There had to

be something more—a groove, a pressure plate, or a recess in the wall opening to another chamber. I started beating the walls, partly to listen for the sound of an empty chamber (nothing but solid stone to my ears) and partly to take my frustration out (at least it helped me warm up). I stopped after having beaten all three sides of the small chamber; plus, my hands were starting to hurt.

I went back to the snake's head and studied the picture more closely. What was it trying to tell me? Maybe it was another clue? I don't know. I just wanted to get out of here. I was starting to feel a little claustrophobic in the tiny chamber and very cold. I did thirty more push-ups. I still had to swim back before Emma left. Emma. I checked her watch. I had been gone for over ten minutes! She must think I was dead by now. No one can swim through water that cold for ten minutes.

I walked to the snake's head and took one last look at the walls. I pointed my light on every square inch of the walls, even the ceiling and floor, looking for any small marker I might have missed, any clue. Nothing.

I looked back at the snake's head and studied every curve, every line, memorizing the image before me. I wasn't planning on coming back here any time soon—or ever, for that matter.

I closed my eyes, picturing the image before me. The shape of the snake's head, every curve below him, their lengths and intersections, the size of the backward C above him. I opened my eyes, taking one last look. Perfect. Time to get out of here, I thought as my teeth continued to chatter. Somehow I knew, even though I was tired and cold, this return swim wouldn't be as bad. I had something waiting for me on the other side. Or, I should say, someone.

"*Max*!" Emma screamed in shock as I broke through the surface, gasping for air.

She grabbed my shoulders and pulled me up the last two steps into the passageway.

"Are you all right?" she asked.

"C-c-c-cold," was all I could say through chattering teeth. Emma laughed and gave me a quick hug, trying to wipe the tears from her eyes without my noticing.

"Where were you?" she asked sternly, drying me with my undershirt. "I was worried sick about you."

I just sat on the dusty floor shivering. It was answer enough for her.

"We've got to get you warm," she said with concern. "You'll freeze to death down here." She hugged me, rubbing my back to warm me up.

The swim had been quicker on the way back because I knew where I was heading, so I wasn't so out of breath. But that second swim was, if anything, even colder than the first.

"Your lips are blue," she said, taking the light to get a better look at me.

"I found s-s-something," I said.

"Shh," she said, hugging me again. "That can wait 'til we get you warm."

It wasn't as warm as a fire, but I'd take it any day, I thought as I shivered in Emma's arms in the ancient tomb under the earth.

After a few minutes, I started to feel better, even though Emma said my lips were still blue. I told her I'd be fine and that I just wanted to get out of here. I got dressed quickly, which helped, and threw my backpack on (the things I went through for this stupid sword). We started down the passageway, heading back toward the surface. I had only gone a few steps before I faltered.

"Are you all right?" Emma asked, sticking her arms out in case I fell.

"Yeah, I'm fine," I said. "I banged my foot on the way down—or up."

"Or up?"

I smiled. "I don't really remember which way I was going anymore."

"Let's just get out of this dark place," Emma said.

She was clearly not in the mood to hang around any longer than she had to. Funny, I hadn't noticed how dark, small, or quiet the passageway was. After swimming all that unknown distance and emerging in that tiny room, this place looked like a palace, with plenty of room to run around too (not that I would want to—there was still a chance of getting a stray dart in my butt).

We set off again, me being a little more careful on my foot, and before we knew it, we were back at the staircase heading up to the Hagia Eirene. It seemed like a lifetime ago since we had left.

"That was a really stupid thing to do, Max," Emma said, breaking the silence.

"Yeah, but hopefully it'll be worth it," I replied.

We were about halfway to the top, the gray light above us growing larger. I swear, try being underground in the pitch dark for any length of time and you'll know what dark really is. The gray light at night was like a well-lit city after that. I, at least, had had the light; Emma hadn't.

We approached the church quietly from underneath. There was no way someone hadn't come to check on the church after all that racket I had made to uncover the stairs, not to mention breaking the lock to get into the church or defiling (destroying would probably be a better word) the floor to uncover the hidden door. There was *no way* the Turkish military was *that* lax on security. They would have to be the laziest military in the world.

Emma grabbed my arm as we slowly took the last few steps. I think she knew we were about to be arrested. We emerged from the staircase.

What do you know? The Turkish military is the laziest in the world.

We looked at each other in surprise. I couldn't *believe* our luck so far. It was about time it changed for the better.

"Hey, what do you know, nobody home," I said, dropping the trapdoor with a loud bang after Emma, the sound vibrating off the church walls.

Suddenly we heard shouting outside.

"Nice," Emma said. "Could you be a little louder? I don't think the prime minister heard you."

"Sorry," I said.

Someone started yelling in Turkish outside the church doors. They didn't sound too happy.

"Know what they're saying?" she asked.

"Time to run," I answered. I grabbed her hand and pulled her toward the right aisle.

"Why are we always running away?" I heard Emma ask. I didn't bother answering as I led her toward the spiral staircase tucked in the back corner of the church. It was true though; we were always running away from someone. For once I would like to *chase* somebody for a change of pace.

We ran up the staircase to one of the old choir lofts over either end of the church. I don't know where we were going, but I was in no mood to be interrogated by the Turkish military, especially after they found that hole in the floor.

I heard a great bang from below as the church doors were thrown open, the sound bouncing off the church's ancient stone walls.

"Max! What are we going to do?" Emma asked, looking me in the eyes.

What were we going to do? I didn't know. We had to get out of here. All I wanted was to find a nice warm bed and go to sleep. We couldn't go through the front door. We couldn't fly out the wind—

The window! I looked at the lattice-covered windows. It was cheap, thin wood, but we could easily break it. We might break our legs, even if we rolled, but it was either risk that or take our chances with angry MPs. I didn't think they took too kindly to people who broke in and desecrated their ancient monuments. I made my decision.

"We're going have to jump!" I said to Emma, backing up to the stone railing for a running start.

"What! Are you insane?" Emma yelled. I could hear the military storming the nave below us. We were running out of time.

"Well, you got a better idea?" I yelled back. Honestly, they would probably shoot us on sight, and she was looking through her purse like there was some rope in there or something. We had to take our chances and jump.

"Look, unless you've got some...*rope*," I finished in shock as Emma pulled out a short, thin length of rope from her purse.

"You were saying?" she said triumphantly. I took back any bad thing I had ever said about her. This girl was amazing.

"Here," she said, throwing me the rope. "Tie it off."

I hurriedly tied the rope around the railing as Emma did her best to kick out the lattice frame from the window. I heard the soldiers yelling downstairs. I think they knew we were up here. Luckily they were so busy screaming they hadn't heard us, but it was only a matter of seconds before they searched up here. It was a rather small church after all.

"Let's go," I said, throwing the rope through the small hole she had made. "You first."

I handed Emma the rope. We looked at each other one last time, and then the sounds of military boots running up the metal staircase brought us out of our reverie.

"Go!" I yelled.

I held the rope as Emma slid down it as fast as she could. Luckily we were only on the second floor, and there weren't any soldiers patrolling around the church yet. I couldn't help thinking how sloppy that was. Emma hit the bottom and held the rope steady for me. The soldiers were almost at the top. I practically threw myself out of that hole and then scrambled to the bottom as fast as my body would take me. I could feel my hands burn a little on the thin rope.

I hit the bottom and looked up. There was a head sticking out, watching us.

"Let's go!" Emma screamed. I took off right behind

her.

Then the bullets came.

With the ground exploding around us, we ran. Clumps of earth flew up on our left; leaves and small branches fell down on our left, the steady *bang bang bang* of automatic weapon fire behind us. We ran as fast as our legs could carry us.

The pain in my foot was forgotten. The cold I had felt only minutes before was gone as adrenaline flowed through me. I think I heard Emma scream once as a pile of earth flew up beside her. I threw my hands up as twigs and small branches rained down on my head.

Two days. Two gunfights. No fancy Porsche to help me get out of this one. Thank God, or whoever was watching over us, that we were only in the First Courtyard, the entrance only a few hundred feet away.

It looked so close—could we make it? Surely there would be guards there; surely we would be struck down in a hail of bullets. There was no question of that. The only question was, who would get hit first, Emma or me?

I hoped it was me. I hoped she would keep running. Maybe they would stop after they had shot one person—a scapegoat to bring to their superiors, tell them there was no one else. I didn't think so.

We ran through the arched Topkapi Sarayi Müzesi. The bullets had stopped, but we continued running through the streets of Istanbul into the night.

CHAPTER SEVEN

# VESTAL SECRETS

Where were we? I was sitting in some sort of lobby, I think. I couldn't remember. There were some reds and blues. I think the couch I was sitting on was black, or was it gray?

"Come on, Max, time to go," a soft voice said. I got up. *Pain!* It shot across my arm, protesting the movement. My world became slightly clearer, a little less fuzzy. I had a stained, dirty, old jacket over me. It smelled like garbage, or was it cabbage? I couldn't tell. This wasn't mine, was it? I should clean my things more often. I looked under the jacket at my arm. Why did it hurt so much? What was wrong with my head? My left sleeve was soaked in blood! What was going on?

"Come on," the soft voice repeated. "Let's go."

I looked for the source of the voice. It sounded wonderful, almost heavenly.

"Emma," I said confused, my eyes focusing on her face.

"What's going on?" I asked, voicing my concern.

"Shh," she said, gently taking my right arm and

leading me toward a small set of stairs. "I'll explain upstairs, hurry," she said more urgently.

"Why is my arm bleeding?" I asked, growing more distressed at the lack of information.

"Shh! Not here," she said sternly. "In the room."

I let her guide me to a door on the second floor. Not much of a room, I thought, just an old mattress on the floor and a sink. Or was that a toilet. My head was swimming. Where was I? What the *hell* was wrong with me?

Emma closed the door. The ground started coming closer to me. How strange.

"Max!" Emma said in distress. Suddenly Emma's arms were around me to catch me, and a flash of pain shot up my arm. "God, you weigh a ton."

I was lying on the mattress. How did I get here?

"We have to stop the bleeding," Emma said. "The wound's not bad, but you haven't stopped bleeding for about fifteen minutes. You're as pale as a ghost."

A fresh shot of pain flew through me, "Ahh!" I yelled as Emma tightened a strip of her shirt over my left arm. My vision refocused, the pain helped with that. "Why am I bleeding?" I asked rather stupidly.

"Don't you remember?"

I thought about it for a minute. Or at least I thought it was a minute. We were in a church. Why were we in a church? Were we praying for something? I didn't say anything.

"We were running away from the guards, remember?" Emma said, sitting down beside me on the mattress.

"Guards?" I asked weakly.

I was starting to get lightheaded again.

"Yes, remember?" Emma asked. She looked worried. "One of them nicked your arm," she said in her wonderful English accent. I liked hearing her talk; she sounded nice. A nice voice to fall asleep to, so I closed my eyes. A few minutes' rest would do the trick.

"Ahh!" A new pain ran through my right cheek. "Did you slap me?" I asked angrily. "Seriously, can't you let me get a few minutes of shuteye? Is that too much to ask?"

"You can't fall asleep, Max," Emma said with tears in her eyes. "You lost too much blood. You can't go to sleep yet."

"I'm tired," I said weakly.

"I know." Emma ran her fingers through my hair. It felt nice. "Just stay awake a little longer, for me, okay?"

"Okay," I said faintly, closing my eyes a little.

"Max!" she said sternly.

"I'm up, I'm up," I said, opening my eyes. I still had enough awareness to remember that her slap had *hurt*. "So where are we?"

"I don't even know. After you started falling behind and I saw you were bleeding, I took you to the first hotel I could find. Someplace they couldn't find us. I wish I had looked a little harder. This one rents by the hour," she said, looking around the tiny room.

"I never knew you were *that* kind of girl," I said softly.

Emma gave a little laugh. "I guess it's your lucky day then."

"I'm so tired," I said, barely above a whisper.

"I know." She leaned over to check the simple tourniquet on my arm. The bleeding hadn't stopped completely.

Emma started to cry softly.

"It's okay." Somehow my head was clearer. I knew what was happening, but I didn't care so much. All I wanted was to comfort her. It was horrible to see her cry like that.

"It's okay," I repeated gently. I reached for her hand.

"I'm sorry. I don't know what to do," she breathed through her quiet tears.

"Em," I whispered. "Tired."

Emma leaned over me, our faces only inches apart.

"Sleep," she said quietly. It was the most wonderful

thing she had ever said. She really did have the voice of an…of an…I forgot the word. I closed my eyes.

My eyes flew open to earsplitting banging on the door. Emma's head shot up in surprise, only millimeters from my face. Why?! Why can't I just go to sleep? Enough running, enough shooting, enough car chases, just enough already.

"Emma! Max!" someone yelled through the banging. The voice sounded familiar. Who was that inconsiderate bastard who interrupted my sleep?

Emma rushed to the door, opening it.

"Professore?!" she yelled in surprise.

"Quickly, quickly," he said, pushing himself in. He carried a large black leather bag with him.

"Professore, what are you doing here?" Emma asked after the shock settled.

He was the last person I had expected to see.

"Un minuto, un minuto," the Italian man said. He sat down next to me and began removing the tourniquet from my arm. "You should have tightened it more," he said to Emma, opening his black bag and removing some bandages, matches, needle, and thread.

"Just a flesh wound. You're lucky, but you have lost too much blood," he said with concern as he quickly cleaned the wound.

"How did you know we were here," I asked weakly.

"That can wait. First, we have to stop the bleeding, then I'll answer all of your questions," Giordani finished, threading the needle and sterilizing it with a match.

"I would give you something for the pain, but you have lost too much blood already," he said, poising the needle over my left arm.

"Just do it," I said. Either let me die in peace or get it over with.

"Max? Max," Emma said, waking me up. I blinked,

the harsh sunlight filtering down from the tiny window into my eyes. I had forgotten what sunlight looked like after our little walk under the church.

The church! The Hagia Eirene! The gunshot! My memory came flooding back to me.

Emma appeared before me, blocking out the sunlight.

"Emma! What…what happened?" I asked. It had all seemed like a dream. "What time is it?" I asked, even more confused. Emma broke out in a large smile and surprised me with a firm hug.

"Oh," I said in surprise, hugging her back. "Glad to see you too."

"It is ten o'clock in the morning," Giordani said behind me. Emma released me, and I looked at the man who had saved my life. "As for what happened, how about you start your breakfast and I'll fill you both in. You need to regain your strength, and I told Emma only a small part of my story to settle her curiosity until you awoke," he said from the chair beside me. The single chair, the mattress I was laying on, and a sink in the corner were the only furnishings in the room.

Emma sat down beside me and handed me a box of…something. It tasted a little spicy, but I would eat anything at the moment. I was famished. "How are you feeling?" she asked.

"Hungry," I replied.

Giordani laughed. "We'll that's good sign," he said. "I must say you had us both a little worried for a while Max. We feared you wouldn't make it through the night. I don't know what you remember, but the wound was just a graze. Unfortunately, you went *far* too long without treating it and lost a large amount of blood. You were lucky I found you when I did."

"Thank you, Professor," I said sincerely. I meant it. I owed the man my life. Funny, one professor tries to kill me, and another saves my life.

"Max," Emma said softly. I turned my attention to

her. Tears were forming in her eyes. "I'm so sorry. I…I didn't know what to do."

"You don't have everything in that purse then, do you?" I teased. Emma gave a weak smile. "Em," I took her hand, "you can't be prepared for everything. You didn't do anything wrong." She nodded, still not looking at me. "Hey." She slowly raised her eyes. "It's *okay*." I squeezed her hand and gave her the most charming smile I had.

She couldn't hold her expression and laughed.

"We're going to have to jump," she said, shaking her head with laughter, her sorrow forgotten. I was glad. I didn't like seeing her sad. "Honestly, I thought you were smart. Why are men always trying to impress someone?"

"I wasn't trying to impress anyone!" I said. Emma just laughed again at my response. Right, time for a change of subject and some answers.

"Not that I'm not grateful for everything," I said, redirecting my attention to the aging professor, "but how did you find us?" I started looking around for my backpack, the sword safe inside.

"Is this what you're looking for?" the professor asked, pulling the backpack from behind him.

My body tensed. Maybe I was wrong about him. Maybe every university professor (or at least archeologist) was a psychotic killer.

Smiling, the professor handed the backpack to me.

"Relax. If I had wanted to take it, I would have. The way I see it, this sword was meant for you. You found it, you uncovered her secrets, or at least, part of them, and therefore you should be the one to have it."

I opened the backpack and pulled out the beautifully restored blade. I had forgotten how stunning the sword was. What was it's secret? What had we gotten ourselves into? It was time for some answers.

"I don't understand," I said. "How did you find us? What aren't you telling us?"

Professor Giordani sighed. "Very well. You have a

right to know the full story. To answer your first question, simply put, we have been following you ever since you left my office a few days ago."

I tensed. The Suits! Emma put her hand on my arm. "Max, it's all right. He's not with the Suits. The professore is here to help us."

"Quite right," the professor said. "In fact, we never knew they existed for sure until they began pursuing you."

"So who are they?" I asked, sitting up on the mattress. My half-eaten breakfast lay forgotten beside me.

"We don't know, unfortunately. They were nothing more than a myth, spoken in the shadows. We had no confirmation, whatsoever, of their existence until they started pursuing you. We don't know where they operate from, how they're funded, who's in charge—absolutely nothing. They have no name that we know of. In fact," the professor said with a smirk, "we have been calling them 'the Suits' after you two."

"Well, what do they want?" I asked.

"We don't know exactly," the professor said. "Obviously, they too want to find out the secrets of the Sword of Crocea Mors for their own purposes."

"The Sword of Crocea Mors," I repeated.

"Yes, the sword's true name, one of many throughout the ages actually. I'm sorry I had to keep so much from you and Emma, but I had to be sure you could be trusted, that you were the rightful ones to fulfill the sword's purpose."

"What purpose?" I asked.

"I don't know," Giordani said.

"Pardon?"

Giordani smiled sadly. "Let me start at the beginning and this time with the *whole* truth. Unless," the professor paused, raising an eyebrow teasingly, "you would prefer I tell you quickly how I found you and put your mind at ease."

"I'd appreciate that," I answered. I supposed he could tell I was still a little bit on edge and not as willing to trust him as readily as Emma. I had been shot after all (so what if it was a flesh wound).

"Very well, a quick explanation is due. You see, Max, Emma," he said, looking at us in turn, "I am part of an ancient society called the Order of the Vestals."

"The *Vestals*?" Emma said.

"Yes. We are the keepers of a long and ancient history. We have existed for thousands of years in secret, passing our knowledge on to our children and they to their children and so on and so forth. Unfortunately, being that many of our secrets were passed on by word of mouth, many of them have been forgotten or mixed up with legends and myths," the Italian said sadly. "What we do know is that the sword was once in our possession in the beginning until a dark evil came trying to claim the sword for their own. I suspect a group of our order may have splintered off and tried to take the sword for their own."

"Maybe the Suits are descendants of that splinter group," Emma said.

"Perhaps. I'd be very surprised, but it would explain several things. Anyway, sensing this danger, our order took the sword to the farthest reaches of world to be protected until it was safe again and the rightful owners came forth to claim it. As you may now guess, the sword was lost far off at sea where we believed it to be gone forever. That was almost the end of the order—we had failed to protect our most sacred treasure—but a small group had chosen to remain intact should the sword ever find its way home. I couldn't believe my eyes when you two walked into my office and pulled out the Sword of Crocea Mors. I knew what it was immediately: the Sword of Yellow Death, the Shamshir-e Zomorrodnegar, the Angau Coch, the Agheu Glas, the Sword of Solomon! Take your pick." The professor's eyes fell on the sword still in my hands. "It has many names as well as a long and bloody history.

"I never imagined I would ever lay eyes on it. Some even doubted the history of our order and thought the sword was only a myth, a children's story. But we shall get into that in a minute. To answer your question, Max." He tore his eyes from the blade to look at me. "After my initial shock, I decided it was time for the order to resume its ancient work, to protect the sword and its protector, and to preserve its secrets. After we started our work in the lab, it was a simple matter of contacting my colleagues in the order."

"But you didn't call anyone," Emma said.

The professor gave a short laugh. "I may be old, but I'm not old enough to not know how to send an email."

"You should have told us," Emma said sadly. "You should have told us everything right then and there."

The professor lowered his head. "I know, my dear, and please forgive me. But please try to understand, I had to protect my order. We haven't existed for all these millennia just so we can betray those who came before us by blabbing all of our secrets now. I had to be sure I could trust you both, that you would do the right thing for the right reasons."

"But why tell us about the date palm at all and about the symbol leading us to the Hagia Eirene?" I asked. "If you wanted to protect your order and the sword, then why tell us anything at all about it? Why not just take it?"

Professor Giordani gave a small smile before answering. "Honestly," he said, "I don't really know. I think it was the two of you actually."

"Us?" I asked in surprise.

"Seeing you two in the lab all excited about what the blade was—and scared at the same time, but still willing to go on and not quit. It reminded me of myself when I was a little younger than you two are now and my father started telling me about the mysteries of the Sword of Crocea Mors and of the order."

He laughed.

"I remember imagining myself finding the sword triumphantly, slaying evil, finding out the sword's secrets that had been lost to us for so long, glory, and my father's approval. But I grew older, and still no sign or word of the 'sword that was lost' ever reached us. So I dedicated my life to archeology and Roman history and weapons, like most of my colleagues in the order. And then you two showed up at my door, and all of the old memories and feelings returned."

"So where was the order?" I asked. "Why didn't they help us?"

"Alas, we tried our best. But like I said, we had no idea that someone outside of the order knew about the sword or that they had such influence and funding. You two have to understand, the Order of the Vestals started out as a group of protectors; warriors who would gladly have given their lives to protect the sword and the secrets it carries. Over the years, as the sword passed into legend and there was no longer anything to protect, members of the order began to enter the scholarly life as opposed to a life of combat. They began to study the stories passed down to us and research old texts and records for clues about the sword's history. In essence, we became scholars instead of warriors. And with no money, there was little more we could do besides watch and hope. None were willing to risk their lives uselessly against highly trained mercenaries with a gunship. Nice work, by the way. I was amazed when I received the footage. I'm so sorry, you two. I did what I could."

"What do you mean?" I asked. It sounded as though the professor had done nothing but watch us run for our lives and hope we didn't die. Some order he was in.

"They worked for the order, Max," Emma answered. "That's why you're not dead. That's why we managed to even get in."

"Who?" I asked, even more confused.

"The guards at Topkapi," Giordani answered. "Well, the captain of the Guard, more specifically."

I looked at Giordani in confusion.

"What? They saw us?"

"Of course, they saw you!" Giordani exclaimed. "My god, I thought you were intelligent. Didn't you think maybe it was all a bit too easy?" (I had to admit I had.) "Did you think you could set off fireworks and no one would notice? That you could break into the oldest church in Turkey, desecrate it in the middle of the night, and get away with it? You wouldn't have gotten two steps after those fireworks without my help. If I hadn't informed the captain, he wouldn't have ordered his men to turn a blind eye to the 'training exercise,' and you both would have been arrested on the spot. The Turkish Armed Forces aren't idiots, for Christ sake! They're among the most experienced and best trained soldiers in the world."

"Then *why* did I get hit by a bullet?" I asked.

"It was a graze," Emma chimed in.

"I almost *died*!" I replied.

"I am so sorry, Max. The escape was staged in case anyone was watching, the Suits specifically. The captain ordered his men to make it believable, but some of those boys take their orders too seriously. And they don't like missing on purpose."

"No kidding," I said.

After a few moments of silence, Emma, no doubt happy that we were finally up to speed, asked the question on both of our minds.

"Tell us about the Order of the Vestals," she said.

"And about the Sword of Crocea Mors," I added.

"Well, that is a longer tale, but after all you two have seen and been through, I think you deserve to hear both in their entirety, at least as I know it. Remember, much has been lost over the years since we dare not write down any of our knowledge. First, I will tell you about the sword since that history is a little less complex."

"Tell me, Emma," Giordani said, looking at his former student. "What do you know of Crocea Mors?"

"Well, as you mentioned earlier, Crocea Mors means 'yellow death' in Latin. And I think it was the name given to Julius Caesar's sword," she answered.

"Yes, very good. But before that, it had many more names, one in particular more well known than the others. For this sword," the professor carefully picked up the sword

I had placed between us on the mattress, "is very old, to say the least. We no longer know how or when it was made, but this blade was once, supposedly, the sword of King Solomon himself."

"Wait," I interrupted. "Are you trying to tell me I have been carrying around King Solomon's—*the* King Solomon's—sword in my backpack!?"

Professor Giordani smiled at my question. It reminded me suddenly of that strange old man I had met on my way to the airport before I had even found the sword. It seemed a lifetime ago. "Oh, there's more than just gold in those waters." I don't know why that thought came into my head then, but it did.

"Yes," he answered in amusement. "As far as the order knows, it was made by the hand of God, although some like to think that the Queen of Sheba gave it him."

"Which do you think, Professore?" Emma asked.

"Personally, I prefer the hand of God explanation. Just look at this metal—only a little cleaning and it's perfect! No corrosion, nothing! This metal is as light as a feather, and I'm willing to bet it's stronger than any steel sword ever made. For the Queen of Sheba to make such a sword over three thousand years ago in ancient Ethiopia would be nearly impossible. Ancient China might be a fair guess, but even they never made a blade such as this. Even today I have never seen such a perfect blade. Who's to say it wasn't made by God himself?"

Professor Giordani suddenly held the sword straight up before him; a slight ringing of metal could be heard. "And still sharp," he said softly to himself.

"So what happened to the sword after Solomon's death and the splitting of his kingdom?" Emma asked excitedly. I had to admit again, the man did have a way of sucking you into his stories.

"Well," the professor said, "according to the Persian legend of Amir Arsalan-e Namdar, which is the earliest tale I have ever found after Solomon's time concerning the sword, the sword falls into the hands of a horned demon named Fulad-zereh. Whether he really existed is unknown but important to know. The epic opens with the Banu of Roum, or the Lady of Roum, who is pregnant, escaping the city that is being attacked—by the Romans is my guess from the script—and running for her life. Eventually, the lady marries a wealthy Egyptian merchant and gives birth to her child, Arsalan. Eventually, as you may guess, Arsalan learns of his royal heritage and vows to reclaim his throne."

"And how does he do that?" Emma asked.

"By slaying the demon Fulad-zereh," the professor answered. "Fulad-zereh, which means steel armor, was an enormous horned demon that would fly over the city stealing the most beautiful women in the land to take back to his lair."

"Not a bad job," I joked.

"Quite," the professor said. "Anyway, as the epic goes, Fulad-zereh used to be a noble general of the fairy king, Malek Khazen, who ruled over a land called Zahrgiah—before his mother intervened, that is."

"Fulad-zereh's mother?"

"Yes, a very powerful witch in her own right. As the epic goes, she used a powerful charm to make her son's body invulnerable to all weapons *except* the Sword of Solomon or, as it is renamed in the epic, the Shamshir-e Zomorrodnegar. Naturally, being the only thing that could kill the beast and end his immortality, Fulad-zereh guarded it closely. The Shamshir-e Zomorrodnegar was said to have several interesting properties: When worn, it could protect its owner against all forms of magic, and any wounds inflicted by the sword, no matter how small, would lead to death unless the wounded drank a special potion, one of the key ingredients being Fulad-zereh's own brains."

"Nice," I said. "How does the story end?"

"Well, like all great epics, Arsalan steals the sword and kills both Fulad-zereh and his mother, thus ending the terror of the demon and his mother."

"Did he reclaim his kingdom?" Emma asked.

"No, Amir Arsalan became an important man, but he did not live to reclaim his birthright. He left that duty for his descendants, and the sword became an heirloom to be passed down from father to son. And from father to son it passed until it found itself in the hands of a worthy descendent of Amir."

"Who was?" I asked. The professor looked over at Emma who smiled.

"Julius Caesar," she answered.

"You're kidding, right?" I asked. This story kept getting weirder and weirder.

"No, I believe Julius Caesar was a direct descendant of Amir, which is how he came into possession of the sword."

"Really," I said, at a loss for words. "How did you know that anyway?" I asked Emma.

"The Sword of Crocea Mors earlier," Emma said. "That was the name of Julius Caesar's sword."

I looked down at the sword resting in Professor Giordani's hands. Could it be? Had I carried the Sword of Julius Caesar, of King Solomon, of Amir Arsalan on my back for the whole week? Needless to say, I had trouble believing it.

"So what happened to the sword after Julius Caesar got his hands on it?" Emma asked, wanting the story to continue. It was a good story, whether it was true or not. Probably make a good book too.

"Well, as you know, he used it to expand the Republic, to make his name known in all corners of its lands until he had placed himself in a position of power with the people of Rome behind him and the Senate powerless to stand in his way. As everyone knows, he positioned himself to be the first emperor."

"And what happened to the sword?" I asked, repeating Emma's question.

"Yes," the professor said, getting back on track.

"The Crocea Mors or the Yellow Death was used by Caesar to conquer many of the lands from Gaul to Germania to even Britannia. It was in Britannia, in fact, that Caesar lost the sword. But with so many victories under his belt, he could afford to leave it and still return the conquering hero."

"How did he lose it?" Emma and I asked. We were hanging on to every word the professor was saying at this point. He was enjoying it very much, no doubt.

"When leading his troops through Britannia, Caesar encountered the British Prince Nennius with his troops and allies from London and Canterbury. His men, homesick and tired from the years of constant war, lose the battle and head home to Rome as heroes. But not before Prince Nennius and Julius Caesar face each other in the field of battle in single combat! After several minutes of hard fighting between the gifted warriors, Caesar delivers a small blow to Nennius's head with the Crocea Mors—nothing more than a cut really—but the sword lodged in Prince Nennius's shield. With Caesar without his sword and Nennius injured, the two are separated from the melee."

"But Nennius isn't finished yet, is he?" Emma said.

"No, he is not," Professor Giordani said. "Prince Nennius throws his sword away and removes Caesar's sword from his shield and begins attacking the Romans with a vengeance. It is considered the turning point of the battle, with Nennius killing every Roman who came across his path and inspiring his men to do the same. Caesar retreats back to Rome, the battle lost, but it was a minor loss for him in the grand scheme of things."

"And Nennius?" I asked. "What happened to him?"

"Well, according to the story, Prince Nennius died fifteen days later from his injuries. All records indicate that it was a slow, painful death. Remember what I told you about Fulad-zereh and the Shamshir-e Zomorrodnegar? Even the smallest wound by the blade will kill. Perhaps Prince Nennius's wound was too severe and was never treated properly or just became infected *or maybe—*" Giordani said with a nasty smile, "the sword really was cursed by Fulad-zereh's mother."

"Or God," Emma said.

"Or God," Giordani agreed with a smile. "It is believed Nennius died of a horrible fever, one that made him turn yellow, hence one of the Latin names for the sword, 'Crocea Mors' or 'Yellow Death.' There are many others, which I mentioned, such as the Welsh name for it, the 'Angau Coch' or 'Red Death.' You can guess why they called it that, I think.

He crossed his legs and leaned back in the chair, looking up at the stained ceiling. "Just imagine what Nennius could have accomplished with that sword," he said, lost in thought.

"Let's just make sure we don't cut ourselves," Emma said.

"No arguments here," I said, looking down at the sword before me. I hadn't noticed how sharp the blade still was after all that time in the ocean. How was it possible?

"So what happened to the sword then," I asked.

The professor seemed not to hear, still lost in his thoughts of what might have been.

"Professor?" I said a little louder this time.

The professor tore his eyes away from a yellow stain and looked at the pair of us as if for the first time.

"And now," he said after a moment's pause, "we come to a point in the story where fact and what is written down in the pages of history diverge, to the founding days of my Order. History says that the Crocea Mors was buried with Prince Nennius, the victor of Britannia, near the North Gates in London."

"But it wasn't, was it?" I asked, looking at the sword again. Professor Giordani looked down at the sword also.

"No, it was smuggled out and replaced with a copy to be buried with the prince."

"Who smuggled it out?" I asked.

"The Vestal Virgins," Emma guessed. Professor

Giordani smiled at his favorite student.

"And who are they exactly?" I asked. I was definitely starting to feel a bit like an idiot at my lack of knowledge (and I thought I was *good* at history too).

"Would you?" Giordani asked, looking at Emma. She nodded as Giordani stood up to pour himself a drink of water from the small sink in the corner. I felt like a ten-year-old as Emma took over.

"The Vestal Virgins were priestesses of the goddess Vesta, hence the name. Vesta was the goddess of the hearth and home, and Vestal Virgins were seen as the guardians of the city."

"Yes, the Vestals were first created around 700 BC by King Numa Pompilius," Giordani threw in, taking a sip of water.

"Sorry, please." Professor Giordani motioned for Emma to continue.

"They oversaw the keeping of the sacred fire, which was never allowed to go out and was free for all Romans to take. By maintaining the sacred fire used in everyone's household, the Vestal Virgins were seen as the housekeepers of Rome. If the sacred fire did die out, the people believed that the goddess had withdrawn her protection of the city, and the Vestal responsible was usually punished."

"Severely," Giordani threw in.

"You see, Max, people had begun to think that the chastity of the Vestal Virgins had a direct result on the health of Rome. Vestals were servants of the state and, as such, had certain rights and privileges that other women of the time didn't have. For a Vestal to have sex with a Roman citizen was seen as incest and treason."

"Because to do so would also result in the Vestal being buried alive outside the city in the Campus Sceleratus, or Evil Field," Giordani added, coming back to his chair.

"Right. It was forbidden to spill the blood of a Vestal Virgin in case you inadvertently angered the gods, so the virgin was instead buried alive in a small room with a few days' food and water so the Romans could say she died willingly."

"Politics," I said."

"Yes, at its finest," an amused Giordani added.

"The punishment was rarely seen, but I'm sure that every Vestal always thought of it when they looked at an attractive man," Emma said with a smile.

"Yes, well, anyway," Professor Giordani continued, "by 394 Emperor Theodosius I had disbanded the College of the Vestals and extinguished the sacred fire, which had burned in the city for over a thousand years. He made Christianity the official religion of the empire, making all other religions illegal, including the old gods, which the people had worshiped for over a millennia. The part I always found most interesting was how, after his death, the empire was split in two, never to be whole again. So perhaps there was some truth in the old gods."

"So what happened to the sword and the Vestals?" I asked. Nothing like a good history lesson, but the professor did have a way of losing track of time. He could have gone on for the rest of the morning about Roman history, had we let him.

"At the time of Caesar, the Vestal Virgins were very much alive and active. Being a group of women with a remarkable amount of time, money, and freedom for the time, they had long ago started studying the ancient writings and histories of the empire. It was during the time of Gegania, among the first Vestals, that the history of the Jewish King Solomon's blade was uncovered."

"But they didn't know where the sword was or who had it, did they?"

"No, it wasn't until the time of Caesar and his endless string of victories that a few of the oldest and most scholarly Vestals began to recall an old prophecy told by one of their founders. Gegania foretold the day when the sword of a powerful Jewish king would find its way into the hands of his heir and bring about great change in the Republic. She instructed her future sisters to watch over this great weapon and to keep it in the hands of the Republic at all costs. Since only a handful of Vestals knew this truth, they chose to keep the sword secret and follow Gegania's orders."

"So a Vestal Virgin followed Julius Caesar through his military campaign all the way to Brittania?"

"Yes, Aemilia Severa, a Vestal Virgin during Caesar's time, accompanied him under orders from the Vestalium Maxima, or Chief Vestal priestess. You see, one of the tasks of the Vestals was the protection of the numerous sacred objects placed under the care of their sanctuary. The Vestalium Maximas had long known the history and bloodline of the sword in Caesar's possession. They saw the sword for what it was, and, being rightfully Caesar's, they ordered Aemilia to keep an eye on it and make sure it remained in Caesar's ownership. If, and only if, it fell into enemy hands was she to retrieve it."

"So after Caesar lost it to Nennius, did she steal it back?" I asked.

"Yes, but as to how she managed to sneak into his camp, replace it, *and* escape uncaptured and unharmed remains a mystery even to us."

"So Aemilia took it back to Rome?" Emma asked.

"Yes, she took it back in secret over many days before finding her way back to the College of the Vestals and placing it in the Vestals' vaults. It was nearly one hundred years later before the infamous Emperor Nero ordered General Vespasian with his son Titus to take Jerusalem and her treasures, but I already told you that part of the tale."

Professor Giordani hesitated for a moment before finishing. "What I did not tell you was what happened to all the treasure."

"Wait…what?" I said, looking at Emma in amazement, my heart rate rising. "I thought you said no one knew what happened to all the gold taken from the Temple. That some was spent, some may be under the Vatican or sent away."

"I did say that. I also said possibly all three, which is indeed the case."

"Do you know where it is?" I asked, sitting fully up on my mattress.

Professor Giordani just smiled at me. "No, and even if I did, it doesn't rightfully belong to any of us." Giordani sat back in his chair. "While a small amount does reside in the Vatican's underground vaults, we know that most of the immense treasure was sent away by Constantine after the completion of his de-facto capital, Constantinople. Being a very wise man, he foresaw that the empire would most likely be split again after his death, despite the work he had done to otherwise avoid it. So he recalled a division of the Third Augustan Legion from Mauretania Tingitana—that is somewhere in modern Morocco, I believe—to transport most of the vast treasure for safekeeping until it was deemed the empire was once again stable after his death."

"Who was to deem it safe?" Emma asked.

"Why, the Vestals of course," Giordani replied.

"But that doesn't make any sense. If Constantine was the first Christian emperor, why trust a group of pagans?" Emma asked.

Professor Giordani smiled at Emma. "My dear, most of the empire still believed in the old gods. Constantine couldn't just throw out one thousand years of tradition and belief and expect everyone to do so with him. The Vestal Virgins were extremely well respected and exhibited a large amount of political power. In fact, without their support, Julius Caesar would never have been able to successfully take power. Emperor Constantine, being as smart as he was, placed the secret of the treasure in their hands to maintain their support and, as a result, the people's support.

"So one Vestal was chosen and sent with the division, and they traveled deep into the Sahara, or so we think, to hide the treasure."

"So you think? You mean you don't know?" I asked in amazement. An ancient secret, rooms full of treasure, gold, jewels, priceless artifacts—and no one knew where it was or even of its existence.

"Yes, as I said, one Vestal was sent, and only one returned with the secret."

"And the division sent?"

Giordani shrugged. "Only the one Vestal returned. I suspect Constantine never fully trusted his soldiers. After all, most soldiers only joined for the money anyway. What was to stop them from going back and simply taking the treasure for themselves?"

"But surely one woman couldn't stop a small army on her own," Emma said.

"Don't ask me. I do not have all the answers. How I wish I did."

"So the Vestal?" I asked, eager for more. This story was getting more and more incredible with every minute.

"The Vestals decided that should they all fall, a fact they most likely considered because of the rise in Christianity, their greatest treasure would hold the secret to Rome's greatest treasure. The sword," which Giordani pointed at, "was imprinted, somehow on that amazing alloy, with a series of clues given by that one Vestal Virgin, whose name was never known, that would lead the worthy to the lost treasure of Rome."

"You mean of the Jews," I said.

Professor Giordani gave me another of his kind smiles. "Yes, some of us do choose to call it the Lost Treasure of Israel," he corrected. "But if you trace something back far enough, then anyone can own it, can't they?"

We sat in silence pondering all of this before Emma asked another question.

"But they never believed the empire was secure after Constantine's death, did they?"

"No." Professor Giordani crossed his legs in the old wooden chair. "After Constantine's death, the empire saw emperor after emperor until the empire was finally split in two again after the death of Emperor Theodosius I in 395. In fact, in 391, with Christianity on the rise, he disbanded the Vestal Virgins as well as several other prominent pagan temples, such as the Serapeum in Alexandria and the Temple of Apollo at Delphi."

"So this was the start of the Order of the Vestals?"

Giordani smiled as he scratched his white beard. "Yes, after the closing of the Temple of Vesta, the last Vestal Virgin and Vestalis Maxima, Coelia Concordia, founded our order. And with a few others, they began to teach and pass on their greatest secret to their descendants."

"Boys included," Emma said. Giordani gave a small laugh.

"Yes, boys included. And all was well, until a few of our order began to express wishes a few hundred years later about finding the treasure for themselves and keeping it."

"The Suits?" I asked.

"I suspect, although I'm amazed that any of that splinter group survived."

"They seem to be doing quite well for themselves without any treasure," Emma said.

"Remember what I taught you about the treasures of the temple—the Holy Grail, the Ark of the Covenant, the Sword of Muhammad, and countless other artifacts of great power and priceless wealth. What do those with power wish for above all else?"

"More power," I answered.

"So how did the sword end up in the ocean," Emma said.

"After the splinter group made themselves known, the head of our order decided that she would do like Constantine before her. She sent the sword far away, on a ship to the newly discovered New World. Seeing as no word was ever recieved it was fair to assume that the ship was lost, and judging by the way you found the sword, Max, I suppose we guessed right."

"And here we are today, the sword that was lost has

been recovered, and her secrets are being discovered. So tell us, Max," the professor said, leaning forward in his chair, his eyes sparkling with excitement, "what did you find down there? Emma filled me in on the staircase, but after that, no one knows what you found."

Emma was leaning in closer at the foot of the mattress. Obviously this was the part they had both been waiting for during the last hour of discussion. It was nice to be the one with something to offer. Suddenly one more question popped into my head.

"Why don't you just send someone down to see for yourself?"

"They had to seal the floor back up, Max," Emma answered for the professor.

"What?"

"An hour before daybreak and fresh tourists, bullets being fired—there was simply no time to launch a search. I had to have the captain of the guard reseal the floor and order a complete 'hush-up,' as the Americans say. Our order has not survived for more than a thousand years by leaving loose ends, Max," the professor finished.

"So tell us, what did you see?" Emma asked, the excitement rising in her voice.

"And you're sure there was nothing else, nothing at all, no other symbols or markings on the walls of any kind?" Professor Giordani asked ten minutes later, after I had finished telling them of my narrow escape from death and the strange picture in the little room at the end of my swim.

"No, nothing. Trust me; I checked every inch of that place. Believe me, it wasn't that big."

"And you were gone long enough," Emma added.

"Sorry," I replied. I meant it.

"I know," she said, giving me a small smile.

"Tell me again about the picture on the wall," Giordani said. He seemed rather disappointed at the lack of clues his past Vestal brethren had left him.

"Well," I said, thinking hard on every detail I had

memorized on the wall. It seemed a lifetime ago. "Right in the center of the wall was a small snake head with one of those skinny little beards you see on the pictures of Pharaohs. It also had a crown on its head and large, backward C above it. And right below it were a few curved lines, like I said."

"Can you draw it?" the professor asked.

"Yeah, sure," I said taking the paper and pen Emma handed me from her purse.

"You know, I've been meaning to mention," I said to Emma as I drew what I had seen on the left edge of the paper, "you should think about getting a backpack for all your…*stuff*," I finished for lack of a better word.

"Hey," I exclaimed. Barely a second had gone by before Emma leaned over and ripped the finished picture out of my hand and placed it next to the sword at my feet, ignoring my wonderful advice.

"Look," she yelled as she lined up the left edge of my picture to the third symbol on the sword, which was nothing more then a large capital C and a few curved lines below it.

"Kom el Shoqafa," Professor Giordani said with a huge smile. Emma quickly joined him as realization hit her as well. "Well, done, Emma. You deciphered the next clue. The image you saw, Max, was the second half of the image imprinted on the blade. Without the sword, the picture would mean nothing and vice versa."

I looked at the complete picture, a large circle above a crowned serpent, the curved lines connecting to complete its body.

Emma must have seen my confusion at their sudden glee. "Max, this is the symbol seen at the catacombs of Kom el Shoqafa in Alexandria!"

"Meaning…" I said as the realization slowly dawned. I blamed my slow response on the blood loss naturally.

"Meaning we have another clue to finding the Lost Treasure of Israel!" she exclaimed.

CHAPTER EIGHT

# THE CATACOMBS OF KOM EL-SHOQAFA

"Well, it was the least he could do for getting us in this mess," I said to Emma as we exited the terminal.

"What on earth are you talking about, Max," she replied, her English accent very noticeable to me at the moment. "You're the one who found the sword. You're the one who took it to Kelley and then to Wilson, who betrayed you, by the way. And you're the one who got me into this mess!"

"Hey, I never asked you to come."

"Please, like you would survive five minutes without me. Who saved your life in Oxford? *And* Istanbul? And without me you would never have met the professor."

"Oh, thanks for that," I said sarcastically. "And let me remind you, who saved *your* life in Italy, and who swam the tunnel at Hagia?"

"What's your point?" Emma sighed, tired of fighting.

"My point is we're taking all the risk while he sits back and lets us do all the work."

"The professor is an old man, Max. Do you *really*

think he can handle being chased halfway around the world and getting shot at? Speaking of which, if it weren't for the professor, you would probably be dead. And if it weren't for him, we still wouldn't know what was going on. And we wouldn't have these new passports either, would we?"

I looked down at the new Turkish passport that the professor had been kind enough to get us on short notice. Mine read, "John Simmons." First Frank, now John. Did I really like either? I voiced my concern to Emma.

"What's wrong with them?" she asked with a laugh. "I picked both of those names. They're good, strong American names, aren't they?" Considering she was still laughing and wouldn't look me in the eye, I was pretty sure she was lying.

"Look," I said, lowering my voice as we got in a cab (at least we didn't have any luggage). "I just don't like the fact that he's part of some secret order that's been around for, like, two thousand years, and yet he thinks two teenagers have the best chance of finding the treasure," I finished in a whisper (I didn't think the cab driver knew much English, but after all we'd been through, a little caution wouldn't hurt).

"We're in our twenties, Max," Emma replied, taking in the sights.

Great—after everything I had just said, all she got from that was "teenagers."

"And what makes him and the order all of sudden think it's time to reveal to the world a treasure that's been lost for so long?"

Emma sighed. (I suddenly realized I must have seemed like some twelve-year-old kid. It was time to buck up.) She took my hand and looked me in the eye.

"You were still unconscious when the professor told me; the order is dying, Max. Only a handful of members are left, and most of them are old, unmarried scholars like the professor. The professor and the order agree: You found the sword and protected it, so it's your duty to discover its secrets and return to the world the treasure that was hidden from it so long ago…before the others do," she finished.

I sat silent a moment, pondering this new information. Maybe it was time the world knew the truth. What the hell. We had come this far; no reason to stop now.

"To the catacombs," I said with a smile.

"The catacombs," she agreed. "Oh, and thanks for reminding me."

"About what?"

"You still owe me a new scooter."

"Welcome to the Mound of Shards," Emma said as we stepped out of the cab in front of the catacombs.

"The Mound of what?" I asked, paying the Alexandrian cab driver a large tip. The man could *drive*; I had to give him that. Had he been driving the Porsche back in Italy, no doubt we would have been dead, but at least we would have gotten there quick.

"The Mound of *Shards*," Emma said. "I thought you read the books Professor Giordani gave us on the plane," she said, looking out at the small castle.

Funny, it didn't look very Egyptian. Not many people around either; it was Friday, and most Muslims had the day off for prayer. The place looked more like some medieval castle with a turret on each corner of the square building. In fact, with the stone crenels all around the roof and a few small, arched windows in the building, the only part that looked even a little Egyptian was the color—a typical desert tan shade found in much of Egypt.

It really was a shame the Romans came here and diluted the Egyptian culture, I thought. Although one of the books I had read on the plane did mention that these catacombs had one of the richest blendings of Roman, Egyptian, and even Greek cultures in the world.

"And did you have to tip him so much?" Emma continued. "I thought he was quite reckless. Although I did see you smiling the whole time, so I guess you were enjoying it."

"I did read *some* of the books he gave us," I said with a smile, trying to change the subject. "But I didn't memorize every part."

"Mound of Shards is the translation of Kom el-Shoqafa. It must have said it at least three times in the first book I gave you."

"I may have skimmed it," I said. "Come on; let's see what we find inside."

"Hang on," Emma said, grabbing my arm. "Here, the professor wanted me to give you this."

I stared at the small box Emma pulled out of her small pack (it was about time she lost the purse). She had picked it up from an airport locker a few minutes earlier and quickly stuffed it in her bag.

"What is it?" I asked as I opened it.

"Don't know. He said we might need it," Emma said as I pulled out a revolver.

"Wow, cool! A Smith and Wesson thirty-eight, double-action four-inch barrel," I said, turning over the beautiful, classic revolver.

"Hey, careful with that thing," Emma hissed. "Put it away before someone sees it."

"And here, this was in the box too," Emma said, handing me the leather thigh holster as I put the revolver in my tan rucksack.

"Very cool. How do I look?" I asked Emma, putting it on over my brown chinos.

"Very American cowboy," she answered. "The professor thought you might like it. I'd keep the gun hidden for now though. Where'd you learn so much about guns anyway? Your father?"

"I've been around," I answered, evading the question. "Come on, let's go," I said, making for the entrance into the catacombs. At least the professor had good toys.

"So why does is it called the Mound of Shards?" I asked, stepping through the doorway.

"I'm going to have to give you another history lesson, aren't I?"

"That's why you're the smart one."

Emma chuckled. "Well, the actual Egyptian name of Kom el-Shoqafa is Ra-Qedil. It's supposedly called the 'Mound of Shards' because of the large amounts of broken clay jars found throughout certain parts of the catacombs."

"Guess the Egyptians didn't know how to clean up after themselves," I said as we made our way through the empty funerary chapel on the surface and began our descent down the wide spiral staircase cut from the bedrock .

"Well, actually the jars mostly contained food and wine, and it was considered bad luck to bring them back to the surface from this place of death. Archeologists believe the catacombs were first built for one wealthy Egyptian family who still worshipped the old pagan ways before the Romans came. When the Romans arrived, the catacombs were expanded by the Christians as a burial chamber."

"Did you know there are ninety-nine steps down to the first level," I said, trying not to look like a complete idiot as we wound our way down the spiral stairs. It really was something—a deep shaft maybe six yards wide running straight down into the earth letting the natural light down to the first level. I looked out one of the arched windows we passed as the staircase made its way around the huge shaft. It must have been ten yards straight down easily.

"I hope you learned more than that on the plane, Max. Honestly, you can't expect me to know everything. Neither of us even knows what we're looking for."

"You know, they used to lower the dead through here thousands of years ago," I said, still looking down the shaft.

Emma climbed back up next to me. "You think it's wrong coming here?" she asked.

"I don't know. It is a tomb. Doesn't matter how many thousands of years pass, does it? You think you'd like it if someone dug up your grave and took your stuff?" I asked her.

"No," she hesitated, "but we didn't do it, and if we don't keep moving, the Suits are going to have dig a few more graves, aren't they."

"Yeah, you're right," I said, taking my hand away from the windowsill and starting back down the stairs. "Let's keep going."

"Yes, o fearless leader," Emma said, falling in behind me.

A minute later we finished our ninety-nine steps and emerged from the narrow staircase on the first level in the vestibule, or a sort of lobby, as Emma explained. Although I already knew all of this from my research on the plane, she seemed happier being the smart one and explaining everything to me, so I let her keep talking. I was starting to learn that she was *way* too smart for her own good.

We stopped suddenly when we came face to face with the most peculiar sight a few dozen feet below the surface. Sitting cross-legged before us in the exedra – wearing a striped navy blue suit with a white taqiyah and leisurely smoking a cigarette – was perhaps one of the strangest men I will ever meet.

"It is about time," the Alexandrian man said in…what was that? Some sort of French accent maybe? "You know I've been waiting for hours? With all the trouble you've caused, you'd think you would hurry a little," he said, casually taking a puff of his cigarette as if meeting two strangers in an underground burial chamber was normal. "You know it's amazing you're still alive."

"Excuse me, sir, but who are you exactly?" I asked.

"Oui, forgive me. My name is Monsieur Es-Sayed Aly Gibarah, but you have been expecting me, of course?" We shook our heads. "No, of course, Giordani always did like his surprises, speaking of which," he said as Emma and I released the breaths we were subconsciously holding.

For a second I thought the Suits had had us, but for some reason, this particular smoking Egyptian didn't give off that vibe. "Didn't Giordani tell you to pick up my gun? I told him to tell you. I see you have the holster I added with it," he said, noting the empty leather holster hanging off my thigh.

"Oh, yes, it's in my pack," I replied.

"Well, what is it doing in there? I didn't give it to you to hide, now did I?"

"You don't think we're actually going to have to shoot someone, do you?" Emma asked Monsieur Gibarah.

"Well, these Suits, as you call them, haven't exactly stopped to talk now, have they?" Monsieur Gibarah asked in his heavy French (a very odd accent though).

"Giordani said you were both intelligent," he said as he stood up. "I hope he was not mistaken. Come, I have men watching the entrance, but if there is any trouble, we're on our own." I noticed the holstered Beretta under his jacket as the mid-fifties French-Egyptian man stood. "Here, I also brought these," he said, indicating two scuba tanks behind his feet.

"What on earth are those for?" Emma asked. I don't think she liked the man very much; maybe it was an English-French rivalry thing.

"For the third level?" I asked unconcerned.

"But that's flooded," Emma said quickly.

"Hence, the tank, mademoiselle. What does Giordani teach you in that university of his?"

"Now listen here, Mr. Gibarah—"

"Monsieur Gibarah, if you please. Are you ready, Maximillian? Good, time is short."

I just smiled, picking up the two tanks and avoiding eye contact with Emma. We followed the good man between the rotunda and the Hall of Caracalla deeper into the catacombs, the revolver bouncing off my right thigh. I sort of liked Monsieur Gibarah; he certainly knew how to get under Emma's skin.

"So do you know what we're looking for?" I asked him.

"No. Giordani felt it was too dangerous to send any

type of open message in case we are being watched. He did explain your dilemma and that you were being pursued by some rather well-funded individuals. He said to meet you at my favorite smoking spot."

"Your favorite smoking spot is in an ancient underground tomb?" Emma asked.

"Don't act so surprised, mademoiselle. I have seen much stranger things in the world. Don't dawdle. Shine the light!" Monsieur Gibarah pointed down the steep stairway to the catacombs.

"Giordani said you would know what you're looking for. Let's hope he was right. I don't think it will be long before they notice the catacombs are deserted and being watched. They do have a touch of class by the sounds of it," he said with admiration, taking a puff of his cigarette.

"And were you being watched?" I asked him.

"Oui, I was," he answered. "But I managed to lose them…for the moment."

"So what is it exactly that you do, Monsieur Gibarah?" Emma asked suspiciously.

"Myself? Oui, I am in the import-export business, you could say. I deal in rare artifacts and antiquities for," he hesitated, "certain special clients."

"You mean people with money," Emma stated in mild shock. No doubt she couldn't believe her beloved professor would be in league with such a fool man. She may have been thinking that he was in league with the Suits, but I really didn't think so. My gut told me I could trust him. The order had need of men like Monsieur Gibarah, men who would kiss the side of the enemy, dance in both worlds, as it were.

Monsieur Gibarah's laugh echoed loudly off the stairway's narrow walls.

"Where on earth did you find this one?" he asked me. "Let me give you some advice, my young friend. Never date an English woman. They'll always talk you to death." He laughed as we emerged on the pronaos before the main tomb, the staircase dividing in two and turning back around to dig deeper into the bedrock and head for the third level.

"Now see here, *Mister* Gibarah—"

"Emma! Look!" I exclaimed.

There standing right before us on the second level, flanking either side of the doorway into the main tomb and the catacombs beyond, was the serpent with the double crown and the circle above him, exactly the same as the one on the sword!

"Ah oui, the Agathodaimon," Monsieur Gibarah said, followed by another long puff of his cigarette. "Is this another clue of the Crocea Mors?"

"Yes," I answered, staring at the identical moldings carved from the rock wall itself. "What do you know of this snake?"

"They are called the Agathodaimon in Greek. Since this tomb is of a time when Roman, Egyptian, and Greek culture experienced much mixing, you will see much of that in Kom el-Shoqafa. Agathodaimon means good spirit, and it was often depicted as a serpent. The serpents both wear an Egyptian pschent or double crown."

"And above the crown?" I asked, indicating the tiny faces in the center of the circle.

"It's the Greek shield of Athena. The small face in the center is a Gorgoneion, the head of Medusa by the looks of this one."

"Let's hope we don't turn to stone then," I said.

"And there," Monsieur Gibarah pointed his small light closer to the serpent on the right in the dimly lit room, "it has a Greek thyrus twined about its coils." That wasn't on the sword; maybe it meant something.

"Thyrus?" Emma asked, her thoughts maybe the same as mine, the earlier insult momentarily forgotten.

Monsieur Gibarah took another puff of his cigarette before continuing. "A staff surmounted by a pinecone or ivy leaves. I have always found it quite odd when I look at it."

"Why?"

"Well, the thyrus is very rarely seen pictured with the Agathodaimons. It is usually associated with the Greek god Dionysus."

"What was he the god of?" I asked.

"He was known as the Liberator," Emma answered. "It was said his music, wine, and dance would make his followers euphoric and free them from all fears and self-doubts, all the troubles of the mortal world. Any who partook in the mysteries of his delights would become empowered and possessed by the god himself. He acts like a divine link between life and death, between the land of the living and the underworld."

"Both of the serpents are right in front of the stairs leading to the third level, so what do you say, Monsieur Gibarah? Deeper?" I asked casually, checking the oxygen levels on the two tanks.

"Deeper," he agreed.

"And how do you know that we'll have to dive down to the third level, Monsieur Gibarah?" Emma asked suspiciously. "We have yet to explore the main tomb or the surrounding catacombs. There may be more Agathodaimons there."

Monsieur Gibarah leaned casually back against the wall, took another puff from his cigarette, and surveyed Emma with equal disdain. Those two really rubbed each other the wrong way.

"Ma chère, I have explored these catacombs longer than you have lived, and nowhere else is this symbol found in this necropolis. If this is the clue that the Crocea Mors has shown you, then this is where you must go."

"You said it yourself, Emma. These thyrsus are the symbol of Dionysus—a link between the land of the living and the underworld," I said, pointing down the left staircase.

"And there is one more reason why I believe the next clue is down there," Monsieur Gibarah added.

"What's that?" I asked.

"The third level was constructed below the waterline.

And in my experience, the Order of the Vestals always liked to hide everything a little deeper. They seemed to think that would keep their secrets safer," he said.

"Can't argue with that logic," I said, donning my tank. "You coming?" I asked, picking up Emma's tank.

"Why is everything underwater?" she muttered.

"Do you know what you are looking for?" Monsieur Gibarah asked, helping me down the first few steps.

"No, but we'll know it when we find it," I replied.

"I will fire this into the water if there is trouble," he said, pulling a small flare gun out from behind his back after helping Emma get behind me. "Good luck."

I gave him a thumbs-up and descended into the cold water. Maybe this time we could just walk out of here without someone after us.

The stairwell didn't prove too deep. After only another dozen steps underwater, we emerged in a small room several yards below the ambulatory on the first level. The archeologists had only recently begun exploring this final level and had made little progress. After more than a thousand years, large amounts of sediment had mixed with the water to make visibility almost zero.

I turned my vest light on, and Emma followed suit. I looked at her and shrugged. Might as well swim to the end and see what we would find. Somehow this room felt smaller than the flooded tunnel at Hagia Eirene; maybe it was just the lack of visibility.

We swam beside the right wall looking for any symbols that we might recognize on the sword. While the rest of the catacombs were decorated with numerous Egyptian, Roman, and Greek images, this wall was blank. Had the water washed the paint off? If it had, then our journey was over.

I swam on for several more yards, Emma right behind me. No moldings, carvings, or pictures of any kind. No wonder the archeologists hadn't bothered to pump any of this water out; anything left would be severely damaged by the water. Not much point spending precious expedition money on an empty room.

My outstretched hand touched the opposite wall. Nothing. Was the journey over? Did I have to go back home? I couldn't help feeling a sense of disappointment in the underground room.

Emma swam by me, surveying the wall up close. It looked like she wasn't quite ready to give up yet. I followed, my hands moving over the smooth wall, feeling for even the slightest change.

I saw Emma's light waving around wildly in the murky water before me. She found something! I swam after her, quickly closing the few yards between us. It must have been in the very center of the wall.

There it was again! The serpent wearing the double crown! And the shield of Athena above his head! But the thyrus was missing from the serpent's coils, as was the head of Medusa from the shield. Interesting. The sword was also missing these same details. I thought it was maybe because the order hadn't been able to engrave clues that fine on the blade, but maybe it was done on purpose. What secrets was the Order of the Vestals hiding from us this time?

I looked over at a smiling Emma. I couldn't help returning the smile at the sight of her in goggles and the bubbles coming from her mouthpiece, her hair floating all over the place in the murky water.

I threw my hands in the air (or water in this case). What now? She shrugged.

I took another look at the serpent. There had to be something more here—another clue, another piece of the puzzle, something different about this figure.

The shield.

There were two small eyeholes where Medusa's head should have been and another for its mouth. That had to mean something. I stuck my fingers in the holes—what the hell, we had nothing else. It was like bowling almost. I smiled at the thought and turned clockwise. Nothing. I tried the other direction. Still nothing. They weren't there for decoration. I pulled in frustration, air bubbles streaming from my mouthpiece. The shield shifted a little bit. I put my feet against the wall for leverage and pulled.

To my elation, Athena's shield flew off the wall. It wasn't carved out of the wall like the rest of it. The separate piece was well hidden, no seam at all. Those Egyptians really knew how to build them.

I looked at the shield in my hand; there was nothing on the back of it. Emma tapped my shoulder and pointed to the circular recess where the shield had sat undisturbed for almost two thousand years.

I reached out and ran my hand over two lines of strange glyphs carved into the rock. This was it, I was sure. I had seen several strange glyphs like these on the sword: several circles with lines through them, a series of dots, a few triangles, and a backward E—it all looked like a kid's chicken scratch or…a code. My money was on the latter.

A flash brought me out of my thoughts. I looked back to see Emma taking a close-up shot with her waterproof camera. She did have a way of packing everything one could ever need in *any* circumstance.

She may have smiled, but I found myself distracted by a bright orange light shining behind her near the staircase.

The signal! I looked over at Emma, comprehension dawning on her face. The Suits, they'd found us again. Despite the danger, I wasn't quite as scared as in our last few encounters. Maybe I was getting used to the constant peril. Maybe I was getting overconfident. What was I doing, just standing here (or floating in this instance)? Time to move.

I took off with Emma right behind me. Monsieur Gibarah didn't strike me as the type of man to get jumpy.

We were about halfway back through the murky water, kicking as hard as we could for every ounce of speed. I wished I had some flippers on. I really wished we had had a few more minutes to study the carvings behind the shield. I wished we didn't run into trouble at every corner. Who were these guys? How did they know where we were every single time?

I reached the stairs, slipping on the first step. Emma helped me up as I hurried up the stairs. I could see the light now through the cloudy water. What was I going to find up there? Was Monsieur Gibarah all right? Was he already dead? Were the Suits waiting for us in the anteroom? They already had the sword; I had left it with Monsieur Gibarah. Did they just want to tie up loose ends? Maybe get a little revenge for their dead buddies? Maybe I should have taken the sword down there with me. After all, I didn't really know Monsieur Gibarah, and my gut had been wrong before. It's funny how much you can think of in high-stress situations.

This is it, I thought as my head broke through the water's surface.

I froze at the sight of a revolver three inches from my face.

"Here, take it," Monsieur Gibarah said, holding the butt out to me. He reached down with his other hand to help me up.

"What's happening?" I asked, dumping my tank off while he helped Emma.

"The motion sensors have picked up several signals heading down through the complex," the French-Egyptian said, clicking the safety off his Beretta.

"Motion sensors," I said impressed.

"One learns to be careful in my business, monsieur."

"How do you know it's not one of your men?"

"I gave them strict orders not to enter the catacombs."

"Well, maybe they didn't listen. You should call them to make sure," Emma said.

"No answer on any channel," Monsieur Gibarah whispered, leading us quickly back up the staircase to the first level. "Hurry. If they catch us here, all they have to do is fire down the stairwell."

I checked the revolver, fully loaded. Let's hope I

didn't have to use it. I strapped on my rucksack and followed a worried Monsieur Gibarah up the stairs. I noticed he wasn't smoking anymore.

"Can we make it back to the surface?" I asked Monsieur Gibarah softly as we ran up the staircase as quickly and quietly as our soaking wet bodies would allow.

Monsieur Gibarah checked the small handheld near the top of the stairs.

"Not the way we came," he answered.

"But there's only one way into the catacombs," I said.

Emma silently confirmed.

"Another lesson, Maxwell," Monsieur Gibarah said, looking back at me. "Always have a second way out."

"Oh, and what's that?" Emma asked.

"We go through the Hall of Caracalla," he answered, pointing his gun to the left wing of the rotunda.

"What's that mean?" I asked, nodding toward the urgent flashing on his handheld.

"They are coming."

"How many?" I asked.

"Two," Monsieur Gibarah answered hesitantly.

"You don't sound too sure," Emma said.

"Two are waiting at the vestibule for us," he whispered, showing us the blinking lights on his handheld. "Two more are waiting on the spiral stairway several feet above them. I expect there are more on the surface securing the area. They believe there is only one way out."

"There is only one way out," Emma said, her voice rising.

"Shh! Just tell us what to do," I told Monsieur Gibarah. He didn't look like the type of man who got trapped in a corner very often. I guess that was a prerequisite in his business if you wanted to stay alive.

Monsieur Gibarah raised his Beretta and looked at me. "They will know the second we emerge from the staircase. Just head for the hall and keep firing. And you," he said, looking at Emma, "stay behind us." She nodded her understanding. "On three then. One…two…three!"

We burst out of the stairway onto the first level, firing across the rotunda at the two men holding the opposite doorway.

"Go!" Monsieur Gibarah yelled as he held his ground in the center of the room, quickly emptying his Beretta's clip.

Emma stayed hunched behind me as I fired two more shots, chipping rock from the doorway's corner. One bald man with a goatee stuck his head out and took aim at Emma; I fired a shot, clipping his shoulder, and urged her across the room to the left wing. We ran into the Hall of Caracalla with Monsieur Gibarah following several seconds later.

"We surprised the first one, the second is only wounded. Hurry," he said, slamming a fresh clip into his gun. "More will be coming."

I pushed Emma after Monsieur Gibarah as he took off down the tall, arched hallway, leading us toward an exit that didn't exist.

Where was he leading us? I thought as I took up the rear, reloading my revolver as quickly as possible. Luckily the hallway wasn't exactly arrow straight.

"Max, hurry!" Emma yelled. I ran to catch up with them, looking over my shoulder every five seconds for the slightest movement. Where on earth were we going? I far as I remembered from the books the professor lent to us, the Hall of Caracalla ended in a dead end.

"Where are going?" Emma asked, her thoughts echoing my own.

Without pausing a second from our brisk pace, Monsieur Gibarah answered, "To the exit," as if we were asking a stupid question.

We passed one final Roman archway before coming to a dead end.

Well, not exactly a dead end. A small, collapsed staircase stood before us with a nice pile of rocks jammed neatly into place, ending any chance of our escape.

This must have been the original entrance into the Hall of Caracalla, which was built after the construction of Kom el-Shoqafa. It must have been left collapsed to prevent any intruders from entering—or escaping in our case.

I didn't understand. Why would Monsieur Gibarah lead us here? It would take days of digging to reach the surface, maybe weeks. There was no way we could hold the Suits off for that long. They would overwhelm us in minutes. Maybe we could still make a run for the staircase? Fight our way through the rotunda and to the surface. But what then? There must be more Suits on the surface. Emma and I had caused *way* too much trouble for them over the past week. I knew giving them the sword would only guarantee our deaths.

I headed back down the hallway to see if the coast was clear. Maybe we could retrace our steps and fight our way out.

*"Whoa!"*

I pulled my head back around the corner as several rounds struck the brick corner's edge.

No way back that way. Looks like Monsieur Gibarah had backed us into a corner.

I fired two shots before running back to Emma and Monsieur Gibarah, only to find her yelling at him.

"What are we going to do now! Everyone knows this passage has been blocked for hundreds of years!"

"Any other ideas?" I asked him.

"Oui," he said calmly holding up a small tan brick marked C4.

"*Are you crazy*!" Emma screamed at the top of her lungs at the crazy French wannabe.

I had to admit the scene would have been quite funny if it weren't for the dire circumstance we were in.

"That could bring the whole roof down on us," I said calmly to Monsieur Gibarah. "And I doubt the blast will completely clear a way to the surface."

"That is why this is what you Americans call a…Plan B, and why there is a *second* block on the surface."

"You are crazy," I said to the French-Egyptian. What else could I say? Either this worked and we lived, or it didn't and we'd die anyway.

He handed me his Beretta. "Take her and get as far from here as you can. This is going to be interesting," Monsieur Gibarah said with a cigarette-stained smile. I had never seen him smile before. I didn't know if that was a good thing.

Holstering my revolver, I did as he instructed and grabbed Emma's hand, running back to the arched corner where I had nearly lost my head a minute earlier. Maybe that would have been a better way to go—quick and painless. Better than being buried alive, in my opinion.

What were they waiting for? Maybe until more men arrived? I stuck my head out for split second only to pull back as more bullets came flying, a smoldering section of rock missing where it had been moments earlier. These guys weren't playing around anymore. They meant business.

"Max?" Emma said softly behind me.

"Yeah, Em?" I asked, looking back at her. She seemed to be her old self again—cool, composed, confident.

"Quite a situation we got ourselves into this time, don't you think?" she asked in that magnificent English accent of hers.

"Don't worry, Emma," I said after firing two blind shots around the corner. These guys were just too good. The second I stuck my head out again would be the last time. "Monsieur Gibarah has a wonderful plan to get us out of here nice and safe," I said, throwing my most charming smile.

"You're enjoying this, aren't you?" she asked, laughing.

"Well, I don't enjoy the getting-shot-at part, I can assure you that."

"And you actually like that *Monsieur* Gibarah?" she asked.

"Well, I like his style," I replied, taking two more blind shots before the gun clicked empty.

"And you will too, mademoiselle," Monsieur Gibarah said as he slid in beside us, holding a detonator with a new cigarette in his mouth.

"Ready?" he asked.

I covered Emma's head as my answer.

"Fire in hole," Monsieur Gibarah said with excitement. I was starting to think he liked his career choice a little bit too much as the explosives detonated and a cloud of dust and rocks descended toward us.

"Well, at least the roof didn't come down on us," Emma said in my arms.

"Yeah," I replied, staring into her blue eyes.

"Gun," Monsieur Gibarah said, his hand outstretched.

I handed the empty Beretta to him, releasing Emma.

"You two get going. I'll meet you at the surface. Protect the sword," he said, reloading the Beretta.

"What about you?" Emma asked. I was slightly surprised at her sudden concern for the man.

"I'll follow you. Now *go*!"

I pulled Emma after me, a tiny shaft of light visible through the settling dust.

"You go first," I told her, following her into the narrow staircase. We squeezed our way through the passageway that had been sealed for hundreds of years.

Hopefully, no one would be waiting for us at the top. And *hopefully*, I thought, I would be able to squeeze through the next particularly narrow gap in what was now – thanks to the C4 – more of a steep tunnel than a staircase.

Suddenly, I heard the sound of gunfire behind me as I held my breath to squeeze myself and my pack through the narrow section; this must have been the midpoint between the two explosions. I hoped Monsieur Gibarah wouldn't have any trouble coming after us. All they had to do was shoot into the tunnel.

I breathed in deeper, my face turning red as I pulled

as hard as I could. Please don't let me be stuck!

"Ahh," I yelled as I pulled myself out from two narrow sections of rock.

"Max!" Emma called from above. "Are you all right?" She must have made it to the surface. Maybe I should lose a few pounds.

"Yeah!" I yelled, looking up at Emma blocking the afternoon sun. Only a few more feet, no need to yell.

"Come on, hurry," she said, pulling me up from the hole to breathe in the fresh, dry Egyptian air. Air never smelled so good.

"You don't look so good," I said, noting the small cuts and dirt on her hair and face.

"You don't look so good yourself," she replied with a smile, confirming my suspicion.

Suddenly a large explosion shook the ground far below us, sending a cloud of dust up from the hole we had just climbed out of.

"Monsieur Gibarah!" I called, kneeling by the hole. "Monsieur Gibarah!"

"Ah, oui, oui. I am here." The French-Egyptian coughed as he emerged from the dusty hole. He looked as if he had just fought in World War III compared to us.

"More C4 I take it," I said.

"Oui," he said. "A little present for our friends down there."

"You know, you should be more careful with that stuff," I said.

"Come, we must go," Monsieur Gibarah said, ignoring the comment. As we helped him stand up, I noticed the blood on his left side.

"You're hurt," I said.

"Oui, I'll be fine. We must get off the streets."

Supporting the wounded Monsieur Gibarah, we headed down the street as quickly as we could. His injury looked pretty bad—far worse than the graze I had received in Turkey, and I had nearly died. I didn't think Monsieur

Gibarah had much time before he lost consciousness. We had to get him somewhere safe, somewhere he could rest, but where? We couldn't take him to a hospital; the Suits seemed to have everything monitored. Who were these guys? Who funds an armed assault in an underground tomb?

"Turn right," Monsieur Gibarah said weakly.

"Where are we going?" I asked. He was leaning on us more—not a good sign.

"Safe house," he answered.

"Are you sure it's safe?" I asked. Lately nothing was proving to be safe with the Suits around.

"Oui."

Two minutes later we carried a barely conscious man into a small apartment scarcely two blocks from Kom el-Shoqafa. The apartment wasn't much to look at as far as safe houses go: a bed, a bath, and a large trunk under the mattress filled with enough guns and C4 to blow up three city blocks.

"Whoa! You sure know how to have a good time, Monsieur Gibarah," I said after pulling out the trunk. I rummaged around for the small first-aid kit he asked for; it was buried at the bottom of the trunk.

"I don't know how much of this can help you. You could have internal bleeding. You really need to get to a hospital," Emma told him after removing his shirt and surveying the wound. It looked pretty deep to me; I didn't think first aid was what he needed.

"I agree, but no. They will be watching all the hospitals, and if they catch me, then I will die a slower and more painful death. Do what you can," he told her.

"What can I do?" I asked.

"There," he said, pointing at the worn cabinet across from the bed. I went over and opened it. Yep, this was definitely Monsieur Gibarah's safe house—there was enough bourbon and Egyptian cigarettes to last a long siege.

"I really don't think he should be smoking at the moment," Emma said as I brought him a large glass of bourbon and a pack of his favorite cigs, per his request.

"See what I mean about English women?" he said as he brought a shaking hand to his mouth to light the cigarette.

"Here, let me," I said, taking the lighter to help.

"Merci," he said weakly as I lit the cigarette. He really needed to get to a hospital; he was as pale as a sheep. Now I understood what Emma had felt like a couple days ago.

"Well, that's it, Monsieur Gibarah. I'm sorry that's the best I can do," Emma said tenderly after cleaning and bandaging the stomach wound.

"Merci." The man coughed. I noticed a little blood on his hand. "And call me Sayed, ma chère."

"Sayed," she said softly with a smile, tears forming in her eyes. Who ever thought these two would become friends?

"Tell me," he coughed out. "Did you have enough time to find anything?"

"Oh, yes," Emma answered, taking out her waterproof digital camera. "We found another Agathodaimon and these markings carved behind Athena's shield," she said, showing him the picture she took.

"Ah, oui," Monsieur Gibarah said, his eyes glowing. "I recognize some of that. It is Tifinagh, one of the ancient languages spoken by some of the Berber people, mainly the Tuareg."

"Do you know what it says?" I asked.

"Alas, no, few outside of the Tuareg do." Suddenly, he started coughing blood heavily, the cigarette falling onto the clean sheets.

"Sayed!" Emma yelled. She pushed him back down on the mattress after the coughing ceased.

"Casablanca," he said so quietly it was almost a whisper, his eyes barely open. "Rick's Cáfe. Hamza al-Meshal, find him…he can help."

"Sayed, Sayed," Emma called, holding the brave man's hand.

"Tell Giordani it was an honor."

His eyes closed.

* * *

"*Enough*!" he screamed, banging his fist on the ancient table, his cigar falling to the floor. This was getting out of hand, out of control. To think that this *Max Taylor* and this Emma Atherton, a simple commoner, he thought with disdain, could cause this kind of trouble for the council. What on earth was he doing running around with the likes of her? The boy should know better, live up to his pedigree.

The most powerful men in the world were assembled here, their influence stretching to nearly all corners of the world, and two kids could evade them not once, not twice, not even three, but *four* times. Four times! Were his men that incompetent? He should really look into hiring some better mercenaries. The best ex-soldiers from around the world *foiled* by a twenty-two-year-old American and his girlfriend.

He had to calm down; he had to compose himself in front of the council. To lose control now while so close to completing his father's life work would be unacceptable. He looked down at the old man sitting at his right, surveying him, studying him. He had to reassert control among the council, among the hired guns. Failure was not an option.

He looked at his security chief standing before him, waiting to finish his report. A destroyed helicopter in Italy, a firefight with the Turkish Army stationed at Topkapi as the pair escaped again, and another half-dozen men killed or buried alive as several pounds of C4 brought a tomb down on their heads. And *still* they managed to get away.

It looked as if the Order of the Vestals still had some sting for a bunch of aging scholars. They would have to be taken care of.

All of them.

It was foolish to have left any of them alive. True,

they may still provide some useful information once the key was acquired, but providing C4 for an escape and turning an entire contingent of the Turkish military against them was another matter. For a bunch of old men, they still had some resources.

He looked down at the old man beside him again. How many times was he going to let age blind him into equating that with stupidity?

The Order of the Vestals wanted a war?

He would give them a war.

But first it was time to clean house.

He removed his silenced FNP from his jacket and shot his pathetic excuse for a security chief in the head. The man was ex-British SAS, but that didn't matter much since no weapons of any kind were allowed in this most secretive of rooms.

"What ever happened to your no-weapons protocol?" the old man asked.

"I made an exception," he replied, his Ukrainian accent adding menace to the answer. He did, after all, make and enforce the said protocol.

"Bring in his second-in-command," he called to the attendant at the door.

He wouldn't make it out of here alive either—none of the attendants ever did. The price of secrecy, he thought with a wicked smirk.

"What happened after they fled from the catacombs?" he asked the mercenary who had just entered.

The man looked down at his former commander without emotion before continuing. He was paid well, well enough that the sight of his leader and friend of twenty years lying dead on the floor didn't bother him in the slightest, as long as he didn't fail so miserably.

"We followed a blood trail," the mercenary said, wishing his firearms hadn't been taken from his Armani jacket. He was good, but not bulletproof. "It led us to a small room with Monsieur Gibarah's bloody body lying on the mattress. We believed him to be dead, until our medic roused him."

Monsieur Gibarah, a man with some more *interesting* associations. It paid to have men like him around, men who lived in the darker shades of society. Frankly, it was amazing Monsieur Gibarah hadn't accepted their offer of employment before disappearing. The money was really quite good. Even thieves must have ideals.

"Did he say anything?" the old man asked excitedly.

"All we got before we lost transmission was, 'See you all in hell.' Then a large explosion took the building and half the city block with it. We lost several more men," the mercenary finished. Many of them had been the mercenary's lifelong friends as well. If he made it out of this dark room alive, he vowed to make those two kids pay.

"And do you know what they were doing at Kom el-Shoqafa?" he asked the mercenary.

"We believe they were searching the third level of the complex, but unfortunately the explosion destroyed most of it, and it will take weeks to clear the rubble."

"So we lost them?" the old man asked.

"No, sir," the mercenary replied.

"No?" he said in disbelief.

"No, sir," the mercenary repeated. "I managed to hit the girl with a small tracking bug in the catacombs while they made their escape, just in case they got away."

The man smiled in the candlelit room. Maybe this mercenary wouldn't die tonight; he seemed to have some brains compared to his former commander. He told the man as much.

"Thank you, sir," the mercenary said. Technically it was his commander who had placed the tracking bug on the girl, but he was dead now. Might as well take the credit and live another day to enjoy his ridiculously large paycheck.

"So where are they now?" he asked.

"On a train, headed to Morocco, sir."

CHAPTER NINE

# THE ABDUCTION AT CASABLANCA

"Hamza al-Meshal," I said, taking my seat opposite Emma on the train.

"Yes, what of him?" Emma asked, her face still buried in some book she had managed to bring along.

"Do you think he'll really be able to help us?"

"I'd imagine so. Monsieur Gibarah spent his dying words on him, and I don't think he would do that unless he truly believed he could help us."

"You seem quite taken with him now," I said, smiling sadly at the memory of our last meeting with the man.

Emma put her book down and looked out the window. "Well, one does after seeing such heroism."

"Yeah," I sighed. "He did like to blow stuff up."

"So what does Professor Giordani have to say about all of this?"

"I don't know," she said. "I called several times from the train station, but he didn't pick up."

"Do you think he's all right?"

"I hope so, but he was never an expert on Arabic languages or anything. I do hope he is all right. We would probably be dead right now if it weren't for him. I think this Hamza al-Meshal character is all we have for now, and he'd better be worth it. Did you ask the conductor how much longer it'll be until we reach Casablanca?"

"I tried. And he either said ten more minutes or little pink bunnies."

Emma threw her head back, laughing. "How on earth do you confuse the two?"

"Hey, you try talking to the man."

Emma shook her head in amusement and went back to her book while I looked out over the small town we were passing through.

"Hey, Em?"

"Mmm?" she hummed, deeply immersed in her book again.

"I'm sorry about all this," I said, looking down. "About your scooter. About getting you in this whole mess."

"Max," she said softly, putting down her book and leaning toward me. "It's not your fault." She placed her hand on mine. "Honestly, it's not. It's been an adventure, and I can't wait to see where it goes."

"Really?" I asked, looking up at her piercing blue eyes. "After all this?"

She beamed, her face only inches from mine.

"After all this," she whispered.

"And the scooter?" I whispered back, tilting my head to one side.

There was no need to talk; only millimeters separated us on the bustling train. They may as well have been miles.

"Even the scooter." She giggled seductively, her eyes closed.

"Max Taylor?" a deep voice asked, a heavy hand pushing me back into my seat. Hard.

"Who wants to kno—"

I froze; utter disbelief and fear overtook me. Two men, one with his hand still on me, dressed in tailored Armani way too nice for this train stood right before us, blocking any chance of escape.

"You two have caused quite a lot of trouble for us," the large man said with a slight German accent, each word emphasized with a firm squeeze of my shoulder.

Impossible! After everything we'd been through, they had to find us now! *Now*! They couldn't wait a second longer? Ten seconds longer even?

Then again, considering the number of men they'd lost over the past few days, they probably weren't going to be doing us any favors.

"Some of those guys you killed were my friends," he said, confirming my suspicions and bringing tears to my eyes. Literally. He was squeezing so hard I thought my arm was going to come off.

"Who are you guys?" I asked, partly because I really wanted to know who they were—I was getting tired of referring to them as the Suits (although that was a very nice black Armani suit)—and partly because I wanted to buy some time.

Why had they waited this long? Of course, I thought stupidly, we were close to the terminal; no reason to alarm us until we got there. How did they even find us? We had been so careful to make sure no one had followed us. Why didn't we pay closer attention on the train? Were we that cocky? These guys were professional ex-soldiers after all; it was our own fault we were caught. But what now?

"That doesn't concern you," the large German growled. "No more games." His partner motioned for him to calm down; they were already drawing enough attention without causing a scene.

I threw a quick glance over at Emma and then at the approaching conductor I had talked to earlier. It wasn't a great plan, but I couldn't think of anything else. These guys had backed us into a corner this time, literally (with no C4 to help us out either).

Emma winked in that split-second glance; she understood. If anyone could, it'd be her.

The conductor approached our small group; he was urging people to take their seats as the train began slowing down for Casablanca.

"Pardon, sir—"

"*Now*!" I yelled, kicking the German's kneecap while he was distracted by the conductor. The soldier immediately went down due to the sudden and unexpected blow, which was quickly followed by my best left hook to his head. I knew it would only take him a second to recover, and he was not going to be too happy about this.

Emma's guy, on the other hand, was probably going to be down for a while. She had opted for a more personal attack at the man's groin. I really didn't want to be on that English girl's bad side.

"Time to go," I said, grabbing Emma's hand and my rucksack. "Sorry about that," I told the stunned conductor, making for the next car.

Something grabbed my ankle and stopped me. The well-dressed German, his nose bloodied, looked up in fury. Emma gave him a swift kick in the head.

"Thanks," I said with a smile.

"Max," she said, looking over my shoulder.

I looked back. Two more Armani Suits were pushing their way down the car toward us.

"Definitely time to go," I said, pulling her into the next car.

"I think you're right."

We made our way through the next car, but it was slow going through the crowded train. I stole a quick glance behind me; the two Suits were gaining on us (luckily their guns were still holstered), shoving anybody who got in their way. Pretty soon they were given a wide berth as people began squeezing closer to one another trying to stay out of their way.

This wasn't going to work; we were moving too slow compared to them. We had to get off this train.

"Head up!" I yelled to Emma as we entered the open

area between the two cars. We took the ladder up to the car's roof, the wind slamming into us on top of the car.

"Go, go," I yelled, waving her on as I unholstered my revolver. I didn't have a plan yet, but I knew we were close to the Casablanca terminal. We were already passing through the edge of the city.

I fired a shot above the close-cropped head that popped above the roof; it quickly dipped back down. It was only a warning shot, and the man knew it. No one misses a shot that close unless he does so on purpose. I didn't want to kill the man. I didn't want to kill anybody, but I wasn't about to let him kill either Emma or me. I doubted even giving him the sword at this point would stop them.

Suddenly a Sig Sauer held by a meaty hand appeared above the car roof's edge and began firing blindly. Time to go! I fired two more shots at the hand and followed Emma down the train.

Man, this wasn't easy; running down the roofs of train cars looks so easy in the movies. They never mention the force of the wind pushing you back or how slippery a train car is.

Suddenly, I stumbled forward and landed on my stomach; the train was slowing down. We were almost there.

"*Max!*" Emma screeched. I looked up, and my heart froze. Another suited man held Emma firmly in his grasp.

The train slowed as we pulled into the Casablanca terminal.

A bullet pinged off the metal beside where I lay; the suit with the close-cropped hair was taking potshots at me, clearly enjoying himself and my predicament. Amazingly, I still had my revolver.

I raised it at the man holding Emma and closed one eye. Could I hit him? Not with all the swaying he was doing due to the train's deceleration. Even then, I couldn't risk hitting Emma.

"Max! *Run!*"

Another shot hit the metal beside me; their aim was getting better.

What should I do?!

The trained slowed to crawl, finally pulling into the station.

"*Run!*" Emma cried, desperately trying to fight the man off with no success.

The two Suits behind me were coming closer.

Clearly, they were savoring the close-up kill in case I slipped off the train car and took the sword with me.

What to do?

Three rounds left.

What to do?

"*Runnn!*" Emma screamed at the top of her lungs.

Time was running out.

The train stopped at the station.

No choice—damn it.

I jumped off the train car, rolled to my feet on the terminal platform, and ran.

I hated myself for doing it. But I ran, bullets pinging behind my feet accompanied by the sound of screaming.

I don't know how long or how far I ran. All I remember was the running, the tears streaming down my face as I ran, the residents and tourists all looking at me as I ran through the streets of Casablanca.

I don't know if I was pursued. Maybe I was at the start, but after so many blocks—or was it miles?—they may have stopped. I don't know. I didn't know where I was. I didn't know what I was doing. What was I doing here? I was just a kid, an ordinary college student from the States.

How did I wind up in the middle of this? How did I get in the middle of some ancient war between two secret societies?

This wasn't my fight.

This was all because I found that stupid sword in the Caribbean. It felt like a lifetime ago.

*Why*?!

I turned down an alley and stopped by a filthy trashcan. Panting, I leaned back with my hands on my head in an effort to open my lungs. Distraught, I ripped my rucksack from my back and threw it against the alley wall with a loud grunt.

Sweat pouring down my face, I kicked the trash can over and over again, denting the rusty bucket.

I threw myself down in defeat against the alley wall. Now my foot hurt as well. Stupid trash can.

Was she already dead?

"No," I told myself. She was too valuable alive. She could be used against me, a bargaining chip. That made her valuable enough to keep her alive until they had the sword. That's what they wanted, and until they got it, she would remain alive.

Alive.

"Alive," I said, as if it were a foreign word.

Suddenly, it dawned on me. I was going to get her back. No matter what it took, I was going to get her back. They may have trapped me in a corner back there, but I was going to get her back. I was going to do the unexpected. I was going after them.

But how to find them? I thought.

"Simple," I said.

I keep going and let them find me.

Then I'll get some answers…and some revenge.

It took me the rest of the afternoon to get directions to Rick's Café. I could see why. The place was located at the end of a narrow alley in an older section of the city; it looked like something out of the 1940s. The 'a' in 'Café' was blown out on the red neon sign above the establishment.

The building had definitely seen better days, I thought as I stepped through the studded wooden doors into the joint. A piano player earning his night's keep on an ancient grand piano, whose surface could have used a recoat decades earlier, brought a touch of class to the otherwise disreputable place.

Small tables hidden in weak lighting and bathed in cigar smoke hosted a mix of clientele from around the world. The only things they shared were money and the desire to keep their faces hidden from prying eyes.

Definitely a place I could see Monsieur Gibarah visiting to conduct his shadier dealings.

I walked through the dining hall—if it could be called that, considering I saw far more liquor than food—and entered the main bar through one of a series of tall arches.

If movies had taught me anything, it was that a bartender knows most everyone in his establishment, especially if they were good tippers, maybe more if they were lousy ones.

I became aware of the glances I was receiving from many of the patrons as I walked by. It may have been my attire; despite being a slightly rundown place, it did appear to have some sort of dress code. Many of the patrons seemed to have on loose suits like Monsieur Gibarah had worn or white thrawb robes down to their ankles in the typical Arab style. And a kuffiyya, taqiyah, or even a red fez seemed to be part of the unwritten dress code. I felt out of place in my sweaty navy blue button-down shirt and brown chinos (with no hat either). I felt like a lost tourist in this place of business of flickering shadows of men.

The quiet conversation among the locals seemed to pick up a notch as I took a seat on a worn-out barstool. It seemed the tourist was staying for a drink.

"What are you having?" the bartender asked, cleaning a dirty glass with a rag.

I decided to get to the point. This guy looked like he'd seen it all and was in no mood for games; neither, for that matter, was I.

"I'm looking for a friend," I said, sliding a folded hundred to him.

"Lots of friends here," the clean-shaven Arab said

with amusement.

I grinned at the pun. "I'm looking for a particular friend in this case," I corrected, "by the name of Hamza al-Meshal. Is he around, by any chance?"

The barman nodded toward a man sitting in the corner alone. He seemed perfectly content hidden behind one of several small plastic palm trees strewn around the place listening to the piano player play Herman Hupfeld's "As Time Goes By."

I thanked the barman and approached the man.

He immediately saw me coming (as if I was hard to miss in this crowd); a split second passed as we took each other in.

Hamza al-Meshal. After everything I had been through, everything Emma had been through, he was my only lead, my only hope at getting her back. Anything he needed, anything he wanted—even the sword if it came to that—I would give to him freely. Just to get her back, just for a *chance* to get her back.

The Arab continued to take me in with an intense stare that seemed to reach into my very soul. There was something different about this man, something mysterious. As if he had seen much in his thirty or so years.

I took one more second, noting his blue thawb robe and black turban, before addressing him.

"Are you Hamza al-Meshal?" I asked him, getting straight to the point, no time to waste with pleasantries.

He took a sip of his orange juice, all the while never taking his eyes off of me.

"And who is asking?" he asked in near perfect English, only the slightest hint of an accent audible.

"May I?" I asked, indicating the chair opposite him. He nodded once, his dark eyes continuing to stare at me. Had I seen him blink yet? Somehow he didn't scare or intimidate me in the least. Maybe because I sensed he wasn't dangerous deep down, or maybe because I was too driven, too desperate, to get Emma back to care.

"My name is Max Taylor."

"Yes, I know," he said.

"You do?" I asked.

"Yes," the Arab replied with a smile.

"How?"

"My old friend, Monsieur Gibarah, told me to expect you."

"But…how? Monsieur Gibarah is—"

"Dead," al-Meshal finished sadly.

The waiter arrived with another orange juice and placed it before me.

"Excellent timing, Hamid, as usual," al-Meshal said, thanking the young man with a generous tip.

"To Monsieur Sayed Aly Gibarah," he toasted. "A man dedicated to finding his…treasure."

"But when did he tell you to expect me?" I asked after taking a sip of the cold drink. It tasted wonderful; I couldn't remember the last time I had had anything to drink in fact.

"Why, he called."

"What?" I asked. "When?"

"Shortly after you and your young companion left him at his safe house."

"What!"

"Shh." al-Meshal warned. "We wouldn't want to be overheard."

"But we thought he was dead," I said in horror.

"I believe that to be the case now. During our short talk, I heard several men in the room with him until the line cut out. He was a good man in many ways. I shall miss him. He briefly explained about the sword and asked that I help you and your friend in any way I can. Speaking of which, where is your companion?"

I looked down, hesitating. "She was taken. On the train. I…I…"

"It's all right," al-Meshal said sincerely. "I will help you get her back."

"You know where she is?" I asked. The man must have been some kind of psychic.

"Well, no." My hopes dropped. "But men dressed such as this do not go unnoticed in these parts of Old Casablanca. Surely you must have noticed this," he said with a smile.

"Thank you, Mr. al-Meshal," I said.

"Al'afw," he replied with a smile. "And please, you may call me Hamza."

"So, where do—"

Suddenly the music stopped, and half a dozen Armani Suits forced their way through the doors, pushing patrons out of the way and heading in my general direction. Man, these guys needed to get a life. How did they find me? Of course, like Hamza said, "Men dressed such as this do not go unnoticed in these parts of Old Casablanca."

"Go!" Hamza said. "Don't come back. I will find you."

I kicked my rucksack to him under the table. I don't know why; maybe because I trusted him, or maybe because I knew I might not make it out of this one.

"Keep it safe."

"Go!" Hamza yelled. Several Arab men dressed as he was stood up behind him, ready to protect their leader.

I had guessed right. All those glances in our direction weren't just from curious spectators.

I took Hamza's advice and ran (again).

I was taking an awfully big risk by leaving the sword with a man whom I had met only a few minutes ago. But what choice did I have? I thought as the first bullet struck the wall beside me.

They definitely weren't playing nice anymore. These guys no longer cared if I was brought in dead or alive. They were upset (to put it mildly), and they wanted payback.

It's not like it's my fault their friends are dead, I thought as I ran through the back kitchens of the café. I dashed through the back door into an alley with a volley of bullets ricocheting behind me.

What the hell were those? Submachine guns?

My question was answered as more shots struck the corner I took.

I froze. Four men stood in front of me blocking my path, their weapons drawn, a feel of imminent victory about them.

I turned around to head back the way I came.

My pursuers approached, blocking any possible escape. I could sense their victorious smiles in the dark alley.

"Whoa, boys," I said, holding my hands out before me, feeling inexplicably brave. "You got me. No need to do anything we'll regret."

"Where is it?" someone asked in an accent I couldn't place. Not Russian, maybe Eastern European.

I looked behind me. There, behind the Suits, was a man by the Dumpsters, casually smoking a cigar, his features hidden by the shadows.

"Where's what?" I asked, lowering my hands, playing stupid.

The gentlemen who had pursued me re-cocked their submachine guns.

"Whoa!" I said, putting my hands back up. "Hold on a second. Give me the girl, and I'll give you what you want."

"Sir," another Armani suit said, approaching from the café. "A group of heavily armed Arabs just forced their way out. One of them had the kid's bag."

"And you didn't stop them?" the shadowed man asked.

"Most of us were chasing the kid," he replied. "They killed two of my men."

The shadowed man raised his hand and shot him.

Okay, now I was starting to get scared. Adrenaline only helped so much. If I ever made it out of this mess—how on *earth* was I going to make it out of this mess?

The shadowed man pointed his gun at me.

"Who was he?"

"I don't know," I answered. It was mostly the truth. I knew Hamza's name, but other than that, I knew nothing. Well, at least I knew he didn't work for the Suits. I guess I sounded convincing enough.

"Where did he take the sword?" he asked furiously.

"Honestly, I don't know," I answered. At this point, I was scared out of my mind. I had no doubt this man wanted me dead and I was about to die.

"You just let a stranger have the sword?!" he yelled in cold, hard wrath, his cigar lying forgotten on the ground.

"Trust me, it wasn't part of the plan," I answered to my own surprise, barely a quiver in my voice. I had no idea where this newfound bravery was coming from, but now was not the time to further antagonize the man. Well, if I was really about to die…then why not.

The men around me re-aimed their weapons at my chest. I guess they could sense their boss's growing impatience and my shortening lifespan.

"Where's Emma?" I asked after the moment's silence. If I was about to die, at least I might take that to the grave with me.

To my surprise, the man lowered his gun and gave a short chuckle.

"If she isn't dead by now, she'll wish she were," he answered, waving his gun at one of his lieutenants.

"Where is she?!" I yelled, taking a step toward the man, the dozen or so guns pointed at me forgotten.

A man grabbed me from behind, forcing my arms behind me, his hands nearly breaking my wrists.

"Where is she?!" I repeated. If only he would step out of the shadows and let me see his face.

One of the men in front of me flipped his Sig Sauer around and held the barrel.

"Don't worry, Max. You're about to join her," the man said, stepping out of the shadows, his eyes almost black in the evening light.

The pistol came down, and the world went black.

CHAPTER TEN

# AND NOW YOU DIE

Where was I? What happened? What was that smell?!

Voices. I remember hearing strange voices talking quickly in some exotic language.

Images, flashes of brown… sand, I think it's called.

A desert?

Strange place for heaven.

Heaven? What was that?

Why did my head hurt so much? Why couldn't I think? I wasn't supposed to be here. I was doing something important. Someone was missing. Who?

What was wrong with me?

Was I moving? I was sitting on something hairy, something smelly. Why couldn't I see?

Why was my mouth so dry?

What happened?

The alley! The man in the shadows. The black eyes. The cigar!

Then the darkness.

Was I dead? No, I wouldn't be in so much pain then.

Where was I?

The desert, of course. My head started to clear.

What had I been thinking about?

The weather, something about the weather.

The sun.

I had been thinking about the sun before I passed out.

It was hot.

Yes! That was it.

It was hot. Unbearably hot. That was the single notion that kept invading my thoughts. A blistering heat that encompassed all my thoughts and mind. Never had I known a desert—or any place, for that matter—as this. It was all I could think about. What I wouldn't give for just a little shade and the smallest sip of water.

*Water.*

The life blood of Earth. Seventy percent of the planet was covered in that beautiful stuff, and here I was without a drop for endless miles around me. But I had to keep my head; I couldn't afford to lose my mind now.

She needed me.

She?

Who was I thinking about? Emma! How could I forget? What was wrong with me? Was I losing my mind?

Probably, I thought with a smirk. I suddenly recognized the beginnings of heat exhaustion, my mind beginning to wander. I tried to focus, take my mind off the heat. Or maybe it was a concussion, either way.

Even though it had been several hours since I had last opened my eyes, I knew the scenery hadn't changed all that much beyond my sweat-drenched blindfold. The only thing worse than the nasty piece of cloth, which I'm guessing had never been washed, was the fact that my wrists were tightly bound.

I could barely feel them at this point; somebody clearly had some mommy issues.

But the absolute worst bit of my predicament was my complete loss of time and lack of knowledge. How long had

I been tied up? Where the hell were we going? And who were these men working for? My list of questions had only grown longer since the start of this crazy adventure.

I had spent the first few hours of my captivity trying to loosen the hold of the rope on my wrists but without much success—unless you count the blood now flowing slowly down my fingers. Of course, all the movement of the camel hadn't helped. Come to think of it, maybe my captors did know what they were doing—practice does make perfect. Had there been any saliva in my mouth, I would have gulped. I was really tired of people trying to kill me.

I must have passed out at some point from the heat (or the concussion). What had happened since the alley?

Lost in my dark thoughts, I almost fell off the camel as it slipped down a dune before recovering.

I had already fallen off the smelly thing several times when I wasn't paying attention, especially in the last hour or so (this heat really had a way of getting to you), and had no desire to do so again.

I especially didn't want my captors stopping to throw me back on. One of them—I called him Grumpy (because the others yelled at him a lot and made him do all the grunt work, so naturally he took it all out on me)—wasn't the gentlest creature when he had to stop and throw me back on. And "he had an absolutely horrid smell about him," to quote Emma (it seemed like a lot of things smelled out here—go figure). But then, maybe it was all of them. Or maybe it was just him.

In fact, the only improvement to my situation was the rapport I was developing with my camel. The endless hours on his back had allowed me to fall into a natural rhythm with the camel's movements. He did smell a bit, but he was starting to grow on me (at least he didn't yell at me). It was only when I passed out that I would find myself on the sand or being thrown back on by Grumpy.

I didn't really care about falling off, but the heat was really starting to take its toll on me. I was having trouble thinking clearly, let alone keeping my mind off it. Not to mention I could feel the warm blood coming from my wrists with all the struggling. If anything, my struggles had only tightened the rope further into my flesh.

No, I would have to wait for my opening, probably when—or *if*—this damn blindfold was taken off, I thought with dismay. It had better be soon, before my waning strength was completely gone.

It was just after noon, if the burning sensation on the back of my neck was any indication. Even the camels must have been wishing they were somewhere else by now. I imagined the desert must look just like those pictures in *National Geographic* I had seen; hopefully I would still get the chance.

Unfortunately, pictures can never convey the unbearable amount of heat. No shade, no water, barely any animal life except those few that have evolved over millennia to survive. The ultimate survivors in my book, and no place fit for a human being.

Sure, it may look all pretty in pictures in your air-conditioned house with cold running water, but no words exist to describe a sun that literally burns through your clothes and into your very heart. It literally cooks your brain slowly and evaporates every ounce of sweat as it escapes your body, and the reflection of the light in the sand burns your eyeballs. Endless sand dunes that reach as far as the eye can see, offering no escape, no withdrawal, a prison with no walls. This must have been Satan's backyard growing up.

The Sahara. Man's very own hell on Earth.

I wondered what they'd do with me in this barren wasteland.

It couldn't be that hard to dispose of a dead body. Why was I still alive? Why were they bothering to bring me out here? It must have been at least two days since I had been knocked out, maybe longer if my parched mouth was any indication.

What would I do in their situation?

Probably throw my victim out in the middle of the desert, tied up in the sun, without water. Let the vultures finish him off; let the sand dispose of the body for all eternity.

As if to confirm my idea, the group of men broke out in laughter to something Grumpy said behind me.

"So…mind if I ask what's so funny," I asked in general to the continued laughter.

I already had a pretty good idea of what the joke had been about, but seeing as I didn't understand Arabic and was desperate for something to take my mind off my troubles, not to mention maybe find out some more about my captors, it didn't hurt to ask—unless Grumpy decided to shoot me.

"Why, you, my friend," a man replied in rusty English.

I recognized the voice as the leader of my captors. I thought I had even caught a glimpse of the man during my capture.

He was dressed in a white thrawb and ghutra like Hamza, but cleaner, more expensive looking. I remembered seeing him and the middle-aged man's black beard shortly before I was blindfolded. In fact, the last thing I remembered before that unfortunate event was that crooked smile and the repulsive state of his yellowed teeth, several of which looked to be missing.

I was caught off guard by the revelation that at least one of my captors spoke English and hadn't even bothered to say a word to me these last few days. Honestly, not even a single taunt at my dilemma.

Fortunately, the rhythmic movement of my body swaying with the camel hid any sign of surprise.

"And why, if I may ask, do you find me so amusing…mister?" I asked with a certain degree of sarcasm.

The leader then shouted out in Arabic to his men what I took to mean "shut up," though in not such nice words because the laughter among the men immediately ceased.

"My apologies, Mr. Taylor. How rude of me. Allow me to introduce myself. I am Abdul-Nasir Fadi, and forgive me for not shaking your hand, but you are, after all, a little *tied* up."

"Funny," I said.

"Yes, I thought so," he said. "And the subject of so much amusement, as you put it, is that you do not very often find yourself in the company of a dead man." Abdul-Nasir finished with an extra-loud laugh that only caused me more annoyance, not to mention more fear. Why couldn't they have just shot me in the alley and called it a day?

Unfortunately, my discomfort must have shown on my face, even with the dirty blindfold, because the rest of my captors began laughing as well.

Fadi shouted out, and the convoy slowed to a stop.

"This looks to be far enough, Mr. Taylor. Soon, I'm afraid, our time together will be up."

I began to feel a certain dread build up inside me, something I had never felt before. It's amazing how many unique emotions a human is capable of.

I felt a tightness in my chest, similar to what I felt in the fourth grade when I had to play Robin Hood on stage, but this was ten times worse than anything I had ever experienced. I almost would have preferred to be shot in the alley. It seemed more merciful. Maybe that's why the man with the dark eyes hadn't pulled the trigger; he didn't strike me as the merciful type.

Suddenly, one of the mercenaries—Grumpy, from the smell of him—grabbed me by the shirt and threw me down to the ground *hard*.

This definitely didn't look good, I thought, spitting out the sand. This really, really did not look good at all. I would rather ride that smelly camel all day and night than be here right now.

I had to tell myself to calm down before I had a heart attack (I'm amazed I hadn't died from one yet). In fact, until that very moment with the four or five armed mercenaries laughing around my blind, bound body, I had never felt so scared or so close to death. There must be a way out of this, I thought, something I can do. But what? I was going to succumb to the curse of many young men, that feeling of invincibility, like nothing can happen to you and you're too young or lucky to end up like those stories of dead kids you see on television.

After everything I had gone through to get to this point—the motorcycle chase, the helicopter in Tuscany, the catacombs, all those bullets whizzing by my head, and the other close calls—this was it.

The real end. The end of the line. No daring rescue. No one to save me now. No one for endless miles in fact.

I really was about to become a dead man.

They could at least hurry up about it, for goodness sake!

"So why don't you just shoot me and get it over with already?" I asked Abdul-Nasir Fadi after the men quieted down from their amusement at my misery.

An agonizing minute passed before Fadi answered. I waited for the cock of his gun to signal my demise. No doubt he would finish the job himself.

"You see, Mr. Taylor, you caused a lot of trouble for the wrong people, and I was hired to solve their problem. Lucky for them, I prefer the old ways and do not like guns especially much. That and they pay a large bonus to kill you nice and slow," he said. I could imagine his evil smirk.

The men laughed as Fadi quickly translated our conversation. Evil bastard.

"Nice and slow. Great. Can things get any worse?" I muttered.

"Yes, my friend, things are about to get very much worse for you," Adbul-Nasir answered.

I heard the mercenaries cock their rifles from atop their camels. I wondered what they were going to shoot off me: My arms? My legs? Both? What's the slowest way to kill a man with a bullet?

A pair of legs hit the sand, sending some down to where I now sat in the searing sand.

A body stood silently before me, its shadow offering a momentary respite from Satan's never-ending heat.

My blindfold finally removed, I blinked rapidly as my eyes adjusted, for the first time in who knows how many days, to the glaring sunlight. Part of me wished it were still on as Adbul-Nasir's ugly, evil, scowling face looked down at me.

"So now what?" I asked bravely. The four men on camels had their long rifles trained on me. The lead camel, Abdul's, stood waiting at the front of the line.

Grumpy (I recognized him instantly, though I had never seen him before) sat at the back of the pack. He was a big boy, not in muscle but in fat. Someone clearly didn't believe in fasting during Ramadan, by the looks of him. No bet as to what the others always teased him about.

"Now, my young friend," Abdul-Nasir Fadi answered with a purely evil look of enjoyment, "we leave you here to die."

"Asre'," Abdul-Nasir yelled in Arabic to his men as he mounted his camel. The mercenaries lowered their rifles, ready to set off into the barren desert behind their leader.

"That's it?" I yelled. "You're just going to leave me here?"

Abdul-Nasir turned his camel around to face me. "Yes," he yelled. "There are few deaths worse than one in the desert, Mr. Taylor. The scorpions will feast on you until the sand covers your bones. There will be no trace that you ever existed on this Earth. And it is with this thought, my friend, that now I leave you to your death."

Abdul-Nasir began turning his camel around to follow his men before adding one final piece of news.

"You may even last the day if you are strong enough, but in the end, you will die…they all do," he said before heading up the dune.

"Oh, I almost forgot," he yelled. "I'll be sure to say

hello to Miss Atherton for you tonight. She looks to be a real treat, much spirit," he finished, his malicious laugh echoing in my ears as he disappeared behind the sand dune.

"*No*! *No*!" I yelled in uncontrolled rage. "*You bastard*! *Ahh*!" I hopped around the desert floor, trying to stand up so I could go after them; the rope cut deeper into my hands and legs, the pain forgotten in my rage.

I don't know how long I screamed before my voice became hoarse, but I do know that those were the worst moments of my life.

Being powerless.

Powerless to help the girl who I liked…who I loved. Why did this have to be the moment I realized it? After everything we had been through together. All those near-death experiences. All those laughs we shared.

Was it really over? Was this the end of Max Taylor and the woman he loved?

Was this how it going to end? Killed at the hands of some sick mercenary?

Bastard. God knows how many times he had done this, how many lives he had ruined. How many loved ones he had split apart just for a few extra coins. A perfect performance right there at the end, riding off into the desert—could have been right out of the movies. Maybe even worth an Oscar. Not that anybody would pay to watch a movie with *him* in it. One of these days Abdul-Nasir Fadi was going to get his, even if I had to come back and haunt him for the rest of his days.

I turned my head around; nothing but endless sand dunes as far as I could see. Not even a mirage. Abdul-Nasir chose his spot well. If I didn't get this rope off of me, I was definitely a goner.

I pulled futilely at my arms again, wincing at the pain. If the heat didn't kill me, I was sure to die from an infection—or worse, bleed to death. Abdul-Nasir truly was a monster at his craft. I wondered how much he got paid.

Focus, I thought, blinking the sweat out of my eyes.

Focus. I had to get out of here. I had to get free. And then what? I had no idea where I was, and worse, unlike Abdul-Nasir and his men, I didn't have a drop of water.

I licked my cracked lips. It must have been at least a day since I had had anything to drink. They must have given me some water on the way to make sure I made it here, but not enough to have the strength to escape. Clever.

Focus! One problem at a time. I had to think, I had to get free. If only I weren't so thirsty.

*Focus*! I thought like a moron. I had to get free, but how? I needed something to cut the rope binding my hands. No other way. I looked around for a rock, a stick, *anything*, to get free.

Nothing. Nothing but sand. Abdul-Nasir really was an evil monster, I thought for the hundredth time. I wasn't the vengeful type and the Suits were the ones who really deserved it, but Abdul-Nasir was definitely going to get what was coming to him.

If only I had a knife.

*A knife! Like the one in my shoe!*

"God bless you, Emma!" I yelled in triumph.

Okay, so it was more of a razor blade than a knife taped inside my shoe, but it was definitely a start. In fact, if Emma hadn't insisted upon it after that whole catacomb fiasco, I wouldn't have a chance in hell of escaping my restraints. Even now she managed to save my ass. Of course, it would be best if I never mentioned this situation to her—the ego of that girl.

Well, back to business, I thought, arching my back to slip a sore finger in my shoe.

There it was!

I felt the duct tape that held the razor blade safely against my shoe and began picking at it.

I had a little trouble with the simple task mainly because my fingers were so numb at this point. Why did they have to tie me up so tight?

"Got it!" I yelled in triumph, holding the blade

loosely between two fingers. I was pretty sure the small blade was cutting into at least one of my fingers, but my hands were so numb at this point I wasn't even sure. I had to get my hands free.

After a few minutes I managed to cut one of the coils binding my hands, only to have some feeling and pain return to them.

"Come on, keep going," I told myself, wincing at the pain. Yep, I had definitely cut one of my fingers deep with the razor blade.

I looked up at the ever present sun. How long until nightfall? It was hard to believe it could get cold in this forsaken place. How far ahead were Abdul-Nasir and his band of merry men?

The last coil of rope snapped and freed my bleeding wrists.

"Well, that's probably going to leave a scar," I said hoarsely, looking at my blood-stained hands. They weren't as bad as I had imagined; any tighter and I probably would have had two stumps.

I needed to bandage them. It would be a real waste to free myself only to die from infection, but the smelly blindfold around my neck would have to do.

The last piece of rope fell away from my ankles, and I stood on my wobbly legs for the first time in days, looking out at the tracks left by Abdul-Nasir and his men.

"Allah, please let them stop for the night," I prayed, tying the last knot on my left wrist and taping the razor blade back in my shoe—Emma would insist (not something I'd ever argue again, that's for sure).

"And no sandstorms either," I added, setting off after the mercenaries, hoping my current luck would hold and the tracks would lead me to Emma and our escape.

I don't know which was worse: being tied up and carried though the desert on a smelly camel against your will or walking by yourself without water in the desert. In my opinion, both circumstances are to be avoided, but trudging alone without water is definitely worse.

I don't know how I did it, how I managed to follow those tracks all day in that searing heat, but I did, somehow. I have very little memory of the event. All I remember is the thought of Emma in trouble, needing my help; her being at the end of this trail, however far it was, however far I had to go to find her, to get her back.

The desert is a funny place. It takes from you without you ever realizing it. I could feel it taking my mind. I could feel it taking my strength. With each step, I would sweat, and its dry air would even take that. Abdul-Nasir Fadi chose this place well. This was where people were sent to die. This was where most did die. But this was also a place where a few, only the strongest, were reborn.

I started to feel a little bit better as the day neared its end and night began; a little stronger but very tired. There's only so much that the human body can take, only so far it can be pushed, especially in such a brutal environment.

My luck seemed to be improving. As a full moon rose, I continued to follow Abdul-Nasir's tracks. I hoped he would stop for the night; I had no chance of catching him otherwise. I knew I would never be able to continue this relentless pace tomorrow. I needed food. I needed rest. I needed *water*. Even if I managed to find Emma, rescue her, and escape, we were as good as dead out here without those basic things.

"One problem at a time," I told myself as I wearily reached the top of another dune. "Just one probl— Ah!" I exclaimed, rolling down the sand dune uncontrollably.

I tried spitting the sand out of my mouth when I reached the bottom, but when you have nothing to spit with, it's an almost impossible task.

As I lay on the sand, the moon shining high above, I felt like crying. Honest to God, crying. How did I get here? It was amazing that only a week had passed since I had found the Sword of Crocea Mors. What was I doing here? I should be in school right now, not lying in the middle of the Sahara Desert waiting to die. I wished I had never found the sword. I wished it had never come to me. I wished I had never met Dr. Wilson, who set this all into motion, or Professor Giordani, who used me like a pawn.

I would have cried right there on the cold desert sand if my body had any water to spare. I could just quit. Just lie there and wait for the end. No one said I had to get up, that I had to keep fighting. If only there weren't Emma.

Emma.

I couldn't leave her, not now. I had some idea of what those men would do to her before they killed her. She deserved far better. I had found the sword. I had started this whole mess, yet I was getting off easy. She was the one who had to pay the higher price.

I pushed off, up from the cold sand, my body screaming in protest. I still had some fight left in me. I wasn't done yet. I set off, a newfound sense of purpose pushing my tired limbs one step after another.

"Abdul-Nasir, I'm coming for you."

As the night wore on, I began imagining different scenarios, each one worse than the last, of how I'd find Emma. Was she still safe? Was I going to be too late? How much farther would I have to go? The moon was beginning to fall closer to the horizon, making the tracks harder to see, harder to follow.

I froze at the sound of two faint voices talking quickly in Arabic over the next sand dune.

Could it be? Did I find them? I scrambled up the dune, following the camel tracks, the sand for once helping me, hiding the sound of my approach.

I poked my head over the top of the dune to take a look. At the bottom of a small valley lay three tents, two small ones and a large one. A small fire burned in the center of the camp with four men sleeping around it. Two men were arguing, whom I had most likely heard. I recognized Grumpy immediately against the firelight; it looked like he wasn't one of the lucky ones with a tent to himself.

There had to be more than my five captors here; I guessed there were at least seven mercenaries in the camp. If Emma was here, she was with Abdul-Nasir, and he would have the large tent to himself. The two small tents looked to have been in place for at least a day, judging from all the tracks around them.

Emma had to be here. I was sure of it. Something in my gut told me Abdul-Nasir hadn't been lying; that and the large stake in the ground beside one of the small tents. The empty chain around it made me nervous. Was she all right?

I had to risk it. Even if Emma wasn't there, I needed to steal some water; one of those camels parked behind Abdul-Nasir's tent would also come in handy. The failing moon would help mask my escape; they wouldn't be able to track me until morning. Now all I needed to do was sneak down without being seen and make my move.

A loud yell woke the men around the fire. For a second I thought I had been spotted; then I saw Abdu-Nasir walk out of his tent holding his bleeding nose, much to my (and his men's) amusement.

"*And stay out*!" Emma yelled after Abdul-Nasir. I laughed quietly to myself upon hearing her voice. She was alive!

"Never mess with an angry English woman, Nasir," I said. The bleeding man looked like he had received a good kick in the face. Served him right.

Suddenly a few of the men broke out in a cheer as Abdul-Nasir yelled and pointed at the tent. One of the men, possibly his second-in-command since he emerged from one the small tents, headed toward Abdul-Nasir's tent with a wicked grin on his face and a curved knife in his hand. The men cheered once more and then returned to their beds by the fire, waiting to be awoken for their turn at the girl.

Clearly Abdul-Nasir didn't like his women very feisty. Stupid man. It would take more than being chained to a stake all day to take the fight out of Emma. The nasty black eye his lieutenant sported (which seemed like more of Emma's work) should have been proof of that.

I had to move fast. Something told me that Emma didn't have much time. What should I do? Think, Max, think.

There, by the lieutenant's tent that Abdul-Nasir now slept in, the mercenary had left his rifle out! But one versus seven?! Even if I weren't so tired, I doubted I'd be able to pull that off. I needed a diversion, but what?

I noticed Grumpy was starting to doze off again by the fire.

Fire?

A plan started to form in my tired mind.

I backed off of the sand dune's edge and circled around so I was behind the small tent Abdul-Nasir was now sleeping in. I had to be quick and *really* quiet. If any of them saw me, I was sure to be a dead man.

I took another peek over the dune's edge from my new vantage point. Good. Grumpy looked to be sound asleep along with the rest of the men.

My heart raced at the sound of Emma's short scream, but the mercenaries hardly even stirred. Abdul-Nasir pushed his men hard, too hard, which could work to my advantage. I had to hurry. There would be no better time to make a run for the rifle.

I ran down the dune, the sand once again masking the sound of my approach. Let's hope my luck held.

I quickly came to a halt behind the tent, scrunching my body up, waiting for the alarm and the gunshots to confirm that I had been seen.

Nothing.

I peeked around the tent; all four men by the fire were sound asleep. No one had seen me come down the sand dune. So far, so good.

The rifle was about seven feet away, resting against the stake that Emma most likely had been chained to all day. Fools. Still, I had to hurry. Every second I wasted placed her in further jeopardy.

As I crept along the small tent toward the rifle, an abrupt snore made me freeze in my tracks. Abdul-Nasir was in this tent. He was only inches away on the other side of the thin fabric. All I had to do was reach the rifle and he would be mine. Revenge would be mine.

I grabbed it. Good—it was fully loaded. I pointed at the tent's opening where his feet stuck out. Cocking the weapon as slowly and as quietly as I could, I rested my finger on the trigger. It would be so easy. Just a quick pull and all the pain and turmoil he had put me through the last few days would be over.

"Damn it," I whispered, letting a breath out. I couldn't do it. Well, I *could*…maybe. No, if I shot and killed Nasir, I'd still be surrounded and in the middle of camp with only one measly rifle. I had to continue my plan. I had wasted enough time. Abdul-Nasir would have to wait; there was still a chance.

Now for the hard part, I thought, turning my back on Abdul-Nasir. I headed deeper into the camp, toward the fire and four men sleeping peacefully around it. It would be a shame to disturb them…almost.

Grabbing one of the two burning torches in the ground, I made my way through the tangle of sleeping mercenaries to the large tent—to Emma.

How much time had passed since the lieutenant had gone in with his curved dagger? Two minutes? Three? The silence in the camp was making me nervous.

Something grabbed my ankle, bringing me to a stop. I looked down, expecting hell to break loose. Good-bye, sweet world.

Grumpy! The stupid, smelly oaf had grabbed my leg and was now sleeping against it like a teddy bear! Honestly, this was dangerous enough without having to deal with silly situations like this. I could kick him, but that would just wake him—and everybody else—up, which was the last thing I wanted. No, I needed something to make him let go and quickly without waking him.

God, what was that smell? I knew I smelled little rank, but how on earth did the man manage to make a skunk cringe at the stench.

I bent over and took a whiff of the filthy scarf lying next to Grumpy.

Yuck! Didn't the man believe in any sort of hygiene?

It was perfect.

"Try a little bit of this," I murmured, holding the rancid scarf up to Grumpy's nose.

The effect was twofold: the immediate release of my ankle as planned (luckily he didn't wake up at his own stench), and most unfortunately, a smelly little present of gas as Grumpy turned to show his backside.

This really was the worst day of my life, no contest. Congratulations, Abdul-Nasir Fadi, you're no longer on the top of my list.

Looking at the disgusting scarf in my hand, I decided to hang on to it for a little while longer (repulsive, I know), but I thought it might come in handy for the really hard part.

Torch still in hand, I headed for Emma as quickly and quietly as possible. I prayed I would find her in one piece.

Bursting into the tent, I found her tied to the center pole that supported the large tent.

She looked at me in disbelief. I assessed her condition in a second. She had several nasty cuts on her forearm, no doubt from the nasty-looking dagger Nasir's lieutenant now held over her to keep her quiet, but otherwise she was unharmed. So far.

The mercenary raised his dagger toward me and opened his mouth to call for help—or so he thought.

"Here," I said, throwing Grumpy's disgusting scarf at his face.

In the second it took him to throw the repugnant thing off in disgust, I moved into position to make sure the last thing he saw was the butt of the rifle coming down on his face, knocking him out cold.

"Max!" Emma whispered in shock. Clearly I was the last person she expected to see. "What are you doing here?!"

"I'm here to save you, of course," I whispered back, peeking outside. Everyone was still sleeping. Thank you, Grumpy, for never doing your laundry (never thought I'd say that).

"Are you okay?" I asked, picking up the lieutenant's dagger and cutting her hands free.

"Thank you," she whispered in my ear as she embraced me tightly.

"No problem," I said, dropping my weapons and returning the hug. A solid minute passed as we kneeled in the tent just holding each other in the torch's light. It felt good to see her again. I know it had only been a few days, but it felt more like an eternity, so much had happened to us.

"Are you okay?" I repeated, letting her go and taking my first good look at her. Apart from the fresh cuts the lieutenant had inflicted on her right forearm, she had a severe sunburn, and her lips were horribly chapped. Not to mention she could use a good shower. But to me Emma had never looked so good. Besides, I bet I didn't look much better.

"I felt like I would never see you again," Emma said tenderly, placing her hands on my face and ignoring my question.

"Well, you were stupid then, weren't you?" I replied, grinning like an idiot.

She placed her forehead against mine and surprised me with another hug.

"Thank you for coming," she whispered intimately, looking into my eyes, leaning in.

"Anytime," I whispered back, my hands still around her.

"What's that smell?" she asked abruptly, pushing me back, crinkling her nose in disgust.

"Oh, that would be this," I answered, picking up Grumpy's scarf. I leaned back in for the kiss.

"No," she said, smelling my chest, "it's you. Good lord, Max, what have you been doing for the last few days?"

"You don't want to know," I answered, throwing the scarf away in defeat. Oh well.

"Ouch!" I exclaimed softly. "What was that for?" I asked, rubbing my shoulder where she had punched. Honestly, save someone's life and you'd think they'd be grateful.

"That was for making me wait so long," she answered. Never make an Englishwoman wait, I guess.

"Well, we're not out of here yet. Can you walk?"

"Yes."

"All right," I said, tucking the dagger in my belt and picking up the torch and rifle. "Let's go."

"So what's the plan," Emma asked as we poked our heads out of the tent.

I held up the torch to answer her question. Then I touched it to the tent's fabric.

"Come on!" I whispered, throwing the torch on top of the tent and heading toward the camels. The canvas was already burning quickly. We had to hurry before everyone woke.

"Untie him!" I said, pointing at the nearest camel and covering her with the rifle. "Come on!"

"I'm going!" she exclaimed.

"*Onzor*!" one of the mercenaries screamed, awakening to the large bonfire. To my amusement, the watchman, Grumpy, was still asleep. Here's hoping Abdul-Nasir would throw him in the fire.

Abdul-Nasir. That reminded me.

"Max, let's go!" Emma screamed as she held her hand out from atop the camel.

No time. Abdul-Nasir would have to wait.

I grabbed Emma's hand and pulled myself up behind her. We took off with a burst of speed. I take back any bad thing I ever said about camels. They are absolutely lovely creatures.

I looked back at the sound of gunfire. The mercenaries were roused, and they looked more than a little upset. I fired a few shots in their general direction, but failed to hit anything. You try shooting backward while being bounced around atop a camel being driven by a mad Englishwoman.

The only good my shooting was doing was to keep the men away from their camels. Good. Just a little bit longer and we'd be over the sand dune and swallowed up by the moonless night, unable to be tracked until morning.

Unfortunately, the mercenaries seemed to realize this too. Under the direction of Abdul-Nasir, who had finally managed to get out of bed, they began firing in earnest, trying to kill us before we reached the top of the dune.

"Can this thing go any faster?" I yelled to Emma as she urged the poor beast as fast as his padded feet would allow up the hill.

"Just shoot!" she screamed over her shoulder.

"Out of bullets!" I yelled back.

"Great rescue plan!" she said as we leapt over the sand dune's peak to safety.

"Well, that wasn't so bad," I said as I waited for my heart rate to return to normal. I couldn't help but laugh at that point. I put my tired arms around Emma, content to let her drive us aimlessly in the desert for a little while. I dropped the gun on the sand; wouldn't be needing that anymore.

After a few more seconds, I realized Emma wasn't letting the poor beast rest. He was still racing down the sand dune.

"Why don't you give the poor guy a break?" I asked. Maybe her experience had been more traumatic than I had first realized.

"Are you insane? They're still following us!"

"No, they're not. They can't see—"

I froze. How could I be such a moron? (I blame the lack of water and rest) *They had torches*!

"*Go*!" I yelled. "*Go*! *Go*!"

"What do you think I'm doing?"

Some rescue this was turning out to be.

We needed a miracle.

"How long can the camel keep running like this?" I shouted over a strong gust of wind, aware that the poor animal had to carry both of us. I knew we should have stolen two.

"*What*?"

"*I said, why…*"

What was that howling sound? I could barely hear myself think.

"*Sandstorm*!" Emma screamed at the top of her lungs.

I couldn't see it in the dead of night, but I knew she was right. I guess Allah really was going to give me a miracle.

The mercenaries were only a few yards behind us and gaining. They weren't about to let a little sand stop them from killing us. God, I hoped our luck held just a little bit longer.

Sand started pelting my face, stinging my eyes, trying to work its way into every opening on my body. It felt like sandpaper against my skin, yet I knew this was only the appetizer. I turned my head back to shield my eyes (I really wished I had held onto Grumpy's smelly scarf).

Then I saw him—Abdul-Nasir Fadi leading his gang of men like a pack of wolves. I knew what was going to happen a second before it did.

He raised his rifle, aiming for the two of us, one last shot before they had to retreat from the storm.

I wrapped my arms around Emma, shielding her head against my chest. The pain slammed into my back harder than the sand ever could.

CHAPTER ELEVEN

# SECRETS OF THE TUAREG

"Max! Max!" Emma called out in agony, her eyes filled with tears, her hair and clothes caked with sand in the aftermath of the storm.

"Max!" she coughed out again, feeling the sand around her for any sign of me. "Where are you?"

A loud grunt answered in reply, but it wasn't me. It was our stolen camel, the very same that had led us to freedom and straight into the heart of the storm.

Emma crawled toward the camel's call, mounds of sand falling off her back, hoping to find me close by.

"Max!" she croaked out again, her dry coughs the only reply.

She reached the camel, still unable to see clearly through her teary eyes; Emma grabbed the resting camel's fur gently.

"Where is he, boy?" she asked, resting her forehead against his side for a minute. "Where is he?" she said before closing her eyes.

She was exhausted. Being chained up for three days in the Sahara's searing heat with little food and rest took a lot out of a person. Even the strongest of us can only take so much.

Where was I?

I wasn't far, maybe only a few feet from Emma and the camel. Was it a dream? Did I imagine her calling for me? I don't know, but somehow I didn't think so. If it were a dream, then she would find me, right? And there wouldn't be endless sand; there would be an oasis filled with water. And there wouldn't be pain, so much pain. I was so tired, my limbs calling out for sleep, just a little time to rest, just a little sip of water. Okay, so maybe more than just a sip.

I could see the camel's blurry hump as it lay on the sand, his head looking left and right for some unknown thing. Maybe he was wondering who his new crazy owners were. Maybe he was trying to figure out what he was doing in the middle of the desert still. Did he really just run into a sandstorm against his instincts? Was he going to die? Maybe if I hadn't been so out of it, I would have thought of the simplest answer: maybe he was hungry.

It must be nice to be a camel. Not a care in the world, other than your next meal.

And why was everything so blurry? So much sand everywhere.

And what was that shadow approaching us? Was it a mirage? Was I dead? Or still dying? Sadly, it wouldn't be the first time. I had seen so much in the last week, met so many interesting people, if you count killers as interesting. There was so much I had learned. But was I ready? Wasn't there still so much to see? People to meet, places to see? Love?

The shadow was coming closer. Not only that, it was moving faster, like it couldn't wait to see me.

Maybe it was Abdul-Nasir, here to finish the job. Now that would really make my day.

The shadow was only a few feet away.

Fine, just hurry up. Even if I had still had some strength, I probably wouldn't have bothered to get up, but every ounce of strength was gone, so I had no choice but to simply wait for the shadow's approach.

Why was everything still so blurry?

I tried blinking a few times, but my eyes just stung more. No, better to leave them be and let the shadow do whatever it wanted. I had tried my best, I really had. I had gone down fighting, I really had. No better way to cash in your ticket, in my opinion.

A pair of sandaled feet stopped before me. They were clearer now, but how could they not be? They were only two inches from my face. Was I going blind now too?

The man knelt beside me and rested a gentle hand on my aching back. A shock of searing pain tore through me as I winced in response.

"Easy, my friend," a gentle voice said. "You were not easy to find out here."

"Who—" I coughed as the word left me. My mouth was so dry, the movement sending further pain through my body, but it helped me stay conscious for a few extra seconds.

I tried again. "Who are you?"

"You have been through a lot," the Arab said. "It is I, Hamza," he said, those being the last words I heard before passing out.

"Max. Max," the voice repeated over and over.

"Look at me."

I turned my head. A foggy outline stood over me.

Why is it so hot, I thought?

"Max," the voice repeated in greater distress. It seemed to be a million miles away.

My eyes closed peacefully to the sight of two beautiful, sparkling blue orbs staring back at me.

* * *

"Will he be all right?" I asked Hamza after Max

closed his eyes. He was still throwing a high fever after two days' worth of care, but there was only so much a nomad in the desert could do. Still, he might be getting better. He looked peaceful, so content when he looked at me just now.

"I do not know. He is strong. Much stronger than most in the desert, but he is weak. He has undergone much in the last few days—you both have," Hamza said, giving me a worried expression.

I had only been awake for a few hours after the last two days, but I was feeling better, stronger. A little water and some food went a long way in the desert. If only this dry air didn't mess with a girl's hair so much. And what I wouldn't give for a little Chapstick or something. How was I supposed to kiss Max with lips this cracked…kissing?!

Now wasn't the time for this, I thought, wiping the sweat again from Max's brow. Hamza was giving him more precious water every half hour now instead of on the hour. Max was sweating so much, and he was so dehydrated already. It really was a miracle that he was still alive, and he had had it so much worse than me. I had just been chained up for a few days.

And he came back. I still couldn't believe he came back, that he'd found me, rescued me. I smiled at the thought of his daring rescue, bursting through the tent right when Khalil, Abdul-Nasir's lieutenant, was about to cut me some more, maybe even more than cut. And out of all his weapons—a gun and torch—he chooses to throw a dirty scarf at my torturer. Oh, Max.

Only an American would try something like that. It was like something from the movies, so romantic.

I came back to Earth as Max groaned in his fever-pitched dream. He needed a hospital, some proper medicine. I'm sure Hamza meant well, and he had certainly tried his hardest, but Max deserved better than to die in some Tuareg cave.

"He needs a hospital," I said, again voicing my apprehension to Hamza.

"And I have already told you," Hamza said patiently, "the journey is too far for him by camel. The desert will most certainly kill him if the fever does not. And no car exists to come and get him out here," he finished before I could ask.

"Now come," he said, "help me change his bandages." He handed me the small bowl of water and some rags.

"The best we can do for him," he continued as he removed the bandages from Max's shoulder, "is to keep him here in this cave, give him plenty of water and rest, and let the medicine do its work."

"Medicine," I sniggered. Like scorpion venom is medicine.

"Laugh all you want, but my people have been using this medicine for countless centuries against pain."

"If it doesn't kill you," I replied.

"Yes, if it doesn't kill you," Hamza repeated quietly.

I looked at the Tuareg in concern. "You said it would help him!"

"Only the strongest people can withstand the medicine, which I believe Max can. And if he does, he shall be immune to the scorpion's sting. He shall be stronger."

"What doesn't kill you," I said in frustration.

"A true Western proverb," Hamza answered, cleaning the wound one final time before wrapping the fresh bandage around Max.

He had done a good job fixing Max up, other than the scorpion venom, which I wasn't informed about until after it had been applied. True, removing the bullet was a bit of a challenge, what with only the most basic of medical instruments at hand, but the stitching was top-notch. Clearly, the Tuareg had had some experience with gunfire wounds.

* * *

"Where am I?" I asked, awakening from my dream. It had something to do with treasure. Gold and jewels stacked from the floor to the towering ceiling, a king's fortune.

"Hi," a soft voice said, stroking my mangy hair.

"Hi," I replied, opening my eyes for the first time in days. "Feeling all right?" I asked quietly.

"All right," she whispered. "You?"

"All right," I replied, Emma's deep blue eyes hovering over me.

"Why am I all wet?" I asked, noticing the sweat all over my body. The memory of what had happened in the desert flooded back like a storm.

"You had a fever," a third voice answered. I turned to see Hamza smiling at me.

"Hamza!" I exclaimed. A small pain shot down my back as I tried to get up.

"Easy," the Arab said, gently pushing me back down onto the cave floor. "Your body needs time to recover."

I was amazed to see the mysterious man again. I had taken a huge risk in giving him the sword, but then, what choice did I have?

"Where are we?" I asked, voicing the first of many questions.

"A cave," Emma teased. She looked to be in good spirits, could probably use a shower though (me as well for that matter).

"Yes, I know it's a cave, thank you. I mean, what are we doing here?"

"They are sometimes used by the Tuareg during our travels to rest. Or to evade a sandstorm," Hamza answered with a smile. "We brought the pair of you here after the storm so you could do both."

"And the bullet?" I asked as I sat up. Wincing at the pain, I felt the fresh bandage over the wound. Guess I wasn't dead yet.

"Hamza successfully removed it, using

some…interesting methods," Emma answered.

"Interesting how?"

"It's better that you don't know," she answered.

"Okay," I said skeptically.

I was getting really tired of being shot at. And quite frankly, that last encounter was just way too close. A man only had so many lives, and I was definitely getting close to that limit.

"Rest assured, you will feel like your old self soon enough. You're just lucky that we found you when we did. You were both extremely weak, and you," Hamza pointed at me, "were bleeding rather badly."

"I've been meaning to ask, how on earth did you manage to find us?" Emma asked.

"Why, it was Tin Hinan who found you."

"Who?" I asked, trying in vain to make myself comfortable on the small cave's stone floor.

"The Queen of the Hoggar found us?" Emma asked skeptically.

Hamza looked at her in surprise before returning his attention to me. "My friend, you never told me your companion was a scholar of the Berber people. The Imashaghen are truly honored to have you here and to call you both friends."

"The Imashaghen?" I repeated, more confused than ever. Now I really wanted to know what Hamza had done to me while I was unconscious.

"The Free people," Emma translated.

"You know Arabic?" I asked in surprise.

"It's called Tamajag actually, the language of the Tuaregs. Didn't you read any of the books I gave you on the train?"

I smiled sheepishly.

"Tin Hinan is my friend and named after the mother of our tribe," Hamza continued. He pointed at a beautiful, hooded white-and-brown falcon perched above our heads, waiting quietly for her master.

"She is named after a woman of great prestige, a great queen of my people. She came from beyond the great sea at the head of a grand army carrying an immense treasure. Our stories tell of an endless caravan of soldiers carrying this vast treasure deep into the desert to a place even the Tuareg do not go. A place with no oasis, and no life, where no living thing has ever emerged from."

"Except one," Emma said.

"Except one." Hamza smiled.

"Max. Tin Hinan must have been the Vestal Virgin sent with the Third Augustan Legion by Constantine to hide the treasure!" Emma exclaimed.

"Yes, our Queen Mother was the only one to return from the Mal''un Desert. We do not know what became of the great army or its treasure, but she returned alive and well, as if blessed by Allah himself. She stayed for some time and taught the Tuareg many things to make our lives easier. She also told us about the world beyond the Sahara. She taught the Tuareg to be strong and how to defend ourselves. She became a queen among our people, though she never saw herself as one. In return she asked only two things, that we pass on our knowledge and, when the time came, that we aid the chosen one, the one worthy enough to carry a blade of great power and history. She explained that we would know this one by his selfless nobility, his ability to put others before himself in the face of danger, and his unwavering trust in others, even strangers. A warrior of God," Hamza finished.

Then, out of thin air, as if by magic long kept secret by the Tuareg tribes of the desert, Hamza produced the Sword of Crocea Mors, the Sword of Solomon and his descendants.

"I believe, my friend, that this belongs to you," Hamza said, returning the sword to me.

"You showed great faith in entrusting me with such a precious and powerful object. And great integrity in placing your life before others."

I looked over at Emma, who blushed.

"I believe it was you who our Great Mother, Tin Hinan, wished for us to aid in his quest."

Hamza pulled another sword from his robes; the thin, long blade sounded a clear ring throughout the cave as it left its sheath. Tin Hinan, the falcon, swiveled his head toward us.

"And by my life or death, if I can aid you, I will," he finished, running the blade across his palm, his blood dripping onto the cave's floor.

"Hamza," I said, trying to stand without invoking too much pain, "I'm no chosen one. I'm just a man." I grunted as Emma helped me to my feet. "I'm no warrior for God or anything. Just an ordinary man who found a sword lying in the sand and found himself caught up in something he barely understands and just wants to see it to its end."

"My friend," Hamza said slowly, "say what you will about yourself and your quest, but few would have gone through what you have. You are different and do not think as most men, although you don't even realize it. How many would have followed the clues so blindly and faithfully without knowing why? And once you did know the secrets the desert contains, you were willing to give it all up to save another life," Hamza said, indicating Emma.

"He's right, Max. I don't know anyone who would have done would you did to get this far," Emma said.

"And fewer still would follow such a man so blindly," Hamza added. "It is a mark among my people that one who is loyal to his friends, even through all his hardships, is a great man indeed."

"Well, woman," I corrected.

"Thanks for noticing," Emma replied.

"So, am I to accompany you?" Hamza asked.

I looked at Emma for an answer.

"Hey, don't look at me. I'm not the chosen one."

"Well, we've come this far. How about we finish it?"

Emma replied with a simple nod.

"Very well, Hamza. How do we get to the Mal''un Desert?" I asked.

"That is very simple," he replied.

"Why?" Emma asked.

"Because we are already in it."

"Of course we are," Emma said.

"So there's no water?" I asked, heading for my rucksack, which Hamza had set near the mouth of the cave. I was down to my last shirt. Here's hoping I would be able to buy more in the future.

Emma came over to help me as I struggled to get the dark blue, button-up shirt on.

"Thanks," I said as she pulled it over my sore shoulder and began doing the buttons. She looked up at me and smiled warmly.

"I'm afraid the only water we have left is what we brought with us," Hamza answered from the rear of the cave, bringing me back to reality.

"And how much is that?" I asked, heading back to him after Emma finished.

The nomad stopped his packing and looked at us.

"Two days. No more."

"*Two days*," I repeated in disbelief.

"You were both very weak, and we have already been here far too long, Hamza elaborated. "Two days, that is all the water we have for ourselves."

"Then why don't we go back to your people and refill?" Emma asked.

"By now they'll know we escaped," I answered. Hamza nodded in agreement.

"Yes, many know me, and some will gladly accept payment from these men chasing you to know who I am and where I live. No, we cannot go back, only forward."

"Do you know where to go?" I asked.

"As I have said, none venture into this accursed desert. My people sometimes skim the edges, but no one goes into its belly. I do not know where to go."

"What about this?" I asked, raising the sword, its blade ringing sharper than Hamza's sword ever could. "Monsieur Gibarah said you might be able to help us."

"My friend, I have told you all I know of our Queen Tin Hinan and the blade the chosen one would carry."

"And the monogram?" I asked.

Hamza looked at me in confusion.

"The last few symbols on the blade. Haven't you even looked at them?" I asked in surprise. Hamza shook his head.

Amazing. I would have expected him to at least pull the sword out and take a look at it. I mean, who wouldn't, considering all the fuss. The man's trustworthiness took another leap forward in my book.

"You never even looked at it?" Emma asked, voicing my amazement.

"The sword was not mine to use. It was given to me only to carry and to protect," Hamza said in bewilderment. "I have done that, and now I return it to its rightful owner."

"Thank you, Hamza." I smiled. "You're a good man. Thank you for everything."

"No, no think nothing of it, my friend. It is I who must thank you for allowing me to participate in this quest long foretold by our Queen Mother."

I simply nodded as a show of respect to the kind nomad.

"Well, this is all very touching," Emma said, "but it still doesn't help us get any closer to the treasure and out of this cave."

"Something tells me you'll miss this cave once we're out in the hot sun."

Hamza nodded. "Yes, that is most certainly a fact."

"So can you read any of these?" I asked, bringing the sword before the nomad and once again placing it in his trustworthy hands.

"Yes, yes," he replied after a few moments passed in silence. "This is the language of the Tuareg. The Tifinagh, your people call it. But this is of a very old dialect, no longer spoken among the Tuareg. Not many, even among my people, can read this. It is only taught among a few," he finished softly, running his fingers along the last remaining symbols on the blade.

I could only imagine what secrets the assortment of simple lines and circles meant. What luck that we had met Monsieur Gibarah, and with his dying breath, he had possibly recognized the symbols' meaning and directed us to one of the few men alive who could still read them. Luck? Emma might call it that, but quite frankly I was starting to believe. Maybe something else was in play here—call it God or Allah or whatever you wish—but something more, something stronger than luck, was keeping us going, keeping us on course, giving us the strength to go on. After everything we had seen, all the close calls we had been through, and most likely some still to come, we were determined to press on.

I could quit at any time, any time at all. All I had to do was say so, and I could go home and pretend that none of this had ever happened and go back to my ordinary life. But something had changed inside of me, or was continuing to change inside of me. I knew I wasn't the same person as when I had first started this wild journey. I was, for lack of a better word, stronger. I had to keep going, to finish this, no matter where it led me. I couldn't explain it. Maybe Hamza was right and I was different from everyone else because most people would have quit a long time ago or would never even have started, but I had to keep going. And if it was God's will and not luck or fate or whatever you call it, then I hoped he would give me just a little bit more strength to keep going to see the end of this and maybe even beyond.

I looked over at Emma with her tattered clothes and soiled hair. Hamza was right about her too; fewer people still would have continued on this journey with a complete stranger, risking their lives for no reason. There really was something different about her, something that set her apart from other people, something…noble. Yes, that was the word; she had a certain nobility about her, something righteous and good that few people had these days. I doubted there was anything I could say to make her go home. Even after being abducted by the likes of Abdul-Nasir, she wanted to push on. That spoke volumes about her character. She really was something else.

Emma looked over at me as if sensing my thoughts. I stared into her magnificent blue eyes; that smile, the one I've seen her give only to me, spread across her full lips.

"These symbols are incomplete," Hamza proclaimed, breaking us out of the moment we had just shared.

"What?" I asked in confusion. "How could that be?"

"Max, aren't you forgetting something?" Emma asked.

"What?"

"The other symbols," she answered.

"The other symbols," I repeated in confusion. Of course! My eyes lit up in understanding. After everything we had been through in the last few days alone, plus the train ride, the abduction, the desert, and the gunshot, I had forgotten why we had come to Morocco in the first place.

The catacombs of Kom el-Shoqafa! The strange symbols we had found behind Athena's shield in the submerged chamber!

A sudden despair filled me, and my good mood began to evaporate. After all that, I didn't remember what the symbols were! Monsieur Gibarah gave his life, and several pounds of perfectly good C4, so we could escape with the secret and no one else could get it.

"Looking for something?" Emma asked, waving a badly wrinkled photograph in the air.

Looking at the photograph she handed me, my heart nearly stopped. The digital photograph she had taken with her waterproof camera! How on earth did she manage to hold on to a copy?

"You also owe me a new purse, by the way," she said

triumphantly.

A new purse? Heck, after this I'd buy her a purse factory, and she could fill them up with whatever she wanted with no complaints from me.

"But how did you?"

"Luckily Abdul-Nasir gave strict orders that I wasn't to be touched until he returned. So after he searched me for a weapon, they tied me up outside and left me alone."

"Interesting," Hamza said, looking over my shoulder at the photograph.

"What?" we asked.

"Are you sure these are the correct symbols?" he asked.

"Yes," I replied. "These are the ones the sword led us to. They have to be the correct symbols. Why?"

"Because this is not the language of the Tuareg," he answered.

"So what language is it?" I asked in frustration.

The nomad shrugged. "I am sorry. I do not know what this means," he answered miserably.

"So…what's it say?" I asked to no one in particular.

"It must be another clue," Emma answered.

"How many more clues are there?" I asked with a growing sense of frustration. "Frankly, I'm getting a little tired of all these mysterious clues and all this running around."

"I know, Max," Emma replied softly.

"I mean, how much more could there possibly be?" I finished, turning my back on the pair, trying to calm myself down.

"Max," Emma said, laying a hand on my shoulder. "It's okay. We're almost at the end."

I couldn't help smiling and letting a snort escape my throat. "And then what?" I asked.

"One step at a time. First, let's just finish this," Emma answered.

"She is right, my friend," Hamza added. "We must

stay the course and finish this great journey."

I took a deep breath. They were both right, of course. It was just so terribly frustrating. Finding a clue one moment, only to hit another wall the next moment. It was an emotional roller-coaster ride.

But they were right, I told myself again. We had to keep going. We couldn't turn back; we had to work the problem.

"Hamza?" I said, turning around to look at him. "Does the blade say anything that makes sense to you?"

"Yes," he answered raising the sword for us to take a closer look at. "You see here?" he said, indicating the last few symbols etched onto the blade. "These are two separate sets of symbols. The first set," which he pointed at, "is the symbol used by the Tuareg to represent a sacred monument built by Tin Hinan shortly before her departure across the Great Sea. It was built by Tin Hinan herself, with the help of a few Tuareg deep within the Mal''un Desert, and has become the site of our most sacred pilgrimage. Few outsiders know of it, and fewer still of the Tuareg venture to the monument to pay homage to our greatest queen."

"Have you ever been there?" Emma asked.

"Twice," Hamza answered. "Once as a young man to prove my strength and my faith. And once more, a few weeks ago after my vision."

"Vision," I repeated.

Hamza smiled at my skepticism. "My friend, it is not often I find myself in the city of Casablanca. My people are of the desert. It is our home. Shortly after my pilgrimage, I received another *dream*," he corrected with amusement, "and arrived in the city only to be contacted by my old friend, Sayed, and to have some of my questions answered. And now, as I have said, either by my life or death, I will help you."

"Very well." I smiled. "And the other symbol?"

"One word: 'up,'" he answered.

"'Up?'" I repeated in confusion. That's it? I was

starting to doubt Hamza's translation abilities.

"Up what?" I asked, hoping for a little more.

"That is all it says, just 'up,'" Hamza said.

"Well, that's helpful," Emma said.

Maybe I wasn't the only one who was getting frustrated by this adventure ; she was just better at hiding it. I wondered what would happen to the two of us after this journey was over. Over? Was I being foolish in thinking that there would be some great happy ending? What was bound to happen? We would get lost and die in the desert or maybe the Suits would find us first and finish us off once and for all. Or maybe we *would* find the Lost Treasure of Jerusalem and live happily ever after. No…the chances were pretty good that we would end up getting shot (and it would be much worse than a bullet in the shoulder).

Still, like Hamza said, we couldn't go back—that was a way to certain death. We could only go forward.

And see where chance took us.

"So what do you think? What's our next move?" Emma asked me.

I looked up at her and Hamza, waiting for my answer.

Really? Wasn't it obvious?

"Simple. We go on a pilgrimage."

What other choice did we have? Where else could we go? The sword had told us to go everywhere else, and now it was telling us to go to Tin Hinan's monument. She must have built it for a reason. She never considered herself a queen, and nothing the Vestal Virgins did was ever done for no reason. No, the monument must hold another piece of the puzzle, and we were going to find it. And just maybe, find out the meaning of the catacombs' mysterious message and what on earth the Tifinagh word "up" meant.

"How far until we get to the monument?" I asked Hamza that evening as we loaded up the two camels with our meager supplies.

"We are already rather deep in the Mal''un Desert, which will save us some time. Also by traveling at night, we will make better speed, but we still won't reach the monument until the second night."

"Our water will be gone after that," I mentioned.

"You are lucky, my friend. If I had not gone on pilgrimage this way several weeks ago, it would take me more time to find the place in this endless desert. It is truly a blessing by Allah that I went this way following my vision."

I don't pretend to know anything about visions, but good luck was definitely something that I had seen more than my fair share of in the last few weeks. Hopefully, it would continue to hold.

"Is there any water beyond the monument?" I asked.

"Not that I know of," Hamza said, tying a strap down on the camel. "But few have ever traveled deeper within the Mal''un Desert, so anything is possible."

"And why was it built so far away from any of your people?"

Hamza stopped petting the camel's head and turned to me, grinning. "That is something we may finally find out, my friend."

"Are you sure it's safe to travel at night?" Emma asked, wrapping a black shawl around herself as she emerged from the cave.

"We will travel much farther at night and drink less of our water," Hamza answered. "It is our best chance."

"Unless you'd rather wait for the sun," I teased.

"Very funny. At least I'm not a warrior for God," she retorted.

I just shook my head. Me…a warrior for God. Go figure.

"Everyone ready?" Hamza asked a few minutes later.

"Ready," Emma said, gripping my waist tightly. Unlike me, she hadn't developed a rapport with the animals. Unfortunately, the unpleasant odor she had picked up while standing behind Stanley hadn't helped the situation much.

(Stanley was the name I had given our camel after I had given up trying to pronounce their Tuareg names; Sheila was the name of Hamza's camel.)

"Very well, then. Off you go first, my friend," Hamza said, giving the falcon a caress along her wing before releasing her off his arm.

"She will carry a message to my friends, letting them know where we are," he said from atop Sheila. "Hopefully, they will leave quickly and help us if they can. Our lack of water will be our greatest enemy. That, and time."

"Do you trust them?" Emma asked. We both shared the fear that one or all of them would betray us to the Suits. The Suits had proven themselves to be extremely resourceful at getting what they wanted and not holding anything back in trying to get it. No level of brutality was beyond them, in my mind.

"They will not betray us," Hamza answered confidently, motioning for Sheila to take the lead. "I trust them all with my very life."

"Good enough for me," I said.

We hadn't traveled far in the early moonless night before the temperature dropped low enough for me to see my own breath. The Sahara truly was an amazing place, a place of opposites, filled with sweltering heat and freezing cold, eternal sand and remote water, a place of life and death.

I handed Emma my blanket to combat her shivering. It'd be a bit ironic to die of hypothermia in the desert, but it could very well happen on a night like this. Probably even more ironic would be dying in the desert from hypothermia instead of a bullet, which was looking more and more like our ticket out of this party. Although I had to admit it had been one hell of a party so far.

"Thank you," she said drowsily, draping the extra blanket around herself without protest (she must have been really cold) and resting her head against my shoulder, letting Stanley rock her gently to sleep as he trudged faithfully across the sands. I, too, fell asleep shortly after.

The night continued on peacefully for several hours, filled with brief periods of sleep from which we would be jerked awake by the slightest noise – a camel's cry, the slashing of our water container – or an unexpected dip in the sand, or just our own paranoia.

Except for the occasional breeze shifting the ever-moving sand below us, the Sahara was a quiet place at night, almost eerie. I started to miss the sounds of the insects and the birds and of a more habitable land in general.

"Do the Tuareg usually travel at night?" I whispered to Hamza, not wanting to wake Emma from her latest attempt at uninterrupted sleep.

"Very rarely, my friend. We prefer to travel during the day, see where we are going, and avoid any dangers that may lie before us," he answered in a similar whisper.

"No moonlight must make it more difficult," I said.

"Yes, but it will also shield us from any unfriendly eyes. Had I not made the journey so recently, I would not be able to guide us this night. We are most fortunate."

"Thank God for visions," I murmured.

"Indeed."

We spent the following day trying to conserve our strength, and our water, for the next night's journey (and those beyond). After only a few minutes lying under the open tent, we were both asleep, with Hamza keeping the first watch. Our fluttering roof had been sand-blasted so much that it matched the color of the surrounding sand perfectly. Indeed, no aircraft the Suits had in their possession (no, I most definitely hadn't forgotten that little attack helicopter they had sent to kill us in Italy) would be able to spot us from even five feet away.

The shade of the tent provided little relief from the blinding sun and heat. Truly a land of opposites, from freezing my ass off one second to almost burning it off the next, I was amazed at both Hamza's talent and the camel's natural ability to take these wildly changing elements with such ease. I wondered if Emma and I were up to the task before us. True, we had both survived our separate encounters in the desert thus far, but every man (or woman) had their breaking point. I wondered if I was reaching mine without even realizing it.

Looking over at Emma sleeping restlessly beside me, I worried that she was reaching hers. Despite the extra blanket and lying against, she had continued to shiver for most of the night and, to top it off, had slept maybe only an hour or two atop Stanley.

And she didn't look to be getting any better. I wiped the small beads of sweat off her forehead as she tossed and turned on her sleeping mat.

"Here, let her drink some of this," Hamza said as he crouched beside me, holding a small bowl filled with a milky white liquid. "It will help her fight the fever," the Arab said to my questioning look.

I took the bowl from him and, gently raising Emma's head, tipped the liquid to her mouth, letting her drink the peculiar concoction until she emptied the bowl. She wasn't getting enough water out here; none of us were. Hamza's rationing was taking us all to the edge. It wasn't enough to conserve it until we reached the monument; we still had to figure out its secrets (if it had any) and keep moving, either deeper into the Mal''un Desert or back to civilization in defeat.

"She's not doing so good, is she?" I asked the nomad, my voice filled with concern.

"No," Hamza answered. "But you were in a worse state when I pulled you out of the desert, and she is stronger than us both. She will fight."

I smiled at the kind sentiment. She was stronger than both of us, wasn't she? Always pushing me on, no matter the danger, comforting me, and being a bit of a know-it-all, but I wouldn't change a singe thing about her. Emma was the strongest person I had ever met. She was a fighter, and somehow she was still too stubborn for even the Sahara to claim her.

"What was that you gave her, Hamza?" I asked as the Arab placed a strange melon back in his pack.

"It is what you would call a gourd, a rare plant for this time of year found in the Sahara. Hopefully, it will help her to fight the fever quickly."

We exchanged few words as the day wore on, each taking turns to keep watch. Past experience had taught us to be careful. The Suits had proven time and again to be very resourceful, and as Hamza often repeated, the desert was home to many dangers, a few of which we were already familiar with.

"It is time," Hamza said to me as darkness fell on the second night, our camels reloaded with their gear minus the passengers. Emma had slept most of the day and was already showing signs of a speedy recovery. Trust an Englishwoman to not even let a little thing like sickness slow her down.

"That gourd of yours is an amazing little plant," I remarked, wanting to give Emma a few more precious seconds of sleep before I woke her for the night's journey.

"The desert is full of many dangers and wonders. But come," the nomad urged, recognizing my ploy, "we must hurry if we wish to make it by tonight."

"Em," I said, gently giving her a shoulder the smallest of shakes.

"Mmm?" she mumbled from that place between worlds.

"Time to wake up," I said, giving her another shake.

"Is it my watch?" she asked groggily.

I smiled. She had wanted to be awoken for her watch, but Hamza and I had felt it would be better if she rested instead and regained her strength for the night's journey. She would be upset, but that was something I could live with.

"No, it's time to go," I said.

"What?" she said, opening her eyes.

"It's nighttime. We have to keep going."

"You said you would wake me," she said softly, a hint of anguish in her voice.

"I lied," I replied with a grin.

"Is it really time to go?" she asked.

"Yep," I answered, giving her a drink of water.

"Thank you."

"Ready?"

"Let's go," she said eagerly, her sense of adventure returning as quickly as her strength.

I helped her up, and together we set off into the night to uncover Tin Hinan's next secret.

"Do you feel better?" I asked her.

"Yes, loads. But I'm still tired."

"It's probably from the medicine. Try to get some sleep."

"Medicine? What medicine?" she asked.

"Just something Hamza gave you," I replied mysteriously, giving her a taste of her own medicine.

"Max. What was it?" she said, the concern in her voice growing.

"Trust me, you don't want to know," I replied in amusement.

"Not another scorpion," she said.

"What? No!" I answered, looking back at her smiling face. It was a good sign, seeing her sense of humor return—not that scorpions were funny (what a weird sense of humor she had sometimes).

We continued on for several more hours, the cold desert night discouraging any desire to talk. Emma slept more peacefully this night with hardly a shiver escaping her.

"How much farther do you think, Hamza?" I asked, the horizon showing the signs of a new dawn approaching.

"We are here, my friend," Hamza replied, pointing straight ahead.

"Where? I don't see it."

"You will in a moment," he replied.

And then the first rays of morning light broke across

the desert, illuminating the smallest, most unimpressive structure I had ever seen.

"That can't be it," I said in shock. It was nothing more than a small mud block with a dome roof, maybe a yard tall and two yards or so wide. This couldn't be it. Was this the best the Tuareg could produce after two nights' hard travel through one of the most brutal deserts on Earth?

"Were you expecting something more?" Hamza asked me.

Honestly, I was. After everything the Vestal Virgins stood for, all the secrets they had left in some of the most famous monuments on Earth, was this the best they could do? Some mud block, not even tall enough to stand in? Somehow I had expected more from Tin Hinan, something a bit more grand. I let Hamza know my disappointment.

"My friend, the Tuareg are a poor people, a desert people. We are nomads. We travel the desert and trade for any goods that we may need. We have no desire for great monuments and statues, symbols depicting our might. We simply wish to live how we always have: free among the desert to do as we wish. Tin Hinan understood this; she understood our people and our way of life. This monument was not built as a monument to her greatness but as a simple symbol of freedom—that the Tuareg may always live free and travel wherever they wish, be that to the farthest corners of Earth if they so wish. Alas, for a long time this monument marked the end of the road for Tuareg, for none before these modern times knew what lay beyond this endless desert, except from the wildest tales from beyond the barren sand," Hamza said.

"So what's inside?" I asked, willing to give him the benefit of the doubt.

"Nothing," he replied with an almost sinister smile.

"Nothing?"

"Almost."

"You will see," he said to my questioning look.

"Emma?" I said softly over my shoulder, the early-morning light illuminating her deep blue eyes as they opened.

"We're here?" she asked.

"Take a look," I said, pointing to the small mud...*hut*, for lack of a better word.

"That's it?" Emma asked.

"Yep. That's it. Tin Hinan's great monument."

"I never said it was a great monument," Hamza said, climbing off Sheila and tying her to the mud hut.

"Come," he said, crawling into the small opening that reminded me of an igloo. "We will rest inside."

"Let's hope this wasn't for nothing," I said, helping Emma off Stanley.

"Let's hope," she said.

Inside the small mud hut was, as Hamza claimed, nothing. Well, almost nothing.

Carved on the wall was a small symbol, identical to one found on the sword. The only word of Tifinagh that I knew from the strange symbol: the word for "up."

"You've got to be kidding me," I said, rubbing my hand over the symbol.

"Yes, 'up,' but up what?" Emma asked, crouching beside me in the small mud structure.

"That was carved by Tin Hinan herself. Yet after almost two thousand, years none of us knows what she is referring to," Hamza said from behind us.

I looked at the Arab as he laid his sleeping mat down so he could rest from the long journey. Did he really have no clue what the message meant? I didn't think he would lie to us after all we had been through together, but still, why did we come here? We were no closer to deciphering the meaning to "up," and we were growing short on water.

"What are we going to do now?" Emma asked, voicing my concern.

"Sleep," Hamza replied. "We are all tired, and there

is nothing we can do now to find the answer. Sleep, rest, and Allah will provide the answers that we seek."

I decided to listen to the man without question. I was tired, and a little bit of sleep sounded really good right now. We could brainstorm all we wanted to in the evening. And if we still didn't find anything by tomorrow night, then we would have no choice but to turn back, back to the water.

"What are you doing?" Emma asked in disbelief as I lay down beside Hamza in the small mud hut.

"Going to sleep," I replied.

"But Max, what about the clues?" she asked, pulling out her photo of the strange symbols we had discovered in the catacombs.

"Hamza's right, Em. We'll be able to think much better after some sleep, and if we think of something, we'll keep going."

"And if we don't?" she asked, already knowing my answer.

"Then we'll just have to go back and think of another way out of this mess," I answered, closing my eyes.

I waited for common sense to set in on her and for her to lay down beside me for a few hours of shut-eye, but instead I heard her heading through the igloo exit.

"Not tired?" I asked, not even bothering to open my eyes.

"No. Someone has to keep watch."

And with that she was gone.

"A very spirited woman," Hamza said from beside me.

"Yes, *very* spirited," I replied with a smile.

Several hours later, Hamza silently woke me for my turn at watch.

"Busy day?" I asked him.

The desert nomad motioned at Emma sleeping peacefully beside me and for me to be quiet. I nodded and started to make my way out of the mud hut.

I stopped and looked back at Emma. Judging from the wrinkled photograph in her hand, she had fallen asleep while contemplating the meaning of the strange symbols taken in the catacombs and their relation to the sword and Tin Hinan's curious meaning of the word "up."

I snagged the photograph and headed outside to do a little bit of my own contemplation.

Resting my back against the cool mud wall, I looked out over the voiceless desert, that endless void in the middle of the world. What secrets did she hold under her shifting sands? I shivered at the thought of being one of them—the memory of Abdul-Nasir and how he had left me to rot invaded my reflection. How many treasures, how many fortunes lay here? How many evils lay buried here? How many atrocities?

My eyes drifted to Emma's photograph, and I studied the four dots that made a square. A tiny line was placed neatly between each pair, but not touching. Then three more dots were placed above this first square of dots, almost lined up in a straight line if the center dot was moved a few inches to the right. What did it mean? What was the secret? What were they trying to tell us?

Night began to creep on the desert as the long day drew to a close. We would be setting out soon, but which direction?

I leaned my head back against the mud hut, my mind beginning to go a hundred miles an hour in a hundred different directions. What were we going to do if we had to head back? It's not like we could just go back to our ordinary lives. I smiled at the thought of Asher. It seemed like a million years ago since I had set foot there, another life.

What would Emma do if this adventure ended right here, right now? Would she go back to England and back to school? Would we ever see one another again? Would we ever talk to each other?

Somehow I didn't think so. I just didn't see myself

going back to school, at least not here, not now. The adventure couldn't be over, it just couldn't. We had to be missing something, some clue, something that would allow us to go on.

Go on. I smiled at the silly thought. Two weeks ago I would have given almost anything for the quest to be over. No more guns, no more chasing, and no more secret passageways. Now I would give almost anything for it to go on. The danger had become so constant I could barely imagine a day without it. This was living, there was no denying that.

But where to go now? I looked at the photograph once more, the seven dots with their silly little lines almost mocking me. What was their secret? What was the code?

Letting out a breath of frustration, I once again lay my head back against the cool mud wall and looked up at the stars that were beginning to make their presence known, trying to take my mind off of it.

The stars were vivid; the lack of light pollution showed the night's true potential. I'd have to wake the others soon. We'd have to make a decision: to stay or to turn back. I quickly found Orion the Hunter with his signature belt of stars, the red supergiant Betelgeuse shining brightly as his club. I looked around for other constellations that I might know, not remembering the last time I had had the chance to gaze up at the night sky.

I quickly spotted the Big Dipper and looked for its smaller twin.

There it was, with its handle pointing directly to Polaris, the North Star.

I froze in shock as the idea hit me, the connection finally being made in my slow brain.

It was so simple.

"So simple!" I yelled in triumph.

The adventure wasn't over. Not by a long shot.

"What is it?!" Hamza yelled, his rifle barrel poking out of the mud hut.

"Max!" Emma yelled, scurrying out after the Arab. "What's wrong?"

"Look *up*!" I yelled in excitement, pointing to Polaris. Hamza and Emma looked at each other as if I had gone wild with fever.

"Yes, stars, Max," Emma said as if I were losing my mind.

"No, *look* – UP!" I said in frustration, handing her the picture and pointing at the Little Dipper.

It took only one look before realization hit the pair of them, and they soon joined in my elation.

"Oh, Max, you did it!" Emma screeched, hugging me so tight I could barely breathe. "This is why Tin Hinan built this silly mud hut. That's what the sword meant by 'up'—*look* up! She knew the Tuareg would always look after it. This is the place you follow the North Star from! How could I be so stupid? So many ancient cultures relied on the stars for navigation. All we have to do is set out north, and we'll eventually find the treasure!" she yelled in her excitement, once again hugging the air from my lungs.

"Well done, my friend," Hamza added, shaking my hand. "Such a simple solution, and yet so complex. Come, we must set out at once. It may be many days into the Mal''un until we find what we are looking for."

"Or if," I noted.

CHAPTER TWELVE

# THE GREAT JOURNEY

On our second night after leaving Tin Hinan's monument and figuring out the next clue, our situation was looking dire. Our water supply was running dangerously low, with maybe enough to last the three of us another day, maybe two if we rationed our supply even further. Not a smart thing to do in the desert, but what choice did we have?

We no longer had enough water to turn back; all we could do at this point was to keep going and hope our luck changed. We now had a new moon to guide our way, but even that small ray of hope didn't do much to elevate our spirits, especially Hamza's. A traveler of the desert for all his life, Hamza knew what it took to survive in this barren landscape, he knew better than most folks, and his dampened spirits really began to worry me.

But what else could we do? We couldn't turn back, not now. We had to keep to the path, keep our faith, pray that whatever we were looking for would make its presence known—and soon.

I looked over Emma's shoulder; she was taking a turn at leading Stanley, her eyes never wavering from the compass in her hand. She was dead set on heading as true to north as possible, and frankly, her concentration was impressive, just as impressive as her quick recovery. True, she still slept more than the rest of us, but each evening she grew stronger, while Hamza and I grew weaker from the little water and food that we allowed ourselves so we could manage to go just a little bit farther.

"What do you think we'll find?" I asked Emma for what felt like the tenth time. It was a topic that I was not growing tired of talking about.

Thoughts of giant rooms filled with gold, jewels, and statues filled my dreams, and even my daydreams. What would we do with all that treasure? Where would we go? That much money would be more than enough to satisfy any man for a hundred lifetimes. I began to see why the Suits wanted it so badly and why the Vestals had protected it so. That much money, especially in those days, could pay armies, even conquer the world; well, that was what the Romans had tried. The old axiom "Ultimate power brings about ultimate corruption" suddenly entered my mind. Maybe I would give some of it away. After all, I had said that that much money was more than any man could spend in a hundred lifetimes; a lot of people could benefit from it.

"I don't know, Max. Will you stop asking me that," Emma said with mild annoyance (I really had asked that question about a dozen times by now). "For all we know, the treasure might not even be there, or we may be going in the wrong direction. Even if we're just a degree off, we could end up missing it by miles," she finished, her eyes darting back to her compass.

I wondered what Emma would do with her share of the treasure. I couldn't picture her as the type to settle down early and play the role of a rich heiress. She loved all of this adventure; if she didn't, she would have called it quits after her abduction. No, Emma was the type of girl who would do this for free, despite the danger (that just made it more fun for her, I suspected), but that still left me to wonder what she would do with her share.

No point thinking about that, I told myself. First we had to find the treasure. And no one said it wasn't buried under several tons of sand. We could be walking over it right now, and we would never even know it. Besides, even if we did find it, we were still trapped in the middle of the desert. With no water.

"What's so funny?" Emma turned to ask.

"Nothing. I was just thinking how funny it would be to actually find the treasure and still be trapped in the middle of the desert," I answered.

"I hope you don't think you're actually going to keep any of it," Emma said.

"And why shouldn't we keep it?" I asked. "We found it. No one else did."

"Max, anything we *do* find belongs in a museum. It isn't our money in any way."

"Not ours?" I asked perplexed. "But we're the ones who have gone through everything to find it. Why shouldn't we keep it? At least some of it?"

"Because it isn't ours to keep," she answered. "It doesn't belong to us. Besides, what would you even do with all that money?"

"I don't know," I answered. What on earth would I buy? I had thought about the question a little bit, but nothing ever came to mind. What did a man need that much money for anyway?

"You can't think of anything, can you?" Emma asked, smiling.

"No."

"Then why are you still here?"

"What?" I asked, confused.

"Why are you still here?"

"I don't know," I answered. I had asked myself the same thing several times over the past few weeks, and I never *really* knew why.

"Because you love it, just like I do," Emma said.

"Love what?" I asked, a bit more confused.

"The *adventure,* Max. The excitement. Don't you feel it? This is why we are both here, risking our lives for something that may not even exist. How many people would risk their lives further after being hunted down and shot at, kidnapped, and left in the desert to die?"

I smiled at our like-mindedness; it hadn't occurred to me that she would be thinking some of the same things as me. Silly really, since we were both going through the same thing.

No, few indeed would continue to risk it all after all the crazy things we had seen.

"Not many," I answered.

"People like us could never be happy with a large pile of money, Max," she said, looking out over the Sahara. "People like us only know one thing."

"And that is?" I asked.

"Freedom," she answered. "We love our freedom, to go where we choose to go, to see what we wish to see, with no one to tell us otherwise, no one to tell us what to do, how to act or behave, or how to live. We both chose to be here on this adventure and to see it through till the end. No amount of money back in the real world would ever make us live here, this moment right here. Right now is what it's all about. This is what life is all about, this is freedom," she finished, looking back at me with a smile that spoke volumes.

She was happy here, right now, this moment, this was all Emma had ever wanted in life, and she intended to enjoy it while she still had the chance. I understood her a little better at that moment, something more about her life and her desires, her passions, what made her tick, you could say. Who would have guessed that colliding with her in that little alley back in Oxford would be the start of one of the most amazing adventures of both our lives.

This really was freedom.

Dawn was beginning to show its first rays when we heard a sharp screech in the sky. My heart rate shot up for a split second, fearing the worst, before I realized it was Hinan, the falcon, returning to her master after a long flight over the barren desert.

That was the way to go without a doubt. Why couldn't we have gone in a helicopter? We would have covered a vast distance in only minutes, plus we wouldn't smell like camel. I gave Stanley's rump a friendly tap, letting him know not to worry about the falcon (not that he gave the slightest sign of being intimidated by the bird). No, this was just another experience, another part of this great adventure, as Emma would put it. Besides, I actually loved Stanley; he was a wonderful and considerate camel, always being careful to spit somewhere other than on us. And Emma was starting to take a shine to him, and him to her; sometimes he would follow her until she gave him a little scratch under his neck. I wondered how the pair would be able to part from one another.

I shook my head at the silly train of thought I was experiencing. What was I talking about? I hoped this wasn't the beginning of dehydration; that was the last thing I wanted now. Couldn't we get a break for once?

Maybe Hinan would deliver some good news, I thought as the falcon gracefully descended from the sky to land on Hamza's arm, her message now delivered. Now the poor bird could rest a while before the dawn, before she was sent out again.

"Are you sure we can spare it?" I asked, hating to be the bad guy as Hamza held some of our precious water out for the bird to drink. Our situation was getting so desperate as to deny a small bird a few sips of water.

"No, but she will die without it, and Hinan is our lifeline to the Tuareg. Without them, we will most certainly die."

"Are they close?" Emma asked as Hamza removed the small scrap of paper from the bird's leg and read the message.

"No," Hamza answered softly. The magnitude of that answer hit me.

"It took time to round up the necessary supplies for a journey into the Mal''un. My people both fear and respect this place and would never dare undertake a journey without them. They also, at my suggestion, took precautions to leave the village quietly and without suspicion. No, my friends, it appears we will be alone for a little while longer," Hamza finished sadly.

"Well, we may as well set up camp," I said, trying to lighten the mood. "Get some sleep."

"Yes, I will prepare a message for Hinan to send after she gets some rest," Hamza replied, dismounting from Sheila.

"What do you think?" I asked, helping Emma dismount from Stanley.

"No choice really," she replied. "You said it yourself—not enough water to turn back, so we keep going."

I smiled at her resilience as she removed our bags from Stanley's back and began to set up camp without a word.

She really was something.

A fighter. No, I corrected myself, an adventurer.

"Can I ask you something?"

"Of course," she answered, not looking up from her work.

"Was it worth it?"

Emma stopped and looked up at me, understanding the seriousness of the question.

"I mean, if we die out here and don't find what we're looking for, was it worth it?" I asked.

"Max," she said, taking my hand. "Before I met you, my days were spent in a library, reading about past civilizations and empires and the men who helped uncover their secrets, about famous archeologists and explorers who pushed back the boundaries of knowledge and set out in the world to make their mark. And then I met you, and in one split second, you changed my life in ways you can't even imagine. You gave me a new beginning, a new purpose in my life. So to answer your question, if we do die, then yes, it was so worth it," she concluded joyfully, kissing me on the cheek.

"You're not the only one whose life has changed," I said. "You've changed me as well. And there's no one else who I would rather have with me right here, right now."

She smiled, an unspoken bond between us. I knew now, without a doubt, that Emma was in this for the right reasons; she truly would go to hell and back for me. I just hoped it wouldn't come to that.

"Come, we must hurry before the sun rises," Hamza said, standing up holding his finished note in hand. Hinan sat peacefully atop Sheila watching us. Silly bird must have been watching us the whole time. I wonder what she made of the pair of us. Hell, I wondered what to make of the pair of us. It seemed like something always happened to interrupt us. Why couldn't we ever get just a few minutes alone?

"How much longer will our water last us?" I asked Hamza, taking my morning sip of water before bed. It really was barely more than a sip of water these days; my lips were becoming so cracked it actually hurt to open my mouth and talk. And we were down to our last water jug, which was becoming increasingly lighter.

"We will be out before tonight," Hamza answered, the concern apparent in his voice. He may have vowed his very life to protect us and to see Tin Hinan's prophecy fulfilled, but I could tell he didn't want to die in the desert, at least not like this. It must be the worst kind of death for a man born of the desert, to know the dangers of having no water and its effects and still traveling on – must be crying out against his instincts. But then, he had made his choice; we all had made our choice at Tin Hinan's monument to carry on and pray for the best.

"And how far will we be able to go?" I asked,

making sure Emma had already fallen asleep.

"On the camels we will be able to continue until the following morning. After that, it is all up to Allah. We have already been traveling with too little, and sharing yours with Emma will only buy her a few more hours," Hamza said with discontent.

He hadn't been happy when he caught me pouring some of my own water ration into Emma's container; he claimed it wouldn't do her any good if I dropped dead on my feet. But she had been ill at the time, and I knew it wouldn't do me any good either if she dropped dead. What could the man do? It was my water, and if I chose to give it to her, then that was my business. Luckily, Hamza had promised to keep it quiet, and true to his word, he had.

"Can the camels offer us some more water?" I asked, again hating myself for asking. Stanley and Sheila were both wonderful animals, and I hated the thought of killing them for water, but these were fast becoming desperate times, and desperate times called for desperate measures.

"Look at them," Hamza said, indicating the pair kneeing in the sand.

They looked tired and already had their tongues out as they began to sweat through the Saharan morning, but maybe that was normal for a camel. Quite frankly, I didn't know very much about camel anatomy, and it was hard imagining the ultimate desert survivors dying before us in this environment. If the camels were near the edge, then we really were in trouble, I thought as I tightened the scarf around my head. It was really starting to sink in at this point—with no water, everything dies in the desert.

"They will not last another two days, and they have no more water left to spare us. I hurried in my effort to find you, and in my haste I may be the one who ends up killing us all," the nomad confessed sadly.

I knew something had been bothering him. I had assumed it was the notion of dying from dehydration in the desert, but I had been wrong again. Hamza felt responsible for us, felt our lives were in his hands. And in many ways they were; without him, we both would have died in the desert long ago.

"Hamza," I said, placing my hand on his shoulder, "It's okay. It's not your fault. We both chose to come out here, to keep going into the Mal''un. You warned us of our water situation, of the dangers of the desert, of the risks of coming out here, and we accepted them, and yet, we chose to go on, just like we choose to still go on. You are our guide and our friend, and I would follow you into whatever evil, whatever desert," I added with a smile, "that you choose to enter. You are my friend, and I am glad for it."

"There truly are none like the pair of you. May Allah bless you," Hamza added joyously, giving me a quick hug of friendship, his spirits renewed. "Go sleep. I will take first watch, and tonight we will carry on until our bones can go no farther. And if we die, we die knowing we tried our hardest, till the end."

"Till the end," I said, shaking his hand. The man was right. We had known the risks and had still persevered, still pushed on, and still we would carry on, even if it meant our very lives.

I had never known what it meant to find a purpose worth dying for. I mean, what was worth dying for? What would you die for? People often said things like, "I would kill for that" or "I would die to get those," but they never meant it. Now I knew, knew what it meant to find a purpose in life worth dying for. The Vestals deserved to have their secret shared with the world, and if we were the ones to share it, then so be it.

I shuddered to think what the Suits would do if they had recovered the sword and discovered her secrets. The treasure alone was enough to accomplish any number of diabolical schemes, but one could only imagine the other sacred relics hidden among the gold and the gems since the time of Solomon. Professor Giordani's story about the Ark of the Covenant, the Sword of Muhammad, and the Holy

Grail came flooding back into my mind. What powers did they hold? What evils could they unleash?

No, this was, if anything was, something worth dying for. And if we did die, one thing Abdul-Nasir did say would come true: The sand would indeed cover our bones for the rest of eternity, us and the sword as well. The Suits could never be allowed to find the Lost Treasure of Jerusalem, and that, quite simply, *was* something worth dying for.

I ducked under the fabric protecting us from the Sahara's morning rays to find Emma fast asleep with only the tiniest of breaths escaping through her delicate nose. Sometimes she could be such a girl, I thought, smiling at the sight.

Luckily, I had the last shift today, so I could sleep a good eight hours during the long, hot day. Second shift, which Emma had today, was the worst; it required you to wake up after a few hours and somehow stay awake and alert during the heat of the day. Not an easy thing to do out here; it was easy to start dozing off without even realizing it. Once, and only once, Hamza had caught me falling asleep during second shift. I had made sure it wouldn't happen again. The nomad seemed to have an uncanny knack for knowing when no eyes were up, watching the landscape for him. After second shift, you could get in a few more hours of shut-eye until the short night finally came and you had to pack up and continue the journey.

No, I didn't envy Emma this day, or really any day since we had entered this God-forsaken desert.

I laid down next to her, looking at the rising sun through the brown fabric that served as our roof, wondering what it was like to die. I had discovered during this leg of our trip that time was one of the things you had a lot of out here. Time to think, time to reflect, time to sit down and just mull over about life and the things you would have done differently, even time to think about death. Yep, one managed to find a lot of time to think in the Sahara.

What was it like to die? I knew getting to that point

sure hurt a lot. Two bullet wounds later, not to mention countless cuts, bruises, and a few other scrapes I had no idea how I had gotten, plus the dehydration and nearly drowning and – oh, how could I forget – the C4, I knew without any doubt that dying could really hurt.

But what was death like after the pain? After you were dead? Who was right? Was there a paradise in a spiritual world beyond our own that so many blindly believed in? Or were the atheists right? Was there really no God, nothing after death—you're just born, you die, and you get by as best you can with whatever you've got? I didn't know, and no amount of time sitting here contemplating death in the desert was going to bring me any closer to the answer. Best to not think about it and keep going. We weren't dead yet, and more than one miracle had happened to us on this wild ride. Maybe there really was some higher power watching over us. I could believe anything at this point.

Rolling over, I watched Emma sleeping peacefully under the Saharan sun. The Sahara. I still couldn't believe we were here sometimes. Could I watch her die if I had to? She had claimed she would go on into the desert, heading as true to north as she could, even if it claimed her life, but could I bear it if it came down to that? Could I watch her die out here, knowing that if it weren't for me, she would never have been here? But then, never meeting Emma was something else I didn't want to consider. I couldn't imagine my life anymore without her here. I couldn't even imagine how I had gotten by not knowing her.

"My friend," Hamza called to me. "Sleep. The desert has its ways of opening your mind to the world, and the time will come for you to do so, but for now you must sleep."

Amazing. Even sitting with his back to me at the corner of our little camp, the nomad knew whether I was awake or asleep. Somehow through the centuries, the Tuareg had learned to be one with the desert; they had learned to be strong.

I closed my eyes and dreamed of the following night, of our last night in the desert, possibly our last night on Earth.

"Max. Max, wake up."

"Huh? My shift?" I asked, feeling rather well rested.

"No," Emma said, smiling at me with her cracked lips.

She didn't look so good; neither of us did. Even with all the protection and scarves wrapped around us, we had pretty severe sunburns, and I could have sworn Emma's hair was a few shades lighter tonight.

Tonight? Something wasn't right. I was supposed to have the third shift; Emma should have woken me up when the sun was still up.

"Why didn't you wake me?" I asked her.

"Hamza never woke me," she answered softly.

"Why?"

"I guess he wanted us both to have a full night's sleep."

"Maybe he fell asleep," I joked.

"I never fall asleep unless I mean to, my friends," Hamza proclaimed as he approached us.

"You were up all night? Why didn't you wake us?" I asked.

"Come, we have far to go, and the night is not growing any longer," he said, ignoring the question.

I looked around, and except for my sleeping mat and the sword, which I still liked to keep by my side at all times, the camp was already packed away on the camels. We were off to an efficient start tonight. I only hoped it continued.

I finished off my last half cup of water, the warm liquid doing little to quench my dry throat.

Emma looked at me in concern as I turned the empty container over.

"Looks like this might be it," she said.

"Maybe," I replied, mounting Stanley and holding a

hand out for her to do the same.

"But we aren't dead yet."

"Will Stan and Sheila make it through the night?" Emma asked Hamza a few hours into our northerly trek.

"Yes," Hamza replied softly. "They will most likely last another two, perhaps three days before their bladders are bone dry of water."

"Us, on the other hand," I said through cracked lips. I had a few more things to say, but that seemed enough. Frankly, it hurt just to talk. My throat felt like it was burning, and my tongue was beginning to feel…sticky.

Was it worth coming out here? I know we had all agreed it was, even if it meant our deaths, but once you're out in the middle of desert, literally dying of thirst (and knowing it too), it's not as heroic of a thing to do as when you say it. In fact, dying like this just plain sucked. Who would choose to go out like this? Were we idiots for doing it without any idea of how far we had to go? And with limited water?

If someone had told me our story, I would have immediately said yes, those people were idiots. But it was too late for buts and what-ifs. We were here and we had made a choice, so best to just keep my mouth shut and keep going. Who knows? Maybe we'd find something. I still held out a small ray of hope.

The hours seemed to pass slowly and quickly at the same time. It was as if the laws of physics, of time, and of space no longer applied to us in this desolate place. We were off the grid, traveling in a forgotten place in the universe. Only the stars moved overhead, the sole indication that this wasn't just a dream, just my imagination.

It seemed like a lifetime ago since Hamza had rescued us in that cave at the edge of the desert, but it had only been, what? Three nights since Tin Hinan's monument? Another two before that? The Bahamas seemed like years ago. The Bahamas. All that water; that really was too much water for one place. Why couldn't Earth share it better? I would have liked to take Emma to the Bahamas; she would have liked it.

I raised my head to look for our desert guide. Where was he?

"Hamza?" I called softly, the words barely wanting to come out of my dry mouth.

No reply. I called again louder. "Hamza?!"

"Yes, my friend," the nomad said softly beside me.

There he was. Why didn't I look to the right? This felt like déjà vu; it was happening all over again. I was beginning to lose my mind to the desert.

I looked back over at Hamza; the Tuareg looked tired and thirsty, but he still looked better then the pair of us put together. It was to be expected, I supposed; the man spent his whole life in the desert; he would last the longest out of all of us. Maybe that was why he had let us both sleep. Did he know something? Did he think we were losing our fight with the desert? Was this the last inning? I was too weak to ask, and frankly, I didn't care anymore. I closed my eyes for a little while, resting my head against Emma's; she was already taking a light nap on my shoulder.

Hamza would wake us if anything happened.

If we awoke again.

"My friend, awaken," I heard. "You are not dead yet. Here, drink a sip of this." A cool, milky liquid inched its way down my dry throat.

"What?" I said confused, my eyes blinking in panic as Hamza lowered my head. "What happened?" I coughed.

"We have stopped. Morning is approaching," he answered, pouring some of the same mysterious concoction down Emma's throat.

"How is she?" I asked, coughing again. The drink had a way of sticking to your throat.

"About the same as you. If we do not find water soon, then…"

Hamza didn't finish, but he didn't need to. We all knew the next part.

I used what energy I had left and slid up against one of the poles Hamza had erected to hold up our fancy roof. This was always my favorite time of day in the desert, and I had yet to miss a sunrise. Emma preferred the sunsets for obvious reasons, but for me, the sunrises were just as good. The calm before the storm, you could say, before the sun's rays became too strong to watch, too strong to even stand in.

A hazy shape suddenly emerged on the sand before me. Mountains? It must be a mirage. Come to think of it, this was my first one. Well, I always believed in trying something new every day; why couldn't a mirage be one of them? Too bad it was so fuzzy and far away—some mirage.

"Max?" Emma croaked.

"Yeah, Em?" I asked, looking down at her.

"Are we dead?"

"No." I sighed, tired of waiting around for the inevitable.

"Good. I thought you would look better in heaven," she said softly.

I chuckled. Even now she had a sense of humor. Did anything ever get this woman down?

I stared at my mirage as it continued to grow in size and clarity. What was it? Not mountains, more like rocky hills. And…a small building? I was starting to lose it.

"Do you regret it?" Emma asked.

"Regret what?" I asked, looking down at her, her deep blue eyes almost glowing in the morning rays.

"The adventure?" she answered.

"No, never."

"You?"

"Never."

I smiled at her, taking her hand.

"It's a shame we never found the treasure," she said.

"Yeah," I replied, looking out over the sand dunes, my mirage still standing before me.

Were mirages supposed to still be there?

"I really would have liked to see where it was, just once," Emma said, giving my hand a squeeze.

I looked at her, realization slowly setting in.

Impossible.

I looked back for Hamza. Where was he?

I must be dying.

He was slowly removing the gear from the camels. Tired and weak, he was still giving us a few precious moments alone together. A true gentleman in my book.

I looked back at Emma and then my mirage, still floating there in front of me for the world to see.

Oh my god.

"Max?" Emma called, concern rising in her voice. "Is everything okay?"

"We made it," I whispered.

"What?" Emma asked.

"We made it," I said, rising to my tired feet. "We made it!" I screamed through my sore, dry throat, my head bumping into our fabric roof.

"Look!" I yelled, pointing at the rocky cliffs. I could see, just barely, what looked like several pillars, mostly buried under the sand (definitely manmade) lying directly north of us.

"La 'iliha 'illallah, Muhammad rasulu-llah," Hamza proclaimed, sinking to his knees, reciting the Shahada.

"Oh my god, Max! We found it!" Emma yelled, her head barely lifted above the sand, taking in the glorious sight.

I couldn't believe it. There it was, nothing but a mist until the morning light revealed it. I just *couldn't* believe it! I…just couldn't…believe it. Was this real? Was it a mirage? No, of course not. Then the others wouldn't be able to see it, unless…

I kneeled down beside Emma, all exhaustion momentarily forgotten as she threw her arms around me in a tight hug.

"Max, what's wrong?" she asked ay my silence.

"*Am* I dead?" I asked in all seriousness. I know it was a silly question, but in light of the circumstances and everything we had been through, I felt I had the right to ask. I mean, the building, the cliffs, they just emerged out of thin air. Things like that just don't happen in real life.

"Ouch!" I cried. "You didn't have to pinch me."

"It's what you're supposed to do," Emma said with a wicked smirk. "Help me up?" she asked, holding out her arm.

"Sure," I replied with a grin. I supposed that's what I got for playing stupid.

"Amazing, isn't it?" Hamza asked, approaching us after his morning prayer.

"And to think we almost missed it," Emma said as we stood at the top of another sand dune, looking out over the morning desert at the small structure north of us. There it was, the treasure. Just a little farther and it was ours.

"How far do you think it is? About half a mile, right?" I asked Hamza.

"More, my friend. The openness of the Sahara has a way of making things appear closer than they really are, of hiding things right in front of your very eyes, as we have seen."

"Well, should we wait until nightfall?" Emma asked.

Hamza looked at me for an answer.

"We go now," I said. "We have no more water, so waiting won't do us any good, and the sun isn't fully up yet. Let's push on and find us some water."

"Hear, hear," Emma cheered.

We were running on steam now, only the joyous feeling of victory at finding the treasure, and the hope of finding some water with it keeping us going. It was so tempting to just lay back down and go to sleep, give our weary selves a break, but it was too dangerous. No, best to push on while we still had some energy.

"Emma, start packing up our gear. Hamza, remove

our tent. I'll take down the camels' tent. Let's hurry before the sun rises any higher," I called out, issuing orders, surprised that the other two followed them without complaint. There was no time for waiting, no time for arguments; the other two knew this too. There was treasure down there, and if God really were looking out for us, there would be some water too.

It took only a few minutes (record time) for us to repack our gear atop the two camels, our exhaustion and thirst forgotten for a little while in our excitement.

"Come on," I said, once again holding my hand out for Emma.

The three of us set out across the sand, the small structure in the distance taunting us with her secrets, daring us to come closer. What secrets were hidden behind her walls? What treasures?

There was only one way to find out.

"I hope the camels don't drop dead beneath us," Emma remarked as we pushed the camels at, well, let's just say it was a bit faster than a walking pace.

"They'll be fine," I responded, giving Stanley's head a little pat. "They'll be fine."

As we made our way up another sand dune, I prepared myself for the sight. From the camp, the building was so far away you could only see a faint outline. What new details would reveal themselves over this ridge? Honestly, after this leg of our trip, I was expecting the next cathedral. With an entire legion at her command and vast treasure under her protection, Tin Hinan must have created an impressive vault for the treasure.

"You've got to be kidding me," I said as we stopped at the top of the ridge. The building looked to be exactly the same distance as before—*exactly* the same distance.

"It is as I thought. Our journey still has some ways to go," Hamza said. "Come," he said, giving Sheila a light tap on her rump, "let us continue."

And there you had it. With those three words we once

again set out into the Sahara, but this time it wasn't night. This time we were setting out into the rising sun.

"I'm guessing this is going to take us a little longer than five minutes," I said, wrapping my scarf around my head. A futile effort, in my opinion, but one did what one could in the Sahara to stay cool. I was already starting to miss the cold nights as the temperature started to climb.

"A few hours, I'm guessing," Emma said.

"She is right, a few more hours," Hamza said dejectedly.

"Let's hope we make it that long," I said quietly.

All the excitement and adrenaline I had felt before was quickly draining away. A few more hours, why was it always a few more hours? Had I made the right call? Maybe we should have stayed at our camp for the day and attempted this at night. But what would we be going on? We had *no* water. None. The longer we waited, the worse we were going to get. But which was the better option? Wait even longer and conserve our meager energy until nightfall or keep going during the hot day and make it in a few hours?

No point second-guessing yourself now, I thought. I had made the call, and for right or for wrong, I was sticking with it. But did I have the right to make the choice for my friends? No, they each had a mind of their own; they made the call, just as I had. Besides, Hamza was a Tuareg, a nomad of the Sahara. If he chose to go on, then I was sure it was the right decision—unless our odds were already so bad that it didn't matter anymore.

I had to stop thinking like that. I had to keep my focus. The desert had shown us the way; now all we had to do was keep our heads and stay the course. We weren't dead yet, not if I had anything to say about it.

I don't know how long I managed to stay focused before the desert started playing its old tricks again. My mind wandered all over the place during those last few hours atop Stanley. The need for a drink was overpowering. What

I wouldn't give for a little drink. The folks back home really didn't know how good they had it. Built-in plumbing? That was a kingly gift. All you had to do was lift the faucet, and you had all the water you could ever ask for. We wasted so much back home, and not just water, but food, garbage, fuel. How could so few people have so much, while others, like the Tuareg, had so little? Yet, not once, not even once, had I heard Hamza complain or rally for his people or request a single ounce of any gold we found. He did this simply because he was a believer and a leader among his people. His forbearers had made a promise to a woman nearly two thousand years ago, and here he was making good on that promise, even though I didn't believe I was any chosen one, or some warrior for God as Emma liked to joke. He still believed and risked his life every day to see a promise fulfilled. The Tuareg were truly a noble people.

"Max," Emma said, shaking me awake. "Don't fall asleep now. We're almost there. Look," she proclaimed wearily, pointing to a large mud structure, mostly buried in the sand.

"That's it?" I asked in disappointment, barely opening my eyes. I was beginning to regret waking up. I didn't even remember falling asleep actually.

"Well, what did you expect? We are in the middle of the Sahara. Things are bound to get a little covered up," Emma said, her voice hoarse from the lack of water.

I tried producing some spit to help quench my thirst, but to no avail. We really were in trouble. Maybe I should just lie down beside the building and take another nap. That would make me feel better.

"No, no, you both must stay awake," Hamza yelled, giving us each a quick slap with his riding crop.

"Why?" I asked, rubbing my arm.

"There is water here," he answered happily.

"What? Where?" I asked, looking out to the dry mud wall ahead of us.

"You need water for any army to build this, Max,"

Emma said in annoyance.

All of our nerves were becoming a little…frayed. We really needed to get out of the sun.

The wall was of Roman design, not that I was an expert or anything, but the portico consisted of four columns carved out of the rock with a plain triangular tympanum on top. The entire structure looked to be no more than about ten yards wide, but the sand had washed right up against it and the rocky hill it was carved out of, nearly burying the place. Given a few more decades, maybe even less, and the entire structure would be buried under the sand forever, with no one being the wiser.

Lucky us.

“Do you think the sand blasted off any decoration that may have been on the tympanum?” Emma asked.

“The Mal’’un has a way of hiding all secrets,” Hamza replied.

Of course the sand had blasted off any decoration. What was wrong with me? Why hadn’t I thought of that? I shook my head to look for a doorway and smiled at my stupidity. How could I see any doorway when only about two yards of the column showed above the sand?

“How deep do you think it’s buried?” I asked.

“Well, judging by the tympanum, I’d say the columns are maybe fifteen yards tall. Who knows what else is buried beneath us?” Emma said, looking down at the sand.

“First things first,” I said, dismounting. “I need a drink.”

“Agreed,” Hamza said, following my lead. “Tin Hinan and her army were in this desert for many months. They must have had a source of water somewhere around here.”

“Spread out,” I said. “Let’s see what we can find.”

“Max,” Emma called several minutes later, finding me behind a rock outcropping at the bottom of the cliffs.

“Yeah, you find anything?” I asked her.

“I think any well here must be deep underneath us,

probably buried next to the entrance of this place."

"What are you trying to say?" I asked, already knowing the answer.

"I don't think there is any water here," she said in defeat.

I pulled her under the cliff's shade. "I think you might be right," I told her, admitting my worst fear. I couldn't believe we had come all this way, just to be stopped by a little thing like water (and a buried entrance).

"What are we going to do now?" I asked her.

"Whatever we want to, I guess," she answered.

"Emma," I said, brushing some of her mangled hair out of her eyes, "It's definitely been fun."

She gave a small giggle.

"Max," she said teasingly. "Now probably isn't the time for this."

"Really?" I said softly. "Because I can't think of a better time," I said, resting my hand behind her thin neck.

"You know my lips are very chapped," she whispered, her hands against my chest.

"So are mine," I said, closing my eyes, leaning in for the kiss.

"My friends," Hamza called joyously, emerging around the rocks. "There you are! Come, come!" He waved happily.

"Water?!" Emma asked, pulling away.

"You will see! Come, my friends," Hamza called, leading Emma away.

"Always something," I said, watching the happy pair leave.

"Max, come on!" Emma called, poking her head around the rock. "Let's go!"

"Coming," I said, following the two, although not quite as cheerily.

"Here!" Hamza said, pointing at a rocky overhang about 50 yards from the building's entrance.

"What?" Emma said, her mood quickly falling.

"The sand is darker," I observed.

"Darker?" Emma asked.

"As in it's not dry," I teased. It was nice being the one with the answers for a change.

"Come, let us dig," Hamza said eagerly, handing us each a small shovel he had brought.

Luckily, we had only to dig for about a minute before water began seeping up from the ground, much to our delight.

"Praise Allah!" I cheered, hugging the nomad, who already had his mouth to the ground, slurping up the delicious water.

We were lucky. What else could I say? It wouldn't have taken long for our strength to give out if that water had been much deeper. Honestly, what else could I say?

Finding fresh water under the sand was beyond lucky, and let me tell you, no drink I had ever had had ever tasted *so* good. I think a whole twenty minutes passed before we stopped taking turns sipping from our little water hole and started talking.

"Thank you, Hamza," Emma said for the hundredth time. "Thank you so much."

"It was no trouble, my friends, no trouble. Of course, I must admit that I did do it for myself mostly," he joked.

"Well, be that as it may, once again thank you," Emma replied happily. "Do you know what? I don't recall the last time I've eaten anything."

"It has been a while," I said.

"Perhaps a small feast is in order," Hamza said, jumping to his feet. "Come, my friend," he said to me.

"We should refill our water sacks as well," I said. "And the camels could really use a drink."

"Yes, yes, all in good time," Hamza replied, removing our food supply from Sheila.

Our feast turned out to be nothing more than some stale bread and some dried camel meat (really, the same as usual), but it was the dried fruit that Hamza had been saving that was the really good part. It may have been dry, and there certainly wasn't enough of it, but right here, sitting against the cool rock wall, drinking fresh water, I understood why this was called a feast among the Tuareg.

"Do you know something? I think I may have had too much water," I said, burping after eating the last piece of fruit.

"Yes, that was quite good, Hamza, thank you," Emma added, refilling one of our goatskins.

"You're welcome, my friends. Yes, it was a difficult journey, but we have made it," he said happily, taking another sip of water from his goatskin.

"Not yet," I replied. "We still have to get inside the ruin. And that means a lot of digging."

"Perhaps not as much as you're both thinking," Emma said.

"Explain," Hamza said.

"Well, you said yourself, Tin Hinan and her men were only out here for a few months. These were mostly soldiers, I'm guessing, not workers or masons. And I doubt they brought much out here with them, other than the treasure of course."

"What are you trying to say?" I asked.

"Well, since they had to carve everything out of this rock, I doubt they put in a door," she said.

"So if there's no door?"

"Then we wouldn't have to dig all the way to the bottom of the place, now would we?" she said smugly. "All we have to do is remove the sand covering the top of the entryway, and hopefully—"

"Crawl our way in," I finished.

"Exactly."

"So what will be waiting for us inside?" Hamza asked.

"Well, if this place is like any of the others, the Vestal Virgins most likely put in place a few extra tricks to make it more difficult for anyone who isn't supposed to be here," she answered.

"By tricks, you mean booby traps, don't you?" I asked.

"After everything else, what's a few more?" she asked.

"Brilliant," I said, standing up and taking my shovel. "Well, I don't know about you two, but I'm ready to dig and find out if all this was worth it."

"Very good," Hamza asserted, also standing up. "I will set up the camp and water the camels."

"What should I do?" Emma asked.

"Sleep," I answered.

"Now wait a minute," she began.

"He is right. We must take turns getting some rest. We will all have a turn to dig," Hamza said, sensing the upcoming battle.

"I hope it's not because I'm a girl," Emma said.

"Trust me," I said, helping her up. "I have no problem with you digging. You can dig all you want."

"Good," she said.

"After you get some sleep."

It was slow going the next two days. We took turns digging alongside the rock wall, inching our way down. I could see why it took a small army to build all of this; in fact, I was starting to wish we had a small army to help us dig.

Speaking of the army, this really was an impressive piece of construction; the doorway alone was probably about two yards high. It was only a matter of time before we would be able to crawl inside.

What would we find? How deep had the Romans carved into the rock? If the treasure really was as vast as everyone seemed to think—the Suits definitely weren't chasing us for peanuts—then this place must be enormous.

But it wasn't the size that troubled me; it was the

potential booby traps. Did I say potential? I meant all but certain.

And if that wasn't something to worry about, then our dwindling food supply was. Isn't that the way it always went? You solve one problem only to have another. You manage to find a little bit of fresh water and not die of thirst only to run out of food. Well, there were always the camels, I supposed. Although Emma did grow rather upset at the idea. Hey, in a survival situation you do whatever you have to. Fortunately for us, we had a real-life Tuareg as our guide who showed us ways of not dying of hunger in the desert.

In fact, after a few days, scorpion tends to grow on a man. We even had snake this evening, which was actually a little better than scorpion, if you can believe it. And ironically, Emma had no problem eating either of them, unlike the camels (and it's not like she had never eaten camel before out here).

On our third day, after eating some leftover snake, my shovel finally slipped through the massive doorway.

"You guys! Hurry!" I yelled.

Finally, after all these shifts digging in the sand, we were almost there. Finally, we were almost in the vault. Finally, the greatest treasure known to man was almost in our grasp.

"Are you in?" Emma yelled as the two ran over.

"Oh, we're in," I said, throwing some more sand out of the hole.

"I will go get the torches," Hamza called, already on his way back to the camels.

"I can't see anything. It's too dark," I said, looking through the doorway on my belly.

"Well, what did you expect?" Emma teased, both of us full of excitement. This was it. Finally, after everything the two of us had been through, we would be going in the belly of the beast.

"Here, my friend," Hamza said, handing me a torch and my rucksack, the sword securely tied on.

"Thank you."

"What do you see?" Emma asked as I lit the torch and stuck my head through.

"Not much. It looks to be one giant room, but I can't see the end." My voice echoed back. "Looks like the sand just barricaded the door mostly. We should be able to just slide on down. Guess you were right," I said, pulling my head out.

"What's new?" Emma teased.

"All right, I'll go down first, see what's up. I'll call for you to follow when it's safe. Okay?"

"Very well, my friend, we will wait for you."

"All right. See you on the other side," I said, looking at Emma one last time before crawling in through the small hole I had made.

"So what's in the bag?" I heard Emma say.

"Just a few supplies," Hamza responded before I tumbled down the sand hill and landed with a dull thump on the dusty floor.

"Max, are you all right?" Emma's voice echoed through the room.

"Yeah!" I called back up, picking up my dropped torch. Not much in the immediate vicinity, I observed, raising my torch higher. This place was eerily quiet. And dark.

"Can we come down yet?" Emma called, the impatience evident in her voice.

"Yeah!" I called back. "Come on down."

"So, did you find anything?" she asked, after she and Hamza slid down.

"No, not yet," I said, leading them deeper into the space.

It didn't take long before we reached the end of the room, where we found a sealed doorway (this one a bit more regular sized).

"Not much of a vault, is it?" I asked Hamza, feeling the closed door for…well, anything to be honest.

"It's not a vault," Emma said quietly, her voice echoing in the enormous room.

"What?"

"It's a crypt," she said, the light from her torch washing over a dozen skeletons.

CHAPTER THIRTEEN

# THE CRYPT

This quest of ours was definitely full of adventures, to say the least. Finding rooms full of gold and jewels would be one thing, but rooms full of corpses was entirely another.

"Who are they?" I asked, my torchlight casting a ghostly orange glow over them.

"Roman soldiers," Hamza answered, casting scraps of fabric and armor aside with his curved knife.

"How many are there?" I asked, overcome with curiosity. I raised my torch higher and surveyed the area; there were easily dozens of bodies around us, their corpses preserved (well, somewhat) from elements outside the sealed room.

"They must have died of hunger. There was only so much food a laboring legion of soldiers could bring out here," Hamza said, still crouching down beside us.

"Maybe," Emma whispered.

I turned my torch toward her, her face cast in that ghostlike glow. I hoped this wasn't some kind of bad omen because I was getting a little uncomfortable in this room.

"You don't think so?" I asked her.

"Well, judging from the small amount of food we've been able to catch along the rocks, they probably did die of starvation first, but I'm not sure."

"Of what?" I asked.

"Well, you said Tin Hinan made it back, right, Hamza?"

"Yes, indeed she did," he said, standing up from his examination to approach us.

"But she came alone?"

"Yes, we are quite sure. No story ever mentioned any soldiers coming back from the desert with her," the nomad answered.

"So?" I asked.

"Well, what if they were ordered to stay here? To die protecting the greatest treasure Rome had ever laid its hands on?" Emma hypothesized.

"I don't know," I said. It was a little thin, a few dozen bodies out of an entire legion.

"Maybe they died of heat exhaustion or an accident while building *this* place," I said, waving my hands around the enormous entrance.

"Maybe," she replied. "But then why didn't any return with Tin Hinan?"

"I don't know," I said again. It was a mystery. No soldier would willingly stay behind to die in the desert, no matter how loyal he was. At least, not *all* of them.

"But it doesn't matter. Come on, let's keep going," I said, leading us back to the sealed door.

"Help me," I said to Hamza. Together we tried to push the door open.

"I don't think it's going to open," Emma said.

"Come on," I grunted. "Push!"

"No, she is right," Hamza said, giving up. "It will not move."

"So does anyone have any ideas?" I asked, breathing heavily.

Taking my torch back from Emma, I scrutinized the

door for something I may have missed. Some secret lever, some small symbol, maybe just a small finger like in Egypt.

Nothing.

"I have one," Hamza said.

"What?" I asked turning around.

Hamza pulled a block of C4 from his pack. Those must have been the supplies I heard him mention to Emma.

"You must be joking?" Emma exclaimed.

"Awesome," I said. C4 really was wonderful stuff – it had gotten us out of some difficult situations before.

"What?! Max, are you serious?" Emma asked, her English accent becoming quite shrill. "That stuff could bring the whole place down on us!"

"Do you know how to open the door?" I asked.

"Well…"

I clapped my hands for Hamza to throw me the block.

"Well, you have until we set this then. Otherwise," I said, slapping the stick on the door, "we blow it."

"And how long will that take?" she asked as Hamza applied the blasting cap.

"Actually, we are done," Hamza replied with a smile.

"Where did you learn that trick?" I asked Hamza as we headed back toward the main entrance to take cover behind the sand hill.

"Monsieur Gibarah and I were very good friends," Hamza answered happily. He was clearly about to enjoy this next part, and for the record, so was I. Emma, not so much.

"I think you should do the honors, my friend," Hamza said, handing me the detonator.

"Thank you. Unless you'd rather do it?" I asked, holding the detonator out to Emma.

Guessing from her displeasure and the fact that she placed her hands on her ears and turned around, I would be doing the honors. Good for me—I had always wanted to blow some C4.

"Fire in the hole!"

I pushed the button.

As expected from an explosion in an enclosed room with very little cover other than a mountain of sand, the deafening blast sent a hailstorm of rock and dust our way. It really was quite extraordinary what a little bit of plastic explosive could do. I bet the Romans never thought all of their hard work could be destroyed in a matter of seconds. I really had to get some of the stuff myself.

"Well, that was fun."

"Here," Emma said, returning my torch. I suddenly wondered how long these things lasted.

"Whatever happened to our flashlights?"

"Ask the Suits."

"Okay," I said. Time to change the subject. "Everybody ready?" I asked, taking out my revolver.

"What on earth do you need that for?" Emma asked.

"Mummies?" I replied lamely.

"Really, Max?"

She really did have an annoying habit of making me feel like an idiot sometimes. We'd have to work on that.

"You have seen too many American movies, my friend," Hamza said with a laugh. "But it is wise to be cautious."

Amazing, even in this dark place, how even laughter had a way of closing in around you, cutting you off. Somehow it just didn't seem right. If it weren't for the small ray of light coming in from the hole we'd dug above us, this place really would feel like a crypt.

"Come on," I said, raising my torch in the darkness and leading the way through the doorway, trying to restore whatever was left of my dignity.

"Time to go into the unknown."

The demolished door opened to a long, narrow corridor. It was impossible to tell how far it delved into the earth because it pitched steadily downward; the torchlight did little to penetrate the blackness. This was worse than Istanbul somehow, worse than the tunnel through the catacombs. This tunnel wasn't worn smooth like in Egypt.

Rather, it was cracked and broken, almost as if it had been done in a hurry unlike the outside and the entrance chamber—almost as if it had been done by soldiers, not masons.

"How far do you think it goes?" Emma whispered in my ear, her hand resting against my back, giving a small feeling of reassurance. It may have been more for her benefit than my own though; I'd probably be doing the same thing if I had no torch. Unfortunately, Hamza had only managed to bring two of them. And between my revolver and Hamza's rifle, we carried the only firearms; somehow both brought a large amount of reassurance in this dismal place.

"What was that?" Emma asked. We all froze. A slight hiss of falling sand could be heard around us—or was it below us?

"I hear it as well," Hamza said.

"Yeah, me too."

"It sounds like sand," Emma whispered, the fear becoming more evident in her voice. Yep, this was definitely a lot more interesting than both Egypt and Istanbul combined.

"Stay here," I said, cocking my revolver. "I'll go check it out."

"Be careful," Emma whispered.

"Hey, I'm always careful." I grinned, taking a step forward before the ground fell away beneath me.

"*Max*!" Emma screamed in the narrow tunnel, her arms thrusting for mine, pulling me toward her, toward the edge of the deep abyss my legs were now dangling in.

"A little help," I yelled, trying to pull myself out of the hole. Emma's death grip on me was beginning to cut into my forearms.

"Come, together," Hamza cried, pulling on Emma's waist, the three of us working together to get me out.

"Well, that was unexpected," I said, lying against Emma to catch my breath.

"Are you okay?" she asked.

I looked up at her worried face. "Never better," I answered.

"You truly are blessed, my friend," Hamza said, lowering his torch into the pit.

Kneeling by the edge, I saw what the nomad meant. Razor-sharp spikes that had been carved out of rock stood menacingly to meet any intruder into this place. The bottom of the pit wasn't too far down, maybe only a couple of yards if the torchlight gave an accurate portrayal; not enough to kill you, but maybe break a few bones. I suspected the spikes were to finish the job.

"It must have lost some of its strength," Emma said, surveying the spiked pit.

"What makes you say that?"

"Well, I doubt it was supposed to collapse the second you stepped on it. When this place was first built, I bet the plates holding this section of floor up killed more than few grave robbers. We were lucky," she said.

"Or blessed," I joked.

"You know, this reminds of an old hunting trick, this pit."

"Fascinating. So how do you propose we get across?" Emma said. The narrow pit was a good five yards across.

"We could always jump," I answered. It would take an Olympic athlete to make *that* jump.

"Here, my friend," Hamza said, handing me a thin rope and his torch, our only one since I had let mine slip (luckily I had managed to hold onto my revolver).

"But what are we going to tie it too?" Emma asked, looking around for some sort of anchor.

Looking up at Hamza, we both knew the answer. I began wrapping the rope around myself, preparing to go down and simply walk through the pit.

"Are you sure about this?" I asked him.

"Yes, you both must go on," Hamza replied proudly.

"Hamza, we couldn't," Emma said.

"It is all right. I will be here waiting," he said, taking the rope to lower me down.

"Thank you, my friend," I said, poised over the edge.

"May Allah protect you," he said.

"I'll see you at the bottom," I told Emma before rappelling down into the dark pit.

Lucky for me, my torch was still burning at the bottom; its light provided a good sense of the distance, and in no time at all my feet hit the bottom of the uneven pit. It was an interesting site for the senses. Looking up, I could see Hamza's torch burning brightly, the rock spikes standing guard like a forest, reminding me of a dense collection of stalagmites. But this was no cave. No, this place was far more dangerous than any cave. This place was built to keep things out and to keep others things in. This crypt, as Emma called it, still had a few more surprises in store for us. I just hoped my hunch was right.

"I'm okay!" I yelled up to the pair. "Come on down!"

A second later I watched as another torch descended into the pit.

"Hamza gave you his torch?" I asked as Emma untied the rope from her waist.

"And his rifle," she replied, unslinging the weapon gracefully from her shoulder. "Plus a few other *supplies*," she said, tapping the pack that held the man's precious supply of C4.

"And I thought you didn't care for it," I teased, holding my torch near her head, her face lit brightly by the glow.

"No time now, lover boy," she said, walking past me, leading the way through the narrow valley of rock spikes.

"Lover boy?" I said, watching her go. That was a new one (and not a nickname I hoped she'd use in the future).

It didn't take long to squeeze through to the other

side of the pit—and when I say squeeze, I mean we really had to *squeeze*.

"Well, how are we supposed to get up?" Emma asked after reaching the other side.

"Not like this guy," I answered, looking at the remains of a Roman soldier who must have slipped on his way down. "Looks like the Romans, when they built this place, shinnied down between this spike," I tapped the rock spike beside the dead soldier and the rock wall, "and the wall to get out of here. They're pretty close together, so we should be able to just climb up."

"I'm sure this guy thought the same thing," Emma said, looking at the corpse.

"We'll just have to go carefully. Come on," I said, pressing my feet against either side of the wall and spike. "Let's go."

"Right behind you," she said, slinging the rifle over her shoulder and climbing up after me.

Climbing up, I began to wonder what other traps Tin Hinan and the Augustan legion had in store for us. To what lengths had they gone to protect the greatest treasure Rome had ever had in its possession?

My right foot slipped for a second as I wiggled up, sending small rocks down on Emma's head.

"Sorry," I called down to her. I was beginning to feel like a monkey with all this climbing.

Suddenly, my left hand reached the ledge at the other side of the pit. It was so dark—my torch barely penetrated the shadows—that I hadn't realized I had reached the top.

"Come on," I said, pulling Emma up after me.

"Are you all right?!" Hamza called from the other side of the narrow pit. Without a torch, he was only a shadow in the night. This place gave black a new meaning.

"Yes!" I yelled back, waving my torch in response, my voice echoing back to me in the tunnel. It was getting narrower, or at least I thought it was. Emma couldn't stand beside me without turning. I wondered what other corners the men had cut?

"I will wait for you here!" Hamza called back. "Good luck!" His voice echoed off the walls.

I gave my torch a brief wave in response. Good luck to you too, my friend, I thought.

"We keep going?" Emma asked with some uncertainty. Clearly, she didn't like the idea of going on without Hamza either. But there was no rock spike close to that smooth wall to squeeze between. Someone had to stay behind to pull us back up, if there was a "back up" from this trip. I didn't envy Hamza at that moment, alone in the pitch dark for who knows how long. At least he was safe; at least he had a sure way out and back to his people.

"We keep going," I said, leading the way.

What other tricks did this place have in store for us?

It didn't take long to find out.

"*Max*!" Emma yelled, once again pulling me out of harm's way as an arrow shot by my head, brushing my hair aside.

"Whoa. Thanks," I said, regarding the metal arrow sticking in the wall.

What was it with me!? Was I a magnet for danger?

"That's twice now you owe me," she said.

"Who's keeping count?" I asked.

"I am."

"Looks like these stones set off the arrows," I said, trying to change the subject. I pulled my foot back, releasing the pressure trigger under the stone floor.

"I would have thought you knew to look for these after Istanbul," Emma said, examining the tiny arrow buried in the opposite wall of the tunnel.

"Guess not," I replied, looking for more arrow ports in the wall.

"I doubt you'll see any in this darkness—until it's too late of course."

"Any ideas?" I asked her.

"Yeah," she answered, sliding by me. "Maybe I should lead."

"Be my guest."

"Okay. Watch my feet, and step *exactly* where I step," she said, slamming the butt of Hamza's rifle onto the ground in front of her. Several tiny arrows quickly buried themselves in the wall beside us.

I wondered if Hamza could hear all of this ruckus echoing back up the tunnel. I wondered what I'd be doing there all by myself in the dark. How long I would wait before giving up and turning back home? Hours? Days?

"You know, this is one of your better ideas," I said, following Emma's steps exactly as we slowly made our way down the tunnel, her rifle disturbing the silence that had permeated this place for almost two thousand years.

"Since when have I had a bad idea?" she asked as more arrows whizzed past her.

I paused to think about the question for a second; only one crossed my mind, and it involved a certain scooter incident from a million years ago.

"Oxford. The day we met."

Emma looked at me with a captivating smile. "Good point."

Amazing how even in a deep, dark underground crypt filled with dead bodies and booby traps in the middle of the Sahara, we still managed to calm each other's nerves and work together.

"That all of them you think?" I asked after a half dozen more steps and no arrows.

"Maybe," Emma replied. "But that probably means there's something else coming up."

"Something wrong?" I asked, looking back up the tunnel with her.

"I was just wondering."

"What?" I asked. I grew worried when her mind was on something.

"Nothing. You don't think they reload, do you?" she

asked, looking at me.

I glanced back down the tunnel.

"This place really sucks."

"Come on, my turn to risk my life," I said, squeezing by her.

"What do you think we'll find next?" she whispered.

"I'm still hoping for some mummies," I whispered back, tapping my holstered revolver. Not that she'd see it in this black.

It was weird. The deeper we went down this tunnel, the more uneasy I felt, like I was disturbing a place that no living man had any right to see, any right to place any part of his filthy, breathing self on. What right did we have to be here? What was this feeling of dread that was washing over me? What was it about this place that was making the hairs on my arm stand erect?

Something wasn't right. We'd gone too far down this tunnel without meeting any resistance. This just didn't feel right. This place felt more like a crypt with every crunching step.

Crunching?

I stopped dead in my tracks.

"Do you hear that?" I breathed in Emma's ear.

She looked down.

The crunching noise. That feeling.

This wasn't a crypt. It was a grave.

A massive graveyard beneath our feet.

"Ahh!" Emma's voice pierced the darkness.

"It's okay. It's okay," I repeated, shielding her from looking at the layer of skeletons we were walking on.

I'm not ashamed to admit I was holding her as much for her sake as for my own. This truly was a horrendous site. No one should ever have to be in a place like this, such an *evil* place.

Who would do something like this? Was this an execution site? Where did all these bodies come from?

"I'm all right. Thank you," Emma said, composing herself quickly. "Just caught off guard."

"That makes two of us," I said.

"Where did they come from?" Emma asked.

"Soldiers," I answered, my torchlight washing over the remains of rusty swords and armor.

"But what are they doing here?"

"Don't know. Let's keep going," I said with some uncertainty.

Emma slowly nodded in agreement. A couple (okay, maybe a bit more than a couple) of dead bodies weren't about to stop us. We'd been through worse, although this probably was the most disturbing.

I just wished I could at least see the floor as we descended deeper into the depths of the earth.

This place really was an impressive feat of engineering. We must have been about twenty yards down into the sandstone rock, if the slight angle in the narrow tunnel was any indication, and maybe a few hundred away from the entrance; it really was a remarkable achievement, especially from an army of soldiers with none of today's modern excavating equipment.

"Yuck!" I exclaimed, pulling my foot up through a collapsed skull. "That's disgusting."

"Shh!" Emma said, placing her hand over my mouth. "Did you hear that?" she asked, her mouth by my ear.

"What?" I asked, looking back up the pitch-black tunnel.

"I thought I heard something," she whispered, raising her torch in the gloom. "Do you think it was Hamza?"

"No," I said, still listening. "Hamza would say something. Maybe it was just some of these bones."

"I suppose."

"Come on. Let's see where this tunnel leads."

It was tough going among the remains. With no clear ground to walk on, we were forced to pick our way through the long-dead soldiers. For once, the narrow, uneven walls were a blessing as we leaned against them to keep our balance. The last thing I wanted was to come face to face with some dead guy.

I looked back down the tunnel, wondering about the sound Emma had heard. It wasn't like her to be paranoid, although the surprise of walking on a grave hadn't done wonders for her; maybe she hadn't heard anything other than us. But maybe she had. I could only imagine what lived down here.

"Look, Max," she whispered, her torch illuminating a message carved hastily into the wall. A bent-over skeleton still holding his blade lay directly below.

"Do you know what it says?" I asked, looking over the rough marks.

"I think the first line says 'Hinan angel.'" Emma translated.

"Well, that's comforting," I said, my spirits rising slightly. "And the second line?"

"It's a bit harder to read. Probably because I think he died writing this," she said, looking down at the poor soldier. "But I think it says 'of death.'"

"Hinan. Angel of Death," I repeated. "Are you sure?"

"Pretty sure," Emma whispered, the gloom of the place once again enclosing us on all sides.

"Look at him," I whispered, kneeling down beside the fallen soldier. "He almost looks to be in pain."

"He was in pain," Emma said softly.

"How do you know?" I asked.

"All these bodies, Max. Tin Hinan came back alone from the desert after building this place. She killed them. She poisoned them," Emma answered.

"To keep the secret," I said.

"To keep the secret," she agreed.

"We could always turn back," I said.

"No. No, we can't," she said with the smallest flicker of a smile. "We go on."

And with that we continued deeper into the crypt.
Deeper into the pool of bodies.
That is, until we reached a dead end.

CHAPTER FOURTEEN

# THE MAN BEHIND THE MASK

Well, this was most unexpected. After all this, I had expected more than some silly puzzle. After surviving the pit and the arrows *and* the field of bodies just to come to this.

What the hell?

Where was the treasure?!

Maybe Tin Hinan *was* the Angel of Death, as the Roman soldiers had thought.

After following this narrow, creepy tunnel for what felt like hours, Tin Hinan and her men had pulled another trick.

A vanishing one in fact.

They had simply stopped.

For whatever reason, they had just stopped digging.

But the wicked Vestal Virgin had seen fit to leave behind one last clue carved into the solid rock wall. Well, one could only hope it was the last. I swore I would kill that despicable woman if she hadn't already died thousands of years ago.

"Well, this is Latin," Emma said, tapping the familiar characters at the top. The Latin message read:

NATUS OF DIVUS

"Son of God," I translated.

She turned to me in surprise. "Since when do you know Latin?"

"I took some as a kid."

"Why didn't you tell me?" she asked.

"Is this really the place?" I asked, trying to change the subject. There were more pressing issues at hand.

"Well, all of these characters are just the Latin alphabet," she said, giving me one last look before returning to the wall.

"They almost look like buttons," I remarked, touching one of them. There they were, right below that simple message. Every letter of the alphabet, carved onto small stone tablets laid in the rock. It was almost like a—

"Combination," I said softly, finishing my thought out loud.

"What?" Emma asked.

"It's a combination. A code, like for a vault," I said. "All we have to do is enter the right combination."

"So what's the combination?"

"Well," I said, raising my torch to illuminate the top line better, "I'm guessing it has something to do with the 'Son of God.'"

"All right, so let's try entering 'Jesus.'"

"It can't be that simple," I told her.

"Why not? Does God have another son I don't know about?"

"All right," I said, giving in. "Let's try it."

I mean, what else could it be?

No sooner had I pressed the letter J than a large stone door slid out of the ceiling behind us, trapping us.

"Was that supposed to happen?" I asked Emma.

"I don't know," she answered, the concern evident in her voice. "But look," she said, pointing to a small blank square in the corner, "I think this is a reset button or something."

"This must have been the most advanced keypad of its day," I said.

Maybe this would open the solid door behind us because I sure didn't like having it closed and being cut off from freedom. And the fresh air—already I could feel the stale air getting a little thin in this tiny space. I was glad neither of us was claustrophobic, although it was hard not to get a little anxious in this place. I don't think my heart rate had fallen below two hundred beats a minute since we came here.

"Should we reset the lock?" Emma asked, eyeing the *supposed* reset button.

"It could just be the space bar," I half-joked. "Besides, what else are we going to enter?" I asked, reaching for the letter E.

I immediately regretted my decision as the walls beside us came to life, slowly inching their way toward us.

"Max?" Emma asked, her voice quivering. "Want to enter that a little faster?"

"I just finished."

"Max," she said. "Do something."

"What the hell do you want me to do?" I snapped, punching the supposed reset button. I didn't bother to congratulate Emma on her hunch as the letters I had pressed slowly came back out of the walls. Time was of the essence here. In another minute, we were going to end up like a crushed Volkswagen.

"Try something else!" she yelled, pressing her body against mine as the walls started to touch my broader shoulders.

"Son of God. Son of God," I said. "Who else could be the Son of God?"

"Max!" Emma insisted, as if saying my name over and over was going to make me think faster.

We really were in a tight pickle this time. This might

really be the end this time. I didn't know if I preferred a slow death in the desert to the Volkswagen death; neither was appealing. I wondered what it would be like to be crushed to death. Pretty soon I wouldn't have to wonder.

We turned sideways as the walls finally reached us, cutting our time together to a mere minute or two.

"Max," Emma said softly, taking my hand.

Ignoring her, I turned my attention back to the wall. The answer was here. What was it? I doubted I had many guesses left.

This was the time of Constantine. Times had changed. Christianity was legal now, so what else had changed? The Son of God?

The Son of God.

*The Son of God!*

Could it be that simple?! I typed in my answer just as the walls found my chest, the pain mounting with each button I pressed.

The walls stopped their advance.

The floor slid open.

Emma and I screamed as we slid down the massive tube. Where in the world were we going this time? I thought as we tumbled end over end down the smooth slide.

First we were going to be crushed to death, and now we were…what? Where were we going?

Did I enter the right answer?

Suddenly the chute spit me out, with Emma landing on top of me a split second later.

"Sorry," she said.

It's okay," I wheezed. "Can you get off now?"

"Oh, sorry," she apologized, rolling off me. "What happened?" she asked, helping me up. "I thought we were goners."

"I guess I guessed right," I answered, picking up my fallen torch to have a look around at our latest predicament.

"What did you enter?" she asked, looking back up the

chute. "No way we'll be able to climb back up that. It's too steep and smooth."

"We'll have to find a another way," I answered, lighting one of the ancient torches hanging on the wall.

"Looks like another room," Emma said, following my lead and lighting a few more torches lining the walls. "This is *huge* compared to that tunnel," she said happily, our latest brush with death forgotten.

"Anything is huge compared to that tunnel, and especially with that shrinking room," I called across the room. This new chamber really was *huge*. It must have been the size of an Olympic swimming pool.

"So what did you enter?" Emma asked again, running back to meet me in the center of the room. There was no point trying to light the whole place; it was just too big. A moment ago, we had felt compressed and trapped; now I felt small and insignificant in this giant room. It was mind-boggling to the senses.

"God," I answered simply, relishing in her confusion.

"What?"

"The Son of God is also God," I elaborated.

"That's not right," she said, even more confused.

"Remember, this place was built during the time of Constantinople. In 325, the First Council of Nicaea was convened."

"Yeah, I remember that. So?"

"One of the purposes of the council was to create a creed, the Nicene Creed in this case. Jesus Christ is described as 'God from God, Light from Light, true God from true God, begotten, not made, from the substance of the Father.' The whole point of the council was to distinguish whether Jesus Christ was God or his son. To satisfy both parties, Constantine intervened and proclaimed—"

"Jesus Christ was God and God's son, not a creation of God. Oh, Max, that's brilliant," she exclaimed, hugging me. "How on earth did you figure that out?"

"Sunday school?"

"You never went to Sunday school," Emma said. "Where'd you learn that?"

"I may have glanced at one of those books you lent me," I said, leaning in for the kiss with eyes closed.

"Oh my god, Max! Max! Look!" she yelled, turning my head toward the far wall still masked in shadow.

"What?" I asked annoyed.

There, etched into the stone in large letters and illuminated by the soft glow from the torches, was a familiar message. A message I had spent almost every night staring at. A message I had spent almost every waking moment dreaming about:

CLAUSTRUM ACQUIESCO CUM VIRIS DE SPQR

"The key rests with the might of the Senate and People of Rome," I read aloud, my brain doing a complete one-eighty.

"Come on!" I yelled in excitement, grabbing Emma's hand as we raced across the enormous room.

"What now? Was the treasure ever here?" Emma asked, looking back at the enormous room.

"I think it's still here," I said, feeling the thick crack that ran straight up the wall directly through the message.

"Dear Lord. Max, this is it! This must be a door," she said, awestruck at the colossal size of the doors. "How on earth did they do it? How are we going to open it?" she asked, pushing against the wall fruitlessly.

"Looks like you need a key," I answered, pointing at a thick slot in the door seam.

"A key?" Emma repeated. "Where would we get a key?"

"The sword is the key," I said, pulling the ringing metal out of my rucksack. This was it, our moment. The sword felt so right in my hands right here, right now. The blade of Solomon, of Caesar, and all of their descendants was home, about to fulfill its purpose, its destiny.

"The sword was chosen by the Vestals because as Rome's greatest weapon, it would hold an empire's greatest secret. So it was imprinted with a series of clues that nearly killed us," I added.

"But how do you know the sword is the key?" Emma asked.

"The key? Remember what Dr. Giordani said about the 'might of Rome' being gold and not the sword, that the sword was just a means to get gold. What if he was wrong? What if the 'might of Rome' was in the sword, as Emperor Vespasian believed? Then the sword is the key."

"I don't know, Max," Emma said.

"Only one way to find out." I grinned.

This was it. I was sure of it.

I slammed the blade into the slot. The sword fit perfectly, right up to the hilt.

Nothing happened.

"Huh?" I said, perplexed. "That should have worked. I was so sure that would work."

"Maybe you have to turn it, *like a key*," Emma suggested.

I turned the sword.

The ground shook with a mighty roar as dust and small rocks began to fall from the ceiling and a room that man had almost forgotten began to open. Sealed from the world for nearly two thousand years. Once considered too valuable and dangerous for any one man to possess.

The massive doors of stone slid open slowly on their ancient hinges. The work accomplished by an entire Roman legion, a legion that was later poisoned for what they knew, was finally seen by the outside world, recognized for the colossal achievement that it was.

A stream of oil suddenly burst into flame. The flames raced down an *enormous* room of stone farther than the eye could see.

Inside was a world of shimmering gold and sparkling

gems, precious jewels the size of your fist, mounds of glittering diamonds, works of art and pottery made from human hands not of this world. Armor and metals and fabrics decorated the labyrinth. Priceless statues lined the walls.

Huge piles of gold—thousands of tons, endless truckloads—stood everywhere, right up to the mammoth ceiling. Entire fields of rubies, emeralds, and diamonds, all the size of golf balls, glimmered in the light; they had been thrown about the gold coins and bricks like a sprinkling of sugar on a cake. This was a treasure far greater than any Professor Giordani could ever put into words, greater than any man or woman could ever imagine, even in their wildest dreams.

My own words could scarcely describe the sheer magnitude of this room and its contents. Never had my eyes seen such a sight, and never would I again see such a marvel. I knew then and there, as I stood in the midst of all that gold and art, that I had made the right decision in coming here; all the challenges had been worth it.

This was just too much for our senses, too much for any one man. This fortune could not be spent by any man in a hundred lifetimes, in a thousand lifetimes. The pockets of Rome, of the Temple before it, were vast indeed.

Emma and I silently held hands, only pausing to pull the sword out of the open door. We entered a lost room unseen by man for a thousand years, our mouths gaping in awe.

"Oh my god!" Emma managed to cough out first.

"We did it," I said, letting a fistful of gold coins fall to the ground. "We did it!" I yelled, picking Emma up and spinning her in victory.

"*We did it*!" I screamed at the top of my lungs, letting Emma down and running a victory lap around a gigantic pile of gold and precious gems.

"I can't believe it," Emma exclaimed. "Look at all of this treasure!"

"All of this, just from a sword," I said, raising the

ringing steel. "Amazing."

"But where's the Ark of the Covenant?" Emma asked, looking around for the greatest of all treasures. "The Sword of Muhammad? The Holy Grail?"

"It's nice to hear someone appreciate the true treasures," a deep Ukrainian voice said.

A circle of men surrounded us; they had gone unnoticed in our elation. Trained men, silent, all armed, all aiming their weapons at us, all ready for the kill, for their vengeance.

"Drop it," a British-accented Suit said, raising a Sig Sauer to my head as I instinctively reached for my revolver. Emma was likewise disarmed of her rifle, much to her annoyance.

"The sword too," the Ukrainian said, lighting a cigar. "We spent long enough trying to find it. Might as well hang it above my mantle."

"You!" I said in shock, recognizing the man from Casablanca who had captured me and sentenced us both to death. I'd have recognized that foul cigar of his anywhere and those dark, nearly black eyes that bespoke a truly evil man.

"Yes, me, Max," he said, throwing his match at me.

"And to answer your question," he said, redirecting his gaze toward Emma. "You won't find the Ark here or the Grail or the Spear of Destiny or anything else with an iota of power. You could look for a thousand years through all of this fortune," he waved, "and never find it."

"How would you know?" she asked.

"My dear, do you really think Emperor Constantine would entrust all of the empire's fortune to one woman. He knew the Vestal Virgins had their own plans, their own agendas. He entrusted Tin Hinan and the Vestals with just enough to maintain their loyalty. The most precious of treasures—those that you seek, and the ones that we will also find, once we remove all of this, of course—those were scattered to the farthest corners of the Earth by the emperor for safe keeping, but this will suffice for now," he said, examining a large diamond.

"I know Giordani told you all about the Vestals by now and of the council, what little they do know of our organization, that is. Frankly, I was pleasantly surprised by their lack of knowledge. Nice to know that security is tight."

"Professor Giordani would never tell you anything," Emma yelled in distress. We both suspected what had happened to the man.

"You'll be surprised what a man will say, given the right motivation," the Ukrainian snapped.

"*No*! *You monster*!" Emma screamed, making a run for the man. She hadn't taken a single step before one of the massive Suits pinned her against him.

"As expected from a commoner," the Ukrainian said through Emma's sobs, taking another puff from his cigar. "But then, maybe I'm talking to the wrong person," he said, looking at me. "A person of such noble birth such as yourself would understand."

"Max, what is he talking about?" Emma asked, controlling her rage for the moment.

"Oh, you didn't tell her? How charming," the Ukrainian teased.

"Who are you?" I asked, ignoring Emma, overcome with curiosity about the man who had chased me across half the globe and very nearly killed me on several occasions.

"Forgive me. My name is Aleksandr Markovich. I would introduce to my men, but seeing as you killed so many of them," I noticed Emma's captor tighten his grip, "I don't think you would receive the warmest welcome."

I didn't argue that point.

"But you did lead us to the treasure. Very impressive, I must say."

"How did you even find us?"

"It wasn't all that difficult really," Markovich said, nodding to one of his men. The mercenary pulled Hamza out from behind a mound of gold, where he had been sitting tied up.

"Hamza?" I asked in disbelief.

The mercenary removed his gag. "No, my friend. Do not believe them," he yelled before keeling over from the punch the mercenary delivered to his stomach.

"He's right of course. The filthy nomad would never give you away, even when captured in the tunnel. Quite unexpected really. By the way, I must thank you, Max, for unsealing the entrance. It did save us quite a bit of time."

"You're really a piece of work, you know that?" I said.

"Oh, come now, Max. Don't you want to hear the story? You deserve that much for finding this place for us," Markovich said, putting out his cigar on the floor. "You see, it was your friend here," he said, pointing at Emma, "who helped give us the final clue to this place."

"I would *never* help you," Emma yelled, struggling to free herself.

But where would she go? I thought. We were surrounded on all sides by guns. What was the point? Maybe that was why I wasn't restrained yet; Markovich knew we were trapped. No more games. After he said his little piece, that would be the end for us. Best keep him talking; try to figure *something* out—*anything*.

"What do you mean?" I asked Markovich.

"Why, with this little thing," Markovich answered, pulling Emma's waterproof digital camera out of his pocket. The same one we used at Kom el-Shoqafa! He must have taken it after they abducted Emma from the train.

The slippery bastard.

"It didn't take long for us to figure out the meaning of the constellation, the North Star."

"It wouldn't matter," I said. "You would still need a starting point."

"Oh, but we got one, *eventually*," he said with a vicious smirk at Hamza.

"Your people are quite loyal, *Tuareg*. After scouring half of Casablanca, we finally managed to find a man who was willing to tell us who you were—for the right price, of course. It's such an honor to meet a Tuareg prince, by the way. Too bad you and people don't have an ounce of gold to your name."

"Prince?" I asked Hamza.

"Oh yes, didn't he tell you? My, so many secrets among friends."

"My friend, I am sorry I did not tell you," Hamza coughed out after the mercenary delivered another quick punch.

"It hardly matters. A man with no means is hardly a man at all, let alone royalty," Markovich taunted. "And besides, we digress, and my time is so limited," he said checking his Rolex. "To sum up the story, once we knew who *your highness* was, it wasn't difficult to find his people."

"They would never betray me!" Hamza yelled.

"Oh, quite right. Once again I must admit that I was impressed by the savages. But they soon loosened their tongues after we killed a few dozen."

"A few dozen?" Emma said. "My god."

"You really are a piece of work, Markovich."

"Oh, don't sound so upset. They were merely a few poor nomads. No one will miss them. And as I was saying, once we loosened their tongues a bit, they gladly released the location of the monument—really just a pile of mud—but once we were there, it was just a simple helicopter ride to you.

"Wonderful job, by the way, uncovering the place. I should have let you keep the sword from the beginning, but then I wonder if you would have kept at it without my motivation?"

"Sir," a mercenary said, "we've disabled the traps and set up rope for the chute. Ready to start transporting the treasure at your word."

"Excellent timing. Yes, you may begin immediately," Markovich said, elated at the news.

"Yes, sir. But I must tell you it will take months, maybe years, to transport all of this out through that little shaft."

"Well then, we'll just have to make the shaft bigger, won't we?"

"Yes, sir," the mercenary responded with a grin. He motioned for his team to begin filling their sacks with gold; the sight reminded me of a team of worker ants eating away at a small insect.

"What do you need all of this gold for anyway, Markovich?" I asked. "You seem to have more than enough."

Markovich turned back to me. "Come now, Max. What do all men with power want? More power," he answered after seeing my confusion. "And money is the only way to get it. And do you think these little excursions into the desert are cheap? Do you think these men could dress themselves?" he joked, feeling a mercenary's Armani jacket. "Gold – real hard currency, not 1's and 0's on a computer screen. So much new gold on the market has the power to overturn nations and so much more."

"This treasure belongs in a museum. It belongs to the people," I said. "Not in your pockets."

"It belongs to whoever has the courage to take it!" he yelled, upset at my interruption. "And as I have told your little girlfriend, the real treasures have been hidden elsewhere in the world. It will take an immense amount of resources to find the Ark of the Covenant and the Spear of Destiny. Therein lies the true power. The power to topple governments, to rule an empire!"

"You're insane," I yelled.

"Oh, come now, Max," Markovich said, swaggering up to me. A mercenary grabbed me from behind to stop me from punching his boss in the face. "This is real life. This isn't some comic book. You're not the hero, and I'm not the villain. You are going to die, and there is no one who is going to save you now. Your little adventure *is over*," he taunted, his putrid breath making me nauseous.

"Take them to a corner and shoot them please," he said to the mercenaries. "I have had enough of them."

"This isn't over, Markovich!" I yelled.

"Yes, yes, so you say," he said, resuming his examination of the diamond.

"This isn't over!"

"Take them away," he ordered casually before the chamber erupted in hail of gunfire and all hell broke loose.

CHAPTER FIFTEEN

# SO MUCH FOR RETIREMENT

This was absolutely crazy! Everywhere I looked, I saw bullets flying, grenades exploding, sending some of the most expensive shrapnel in the world soaring. It was a battle; some unknown force had come to our rescue, claiming war on Aleksandr Markovich and his Armani-wearing thugs.

"It's the Tuareg!" Hamza yelled in joy and disbelief, his guard struggling to hold him back from running off to join his comrades.

"A bunch of freedom fighters aren't going to save you, kid," the Suit holding me taunted, dragging me away from the intensifying firefight.

"No," I replied mischievously, an idea coming into my head. "No, they're not," I said, right before I slammed the back of my head into his.

The Suit yelled in shock, grabbing his nose to try to stop the bleeding. His mistake. I laughed, running off into the chaos, looking for my two friends and my gun.

"Emma!" I yelled, taking cover as another well-thrown grenade landed near me, sending a heap of gold coins down on my head.

"Emma!" I yelled again, shaking off the gold, a ringing sound present in my ears.

Walking by the crater the grenade created, I cringed at the sight of a Suit and his half-blown body. Lucky for me, it was the same guy whose nose I had just bloodied, most likely trying to recapture me or worse. Unlucky for him was the fact that he had a few more bloody spots to worry about. Not that he'd get the chance. I paused long enough to scoop up his Sig Sauer and to silently thank the Tuareg warriors who had saved my life again.

I checked the clip—half empty; looked like the bastard had fired a few shots at me without my noticing in all this noise and chaos. I would have reloaded, but seeing as he probably kept the ammo in his jacket…well, let's just say whoever had thrown the grenade, whether on purpose or with blind luck, had a really good throwing arm.

"*Max*!" Emma screamed somewhere beyond the mountains of gold.

"Emma!" I yelled back, trying to reassure her, buy some time till I could work my through all the statues and artwork crammed between the utterly ridiculous sums of gold filling this place.

Who needed this much gold!?

And then I saw her and Hamza around the mountain of gold I was skirting. Both were being dragged deeper into the chamber, used as human shields by their captors.

"Emma!" I yelled again as they were pulled away, bullets pinging off the gold in front of me stopping my progress.

I had to keep going, but how? I hunkered down by the mound of treasure, trying to make myself as small of a target as possible. This wasn't a game. One wrong step and, well…game over.

Never before had I realized the kind of pressure a gunfight of this magnitude could place on a man. No, this wasn't a gunfight. This was a massacre.

Everywhere I looked, the Tuareg fighters were overwhelming the surprised Suits. With superior numbers and firepower—a pistol only had so many rounds compared to the Tuareg's rifles and grenades—the Tuareg were quickly taking the fight to the enemy.

And they weren't holding back any punches either. Hard-pressed by their leader's abduction and the massacre of one of their tribes, the Tuareg fought with a spirit of vengeance and ferocity long unseen by their people. Indeed, watching these fierce warriors attack and press on without hesitation was inspiring – without fear of death as the better trained men of Markovich placed round after round into their numbers, still they pressed forward. Something had awoken in them—that need or desire to accomplish, to achieve their goal, no matter what it cost.

No, I realized. It was love. Love that drove them into battle without the slightest thought of fear of death. Love for their people. Love for their leader; complete and unequivocal love for their ruler, Hamza al-Meshal, Prince of the Tuareg.

If they could find the courage to go on, to die if need be for the one they love, then how could I do any different?

And with that one thought, I stood up and raced back into the gunfire to find the one I loved.

"Emma!" I screamed in desperation as more gold coins bounced off the back of my head. The Suits were losing, that much was evident, as they fought back with their final clips of ammunition. The fighting had become all the more dangerous, as when a prey trapped in a corner fights back with everything it has left.

Suddenly I spotted Hamza. His captor was attempting to pull him toward the exit despite his struggles. The Tuareg were much too afraid to fire a shot, should they accidently hit their leader.

Even as I raised the Sig Sauer, I knew I wouldn't fire either; the odds were just too poor. Hamza, in his attempts to pull away from the Suit, made the situation worse by struggling so much and preventing a clear shot. The Suit clearly knew he had only one chance of making it out of this gold hellhole alive. With his muscular arm locked around Hamza's neck and a gun pointed at his head, he most definitely wasn't going to let go. To do so would mean his death.

All of a sudden a young Tuareg burst out amid all the gold. Upon seeing the Suit, he fired the small rocket-propelled grenade launcher he was carrying, much to everyone's horror.

Before anyone could react, the grenade exploded several yards away from the pair, sending mountains of gold and jewels—as well as Hamza—into the air.

"Hamza!" I yelled, running over to him, a distinct ringing in my ears as semi-molten gold coins showered down upon us, burning the back of my neck.

"Yes, I am all right," Hamza responded somewhat shaken as I rolled him over. "But Ali won't be when I am through with him."

Assuming he meant the young Tuareg who had fired the RPG so carelessly, I responded, "He probably saved your life." Unlike the Suit's, whom the Tuareg had quickly punished for holding their leader hostage.

"Yes, so he did," Hamza conceded, collecting himself as I helped him up.

"Are you all right?" I asked as several Tuareg gathered around us, including Ali, who still looked mortified at thought of very nearly killing the man he had come to save.

"Yes, for the most part," he answered, giving Ali a stern look. "I'm just glad we all don't shoot as well as you," he added, his frown turning to a smile of thanks.

"How the hell did your people get here?" I asked, still amazed as I looked around at the smiling faces of the Tuareg as they cheered for their ruler's safety.

"Hinan knows and sees all, my friend," Hamza

answered with an even larger smile on his face.

"Bloody bird."

Suddenly another Tuareg burst into the small crowd, yelling something to Hamza in Arabic. The firefight was dying out as the few remaining Suits ran off into the treasure room trying to evade the Tuareg fighters.

"My friend, we've found Markovich!"

"Where?" I asked.

"He's heading toward the exit…with Emma."

"Which way?" I asked, disoriented in the giant room of gold.

"He will show you," Hamza answered, directing the messenger to take me. "Go!"

I quickly followed my guide through the endless maze of fortune, bodies from both sides lying dead as I flew by them. So much death for a little treasure. Was it all really worth it? Part of me wished I had never found this room.

"That's far enough, Mr. Taylor," Markovich said as we emerged from the maze of treasure, my revolver pressed against Emma's head to reiterate his point.

"Max, stop!" Emma yelled. "He's got a bomb."

I was only half listening to the man. At this point, all I wanted to do was put a bullet in that man's head.

After all the pain he caused, all the innocent people he tortured and killed, if anybody deserved to die, it was Alexsandr Markovich.

"Ah, ah, ah, Max," Markovich teased, shaking the detonator with his free hand. "Any closer and I kill her and bury you all in here alive."

"Just try it," I said, cocking the gun.

"Max?" Emma asked in concern.

"Quiet," Markovich said, pressing the gun harder against Emma's skull and slowly backing toward the entrance. "Don't be a fool, boy. See that device there?" He indicated a large container to his left. "I press this button and you and all your filthy nomad friends will die in here together. Lower the gun and back away, and I promise to let her go."

"Not going to happen," I said, following Markovich step by step, keeping my distance.

"You think you've won a victory here. The council will only send more men who are far more prepared than today. You can't win."

"That is where you are wrong," Hamza said, emerging from the treasure room unarmed, his men taking aim but keeping a respectful distance.

"Do you really think a few poor nomads with a few grenades can hold this place off forever?" Markovich taunted.

"No, of course not," Hamza said. "Get ready," he whispered to me.

"This treasure is far too great for any one man or even one people to own," Hamza said to Markovich. "Such a fortune should be spread equally among the world."

"Spoken like a fool," Markovich replied.

"Perhaps," Hamza said with a smile and nudged me.

I took aim above Markovich's head, hoping no one moved. What was Hamza's plan?

"But would a fool send word to the World News about the greatest discovery ever uncovered by mankind?"

"*What*!" Markovich screamed, taking aim at Hamza.

I fired, hitting Markovich in the shoulder.

The bomb exploded.

"*Emma*! *Run*!" I screamed.

* * *

"Things will never be the same again will they?"

"Perhaps not, my friend, but who knows this? The

desert still holds many secrets, and some she will never reveal," Hamza replied as we looked down on the massive excavation already beginning to take shape.

Reporters from all over the world galloped to and fro like worker ants, marveling at every new piece of art and treasure that was brought up. The level of activity at the site was extraordinary as massive prefabricated buildings were being erected to study and categorize each piece before being delivered to museums around the world. A second helipad had been assembled near the archeologists' living quarters for all the VIPs arriving to see the great discovery themselves.

The United Nations had been remarkably quick to isolate a huge area around the site with security to prevent any would-be thieves. Little did they suspect how futile their efforts would be against Markovich and his organization, but then again, with a society as secretive as his, attacking a UN-sponsored project teaming with reporters would hardly go unnoticed.

But then I suspect with the *real* treasures hidden elsewhere in the world, they would hardly gamble their secrecy for this fortune. Of course, losing a few trillion dollars of gold when it's in your grasp might upset a few of them.

"What are you thinking so hard about?" Emma asked, arriving beside me.

"Oh, nothing really. Just how much money Markovich lost this week," I answered happily, thankful to whoever it was that was watching out for us. Thankful for Emma to still be here after nearly being buried alive by the explosion. Thankful to have found one of the many shafts used by Tin Hinan to lower the endless treasure into the chamber that led to our eventual escape (granted, it did take two days of hard digging before we reached the surface). Thankful for Hamza, my dear friend, and his wonderful family, the Tuareg, and that absolutely wonderful falcon of his that saved our lives more than once.

"And?" Emma asked, seeing more.

"And nothing. Just thankful to be alive."

"You think he made it out?" she asked, referring to Markovich's unknown fate.

"I don't know, maybe. I hope not," I shrugged. "Nothing worth worrying about now."

"Mr. Taylor! Ms. Atherton!" a PR rep called, running up to us. "Your helicopter is on approach to take you back to Casablanca."

"All right," I said. "We'll be right there."

I still felt bad that Emma and I were taking all the credit for the discovery, but Hamza had insisted, claiming that the Tuareg were a desert people and that fortune and glory were not things looked for among them. All they craved was to be left alone in the desert that they loved, the desert that their ancestors crossed, and hopefully, the desert that their children would continue to cross in the future.

"Well, I guess this is it," I said, turning to Hamza.

"Perhaps," the Tuareg prince replied with a smile, "but somehow I think the fates have something different in store for us."

"Then…until next time, my friend," I replied.

"Until next time," Hamza said, shaking my hand.

"Hamza, thank you. Thank you for everything," Emma said, embracing him.

"Do not be sad, my friends. Remember, the adventure is never over. Allah wills it."

And with that, the prince of the Tuareg turned and mounted his camel. The poor beast was weighted down with all the gold it could carry. The Tuareg may have no need for a cavern of gold, but a little doesn't hurt. Even so, it only took a heartbreaking minute for the camel to disappear over the sand dune, taking my dear friend with him.

"Too bad we didn't think to grab some," I said, raising the Sword of Crocea Mors, its shining blade singing in the Saharan wind, this amazing sword that led me on a journey of a lifetime. I couldn't believe it was over. All the clues, all the dangers, and all the ridiculous close calls we faced together to get to this point. It was really all over; time to go back to our old lives.

"And what would you do with all that gold?" Emma asked.

"Probably go have another adventure," I answered "It's almost a shame that it's over."

"Maybe not."

"What?" I asked in surprise.

"Look," Emma said, pointing at a lone camel far to our right. "Looks like Hamza forgot one."

"And not just any one. Stanley!" I yelled, running over to my trusty camel, my dear companion that had led me safely over the Sahara.

"Max!" Emma exclaimed in shock as she looked in one of the saddlebags.

It was filled with gold! Gold and gems the size of golf balls!

"That sneaky Tuareg," I whispered. "What do we do with it?"

Emma looked out over the Sahara in answer. Her desire and love for adventure outmatched my own.

"What the hell," I said, helping her onto the camel and taking a seat behind her.

"Emma, I think this is the beginning of a beautiful friendship."

She smiled at the old joke.

And as we rode off once again into the Sahara, I pulled her hair back and gave her a kiss.

# Afterward

Max Taylor isn't your ordinary adventure hero, your ordinary explorer. There isn't anything special about him (other than his style); he has no special education, no military training (although they both would have helped him out more, especially when in a tight jam). He's just a young man who found himself in an extraordinary circumstance.

He is just like any of us. He did what was expected of him. But then, somewhere along the way, life got a hold of him. It tested him, it tried him, but in the end, it showed him the way. It showed him *how* to live.

Max Taylor isn't a perfect man or a perfect hero. He has his flaws and his strengths just like the rest of us. And like the rest of us, he continues to grow, to evolve as a man, as a human being. And he may stumble along the way, but that's okay. Who doesn't trip every once in a while?

I wrote this story to inspire other people, both young and old, to follow their dreams, no matter how crazy or insane or dangerous they may be. To keep trying, no matter the odds, to persevere no matter the obstacles, no matter the challenges and roadblocks life may throw in the way.

I also wrote this story to inspire myself and to help me realize my own dreams of adventure, to learn more about other cultures and other ways of life.

And lastly, to just tell a good story.

*Attila T. Vamos*

www.ingramcontent.com/pod-product-compliance
Lightning Source LLC
Chambersburg PA
CBHW022142170626
46807CB00005B/2048

* 9 7 8 0 6 9 2 0 9 7 7 9 3 *